Aris Reigns

The Kingdom Of Vampires

"A surprising twist on the vampire trend...Author Morgan weaves together the thrilling history with a contemporary love story that comes together in an action-filled climax—and an enticing cliffhanger—that will leave readers thirsty for more. Blending sensual fantasy and the supernatural, this vampire saga takes a welcome turn."

— *Kirkus Reviews*

"This sophisticated vampire romance with a twist takes readers on a compelling journey deep into...the pull of hypnosis...the possibility of past lives...and the power of dangerous desires."

— *Kindle Nation*

"This is a very grownup Vampire story that is just as sensual as it is supernatural. The reader will not be disappointed with the denouement or the inevitable cliffhanger that entices one to look forward to the next book in the series. Devin Morgan will be one to watch in this genre."

— *Amazon*

"Eloquent imagery and vivid detail—the author does a wonderful job of harmonizing two different worlds together. She brings you into the story quickly and doesn't let you go until the end. Unpredictable (in the best and most refreshing of ways) and delightful."

— *Amazon*

www.TruLoveStories.com
Where Passionistas Play!

BroadLit

Published by

BroadLit ®
14011 Ventura Blvd.
Suite 206 E
Sherman Oaks, CA 91423

ISBN 978-0-9905156-1-6

Produced in the United States of America.

Visit us online at www.TruLOVEstories.com

To Aris, Gaby and Chanelle
The only vampires I will ever love

A huge thank you to Sheri and Jake Faller for all the Sunday afternoon trips with me to the Catacombs and a special thank you to Sheri for all the beautiful food she makes sure I eat while I'm working.

Thank you to Rik Vig (a brother of choice) for all the amazing support he has given to me through the years and the beautiful graphic designs that he has created for me.

Thank you to Judy and Richard Sherman for their advice, support, love and the laughter and teasing when I become too serious.

Thank you to Robin, Ryan and Dylan Rogers for their huge hearts and all the hours they spend listening to me talk about Aris.

Thank you to all my students who support me with such love and confidence in anything that I do.

Thank you to all the wonderful people who make Broadthink such a great publishing house. Each and every one of them has been a part of "The Infinity Diaries Trilogy."

Aris Reigns

The Kingdom Of Vampires

by Devin Morgan

An
INFINITY DIARIES
NOVEL

A BROADLIT BOOK

Prologue

His back was stiff, his stride furious as he paced in front of Sarah, eyes daring her to look away. "I have been many men to you. DeMarco from your human life and De Flores, the vampire King whom your Immortals fear. I am both of these, vampire and one in the same." Menacingly, he stepped closer; close enough for her to feel his hot breath on her face. His skin was pale, deathly white, all of the golden tones of the man she knew in Chicago gone. His wavy black hair, which had always been so groomed, hung in tangles down the back of his neck and over his forehead into his eyes. The boots on his feet were soft black leather. She could see the defined muscles in his legs as they strained against his tight, well-worn jeans. In the dim light of the lanterns, she could see he wore a dark knitted sweater under his black leather jacket. "And, I was yet another to you in a life long ago, a human man. One you seem to have forgotten altogether." He spoke softly in a threatening whisper. "Diego."

"Diego?"

"Yes. Diego." Raising his voice until it echoed against the stone walls. "The gypsy you pledged your undying love. The gypsy whose heart you entranced in that English forest more than five hundred years past, whose body and soul you possessed." Clenching his fist, he squeezed his eyes shut as he fought for control. When he spoke again, his words were soft, clipped and filled with menace. "I have not forgotten you in over five centuries. I have searched the globe to find you. And when at last I do, I find you in love with another. An Immortal." He snarled, hate contorting his handsome face into something monstrous and terrifying. "Your Aris."

Sarah realized she wasn't breathing just before he lunged at her. She gasped for air as he grabbed her by the shoulders; he shoved her toward the window with such force she feared he might throw her through the glass onto the stones below. After only a moment she realized he was pushing her toward a tall wing-back chair hidden in the shadows in the corner of the enormous room. Unceremoniously, he threw her onto the chair as he shouted. "Sit." He fought to restrain himself from striking her; he knew he could kill her with one blow, but that would bring him no joy. He wanted her alive and terrified. He began to pace. When he spoke, his voice was low. Dangerous. "Do not move."

She couldn't move if she wanted to. The shock of being brought before the evil vampire King, the very devil that was leading his troops in war against Aris and his Immortals, in his throne room in the heart of a medieval castle only to find that the bloodsucker holding her prisoner was none other than her Italian ex-boyfriend from Chicago was more than she could handle. She was frozen to the spot. Unable to face him, she stared at her shoes. They were a perfect fit. Her addled brain wondered how her captors knew what size she wore and why they cared. When she was kidnapped from London and the safety of her Immortal friends by the vampire Queen who brought her to this God-forsaken place, she was in bed in a luxurious historical hotel, barefooted. She had fallen asleep on a soft, warm bed only to wake up bound and gagged, bouncing down a rut-filled road in the back of a jeep, slapped around by some crazy vampire woman who seemed to be looking forward to torturing her to death. Now she stood before the vampire King who appeared to think torture was a pretty good idea as well and all she could think about was her shoes. She was sure she had lost her mind.

King DeMarco grabbed her chin, forcing her to look at him. His mouth softened for only an instant before the menace returned. He tore his hand away and continued pacing. "In that time long ago when your father snatched you from Diego, from me, I went mad. I roamed the woods like an animal mourning your loss. When, at last, I returned to the gypsy camp my grandmother told of a vision she had of you in the court of Henry VIII. I set out to follow you to London and there I found you at court. Do you remember?" He stopped in front of her, stooping down, resting his hands on the tufted arms of the chair in which she sat. She felt like a trapped animal. A trapped wolf will chew off its own leg to get free. She vowed she would do whatever it took to escape this wretched place. She remained silent in fear that any word from her might drive him over the edge.

"Yes, I found you at court in London. I came to you. You shunned me. You turned me away. You told me you loved another." There was madness in his eyes as, once again, he gripped her face in between his huge hands. "But I loved you still." Suddenly his black eyes softened as they locked onto her frightened ones. Almost tenderly he pulled her to her feet. Suddenly his body grew rigid, he began shaking. Instantly repelled by his sudden urge to hold her, he threw her back down onto the chair.

Slowly he paced a circle around her as he spoke. "I watched the palace. I followed you to the ship on the day you set sail for Spain when Cardinal Woolsey exiled you to be married. I stowed away, but before the ship cast off, a sailor found me. He gave me over to the captain. Beaten and whipped, I nearly died from the great loss of blood and the infection that set into my wounds." He tore the jacket from his shoulders, pulled the sweater over his head and threw both of them on the floor. His muscles strained with anger. His body looked powerful, invincible. "Do you see this? Wounds so deep even my vampire body retains the scars." He spun on his heel, exposing his nude back to her.

Even in the soft lantern light she could see the long silver scars running from shoulder to shoulder, crisscrossing his spine to his waist and below.

Turning to face her, he picked up his jacket and put it back on, his pale chest a striking contrast to the black leather. "I took a thrashing for you because you once said you loved me. The wounds on my back healed, but the wound in my heart remained open and bleeding. I vowed I would find you, win you back. I was obsessed to have you for my own.

"When I healed sufficiently to work, I signed on to a ship's crew bound for Spain. They drove us like dogs and I grew strong once more in spite of my ordeal. It was only after we landed that I learned you were dead, killed by a storm at sea. Again, I mourned my loss of you.

"Desiring solace, I traveled the countryside unaccompanied and on foot, learning the lay of the land. It was then I found this very castle occupied, in those days, by minor royalty. I secured work inside its walls as an apprentice to the lord's blacksmith. I lived a quiet life, alone and finally at peace, for more than two decades. Then in my forty-second year, the blacksmith died without a wife or child; he willed me his small house and his blacksmith tools. I took pride in my work and made a decent living." He stared out the window, possessed for a moment by human memories. His expression eased and Sarah could finally see DeMarco, the man she had cared for, in this vampire King standing before her.

Without warning his eyes hardened; his spine stiffened. His voice grew gruff as he continued. "One evening as I walked in the forest, I was set upon by two of the fabled undead. I had heard of vampires before but I did not know they truly existed. The two males dragged me to their encampment and there, took my human life." DeMarco paused, staring into a far distant past. After a moment, he continued his story; Sarah strained to hear his soft whisper. "For three days I suffered the fires of hell. When the pain stopped, I knew that I was the same as they, one of the undead."

Again, he stooped down before her, his eyes level with her own, pain clearly visible in his dark gaze. "I knew there was no turning back, no way out, so I quietly accepted what I had become." Tearing his eyes from hers, he stood and began anew to pace. "I lived within the coven, yet apart from it. I learned all I could about vampire lore. As the years passed, I heard tales of the Catacombs. The legends said the Catacombs was a place of great learning; their libraries contained books with the secrets of life and death. Never forgetting for a moment my only true love, my Elizabeth," he spun on his heel to face her, a sneer narrowing his eyes and his smile holding nothing but disdain as he spoke. "Yes you, Sarah, in an incarnation where you loved me and betrayed me." Sarah was shaking, terrified he would end her life any moment.

After an interminable silence, walking away from her toward the window he continued speaking in a soft, measured voice. "But I believed if I could find her, find you, in a future life, I could win you again. I realized if I could get my hands on those books, I just might be able to do it. My deep love for you was my last vestige of humanity, all that was left of my human life and I clung to it like a drowning man.

"I plotted my journey to the vampire underground kingdom in London, concocting a plausible story as to why they should admit me to their society. I heard of others who left Spain for London and had been welcomed and lived there still.

"I set sail for England, working my way across the sea on a merchant ship. It took weeks before I reached my destination, but to a vampire, there is no such thing as time and so I was patient.

"I appealed to the great Council." His scorn was evident when he

spoke the word 'great.' "I told them I longed for a peaceful life, a life
without being a beast of human prey. They believed me and, after
much time and testing, I was accepted. I worked diligently, building
a reputation as an honorable Immortal." He laughed and it was an
ugly sound as it reverberated off the stone walls. "It took centuries,
but, as I said, what is time to a vampire. At long last, I managed my
way into the most elite circle, those who work on the Infinity Diaries,
the very books of life and death that I had traveled to uncover. I was
given primary responsibilities that I readily accepted and fulfilled.
After decades of pristine work, I gained the trust of the Master
Keeper of Records. He gave me what I was looking for, access to the
ancient scrolls. The delicate job of updating and copying the ancient
scrolls was delegated to me; transferring them into current volumes
representing each soul that had ever walked the earth.

"Working with determination, I searched until I found the soul-
chart of Elizabeth Wyatt. It was there I learned about Sarah Hagan
of Chicago. Research is quick and most accurate on the internet so
I found out everything I could about the psychologist and newly
famous author from Illinois. I read your book on reincarnation. It
made me laugh that you believed in past lives yet did not remember
yours. I vowed to make you remember. I vowed to make you love me.
I devised a plan to win you once again.

"I took my leave of the Catacombs, arriving in Chicago where I
found you and courted you as DeMarco Brassi. I hoped you would
feel something when you saw me, remember me. But you did not."

His voice was low, muted with contempt. She shivered as he
whispered, "I became everything you could ever want. I learned
all there is to know about your trade. For all purposes, I became a
psychologist. All that was missing was the university degree. I studied
re-incarnation. I gave you lively debate and intellectual stimulation. I
respected your wishes concerning intimacy. I offered you all the love
and security that you could ever desire. DeMarco Brassi deserved

your love, but you gave it to another. You turned from me yet again and for that second time, Sarah Hagan, you will die."

CHAPTER 1

As if he were looking for something, DeMarco turned to watch from the window, leaving Sarah to stare at his back in silence. The moments ticked slowly by, each second a minute, each minute an hour and all she could think about was Aris. Was he safe? Where was he? She knew a person's whole life was supposed to flash before them in a heartbeat at the moment of their death, yet her memories were only of her life with Aris. The first time he appeared to her through one of her clients, a voice from a distant age speaking to her through Carlos Havarro's therapeutic hypnotic trance. He returned each time she hypnotized Carlos and she grew to know him, to know who he was. Then he shared what he was; vampire, Immortal.

The first time he told her about his race and how different his society was than what humans believed blood drinkers to be. She recalled her disbelief and then her fear when she realized he was telling her the truth. To quiet her fear, he explained about the two races of drinkers of blood, the Immortals and the wild, evil vampires of past legend. If that wasn't enough to take in, when he told her the Immortals were created by the blending of humans and an Alien culture visiting earth on a scientific expedition, she knew she had lost all sense and reason. So she simply surrendered and listened to his story with an open heart.

She grew to be more than fascinated by him as he explained his society in the underground Catacombs of London. He told her of the Utopian life they led. At first it had been hard for her to believe, yet when she met his closest Immortal friends, Gabriela and Richard, she came to know that everything he told her about Immortals was true. They did not take human life to survive. They were much further evolved than the evil vampires that roamed the earth and filled movie screens. She remembered when he first appeared to her as a human. She was frightened at first, but his kindness won her trust. When first he told her of their past love and life together during the time of Henry VIII she scoffed, but through her own hypnotic sessions, she came to believe it was the truth. She believed she had loved him before and she couldn't stop herself from falling hopelessly in love with him again. Now, here she was facing another man from a time centuries ago who said he, too, had loved her and because she had chosen another, was now determined to end her present life.

The sound of the door scraping on the stones as it opened jolted Sarah into the present and sent an icy shiver of dread through her body. At the sound, DeMarco spun to face the arrival of the beautiful female vampire who was stepping into the room. Sarah gasped as she recognized the same woman who had kidnapped her and slapped her so savagely in the back of the kidnapper's car.

"Ah, here is my Queen." The King turned toward Sarah, laughing as he spoke, "Now human, you will deal with Mariska." The female was long and lean, wearing a tight-fitting black business suit. Her strappy black high heels clicked a staccato on the stone floor as she crossed to stand next to the King. Seeing them side-by-side, even in the midst of her fear, Sarah marveled at the dark beauty of the evil pair. In her mind's eye, she had pictured the enemies of the Immortals as grotesque, horrendous, repulsive. The subterfuge of their great beauty made them all the more terrifying.

Mariska stepped closer to their captive as she spoke. "You do not remember me from your past, do you human?"

Her mind cloudy with a thousand disjointed thoughts, Sarah couldn't remember ever seeing the female vampire before the kidnapping. She shook her head 'no'.

Now it was the Queen who paced in front of her. Sarah found herself mesmerized by her movement, breathing in rhythm with her tapping steps.

"Long ago in the gypsy camp you thought you bested me. You used your long, fair hair and pale skin to steal my betrothed." Her black eyes burned a hole through Sarah, a sinister laugh curved Mariska's crimson lips. "Soon I will begin using my dark powers to steal your mortal life. Slowly. Painfully." Her last words were softly whispered and even more frightening because of it.

Sarah's head swam as she did her best to recall some memory of the female vampire who was standing before her. Suddenly, she had a flashback to one of the hypnotic dreams she had during the time she was doing regressions in Chicago with her own psychotherapist. In the dream it was the sixteenth century and a maiden named Elizabeth Wyatt was fighting in the dust with a young gypsy woman who she now realized, resembled the Queen greatly. Sarah's mind began to clear. During her hypnotherapy sessions, she discovered Elizabeth Wyatt had been the name of one of her past life incarnations. Somehow this vampire thought Elizabeth Wyatt had stolen her man in that long-ago lifetime. It was only a moment before Sarah recalled why the two women were fighting and she knew Mariska was right. They were battling in the dirt over the woman's gypsy lover, over Diego, Diego, who now stood before her as King of the vampires. Her head swam as she realized that she and Mariska and DeMarco had all shared a life together in a long-past time. And in that century long ago Elizabeth won, not only the fight but the man. She remembered the curse the bruised and defeated gypsy spat on her as she crept away from the midnight fire.

And now, here she stood, Mariska, Queen of the Spanish Coven. Sarah feared this was going to be a very long night.

. . . .

Three darkly handsome manservants entered the chamber carrying two comfortable chairs and a round, carved wooden table. One built a glowing fire while the other two placed the furniture at a comfortable distance from the blaze. They were followed by a lovely young female vampire carrying two jewel-encrusted golden goblets on a matching tray. As she placed them on the table the gems glistened in the firelight.

Turning from Sarah as if they had forgotten she was there, Mariska and DeMarco moved across the room to sit in the chairs. They raised the goblets to toast one another, their eyes locking with an unspoken hunger more sinister than their desire for blood. They drank; neither paused while there was a drop left. Sarah shuddered, thinking what must have been in the goblets and, even more frightening, what might come after their taste of blood.

DeMarco rose and crossed to his Queen. He glanced at Sarah as if in defiance, then bending to Mariska, kissed her deeply, wildly. She buried her hands in his hair as he dragged her to her feet. Pressing her hips into him, she leaned backward, exposing her throat to his bared teeth. Sarah wasn't sure if it was just the reflection of the dancing firelight, but his canine teeth appeared to grow longer and sharper just before he plunged them into her throat.

Sarah's heart raced as she turned away, shutting her eyes against their blood union. Still she was unable to block Mariska's burning cries of anguish and ecstasy echoing throughout the stone room as her mate drew the venom from her veins. Sarah was terrified, yet fought against an uncontrollable desire to turn, to watch the strengthening of their forbidden bond, to watch the vampire blood-letting. Then there was silence.

Slowly Sarah opened her eyes. Her captors had returned to their chairs. They sat quietly for a moment, staring into the fire. A loud banging on the door brought them quickly to their feet. "Enter," the King spoke. A slender incredibly muscular man walked into the room, his long black hair caught in a braid that touched his waist. "Ah, Esteban. What news?" The King gestured the newcomer to join he and Mariska as they rose and crossed the room to the window.

Sarah thought she heard whispers of spies and war. Breathing slowly and deeply to calm herself, she listened carefully. She knew she heard mention of the Catacombs, but they spoke so softly she was only able to catch a few words. Knowing any information she could glean would help the Immortals, she leaned forward in her chair as if to adjust her shoe. Their words were more clear, yet still she could only hear scattered phrases. After a hurried exchange, the vampire called Esteban hurried from the room as the King and Queen approached her.

The Queen was the first to speak. "You, human, will die a slow and tortuous death." The shadows the firelight cast on Mariska made her face appear to be an eyeless skull. When she spoke, the words came from the mouth of a death's head. "And then the true carnage begins. We march on the Catacombs. We will slaughter their King and Queen. Our army will eliminate every underground citizen." She spoke as an afterthought. "Ah, yes, and DeMarco and I will personally take care of those who mean the most to you. One by one we will slowly eliminate your loved ones. I want you to ponder that as you wait for your own death. And I assure you, human, we will take the greatest care with your precious love, Aris." Sarah's heart raced. She knew she had to escape, to find a way to warn her Immortal friends.

Mariska drew DeMarco to her side. "We will rule in the Catacombs. We will own the Infinity Diaries and know the secret workings of the universe. With the power of the knowledge of life and death in our hands and hate in our non-beating hearts, we will rule the human world and feed on them openly like the sheep they are. We will use the knowledge of the Immortals to find any evil humans who will rally to our cause, who will help us enslave the human race. We will be the most powerful beings on the earth. All will bow down to us. We will begin the next evolution of the human species and we will be its King and Queen." Mariska stared silently at Sarah for a moment more, then shouted toward the door. "Guard."

As the soldiers entered the room, DeMarco turned to stare out the window at the star-studded sky. Without looking toward Sarah, he lifted his arm to wave her away, condemning her to her chamber to await her death. She heard the muffled tapping of stilettoes on the stone floor behind her as the soldiers took her into the hallway and closed the door after them.

. . . .

"*Escape. Escape. Escape.*" Her mind ran in circles as they marched her through the vast hallway. "*But how? How? I only know I'm somewhere in the mountains in Spain. If I can get away, where do I go? I've got to get away. How can I get away? And where the hell do I get away to?*" Her mind ran like a hamster on a wheel, continuously moving, going in circles and reaching no conclusions. "*The bars. I've got to get the bars loose. I'll figure out where to go once I get out of here.*" At least she had the beginning of a plan as the door to her prison loomed in front of her. It crashed against the wall as the soldiers slammed it open and shoved her inside. Stumbling and falling, she hit her head on the cold stone floor. She lay unconscious, a trickle of blood pooling beneath her forehead.

. . . .

The three Immortal comrades, Aris, Richard and Gabriela, quickly concealed the car they had rented at the Barcelona airport with loose brush, then raced through the forest effortlessly leaping over huge fallen branches and trees. They were determined to reach Sarah before it was too late. At last they could see the top of the castle tower in the pale light of a crescent moon. Richard touched Aris on the shoulder signaling him to stop. At the same moment a tall dark figure stepped from behind a tree.

"Simon." Gabriela embraced their comrade, a spy from the Catacombs. It had been years since she last saw him, his most recent life spent in subterfuge in the evil coven. He held her for a brief moment before turning to embrace the males. "Aris. Richard."

Frantic to secure Sarah's safety, Aris ignored the niceties of his ally's greeting. "Is Sarah alright? Where are they keeping her?" It took all of his patience to stand still and wait for a reply. He ached to storm the castle, to free the only woman he had ever loved, but knew rash actions would bring him no victory.

"She is being lodged in the castle keep, the only tall tower left standing." He pointed toward a stone wall atop the stark rocky crest of the hill separating them from her prison.

Aris made to leave but Richard held him fast. "Wait. We are in need of more information."

"I am in need of nothing." He tore out of his friend's grasp. "I am going to find her."

"No, Aris." Simon stepped in front of him. "She's been taken for an audience with the King and Queen. Wait until she returns to her chambers. The castle is close by, we must take care."

"Wait? I wait for nothing." He turned from them, racing in the direction Simon had directed them.

. . . .

Sarah groaned as she opened her eyes. The huge lump on her forehead was throbbing and she was shaky on her feet as she staggered toward the window. She had no idea how long she had lain on the floor, but the sky was still dark. She still had time before morning. Her hand was shaking as she reached to grasp the windowsill. The wind whistled through the bars and echoed throughout the chamber. Sarah's imagination played cruel tricks; she swore the wind called her name. Leaning her aching forehead against the cold metal separating her from her freedom, she heard it more clearly.

"Sarah. Sarah."

Suddenly, long powerful fingers wrapped around the bars and quietly lifted them from their foundation, bending them as if they were made of soft wood. Sarah knew she must be dreaming as Aris leaped through the opening, landing silently before her.

"Aris." It was a whisper. She reached for him as if she were suddenly unaware of where she was, sleepwalking, wanting only to be in his arms.

"Come. We are in great danger. We must hurry." Lifting her as if she were weightless, he wrapped her arms and legs around him. "Hold on tight. The only way out is down." She breathed in his fragrance as he climbed out the window. Leaning her cheek against his powerful shoulder, all of her fears fell away as he made his way, spider-like, down the ancient stones of the tower.

Loud voices and a wolf's howl halted his progress while they were still hidden in the shadows of the fallen foundation stones. Sarah buried her face in his chest to stifle a gasp as three male vampires crossed the courtyard beneath them. One had a huge black wolf on a leash. The wolf strained at the lead, snarling and howling, struggling to get away. He kept turning his huge head toward the escaping couple clinging to the side of the castle, his snout working as he took in their scent.

"What is wrong with him?" the tallest of the three questioned.

"Nothing, he hasn't eaten. Maybe he'll get the remnants of the human when the Queen is finished with her." The animal's handler laughed as he finally gained control of the beast and they walked on.

Aris waited in silence, preventing her attempted query with a tender kiss. "Wait," he whispered so softly she had to strain to hear his words even though his lips touched her ear. She shivered as she felt his warm breath against her skin. "We are still in danger. They are still within ear-shot. When they have gone, we will continue to safety. Once I have you out of harm's way, I will answer all your questions."

As soon as the three vampires disappeared from sight into the castle, he resumed their descent. He carried her close to him as he ran through the forest to safety and the waiting circle of her Immortal friends.

CHAPTER 2

Aris' hands gripped the steering wheel as the car sped toward the distant horizon; the early morning sky glowed with the first rays of the rising sun. Richard spoke quietly into his cell phone so as not to wake Sarah sleeping soundly in the backseat, her blond head resting peacefully against Gabriela's shoulder.

"What was that about?" Aris kept his voice low.

"Simon. He will meet us in London in a few days. Demitri and Alexi will stay on to keep watch on the coven." He checked to see if Sarah was still sleeping before he continued. "It seems Queen Mariska went raving mad when she heard of Sarah's escape. She ordered the male and female who had served Sarah in the castle to be extinguished. Then she single handedly, stone by stone, destroyed the tower, leveling it to rubble. She railed at the King, yet when he remained unruffled, she further demanded he eliminate the guards who had taken Sarah back to her chamber. The King refused. According to Simon, she stormed from the audience chamber, the entire castle ringing with her shouted accusation that DeMarco still loved the human woman."

Aris glanced in the rear view mirror. He would feel much more at peace when they were all four on an airplane heading to London.

"The amazing thing is," Richard continued, "the situation has worked to our best advantage."

"Our advantage? How so?"

"The Queen ignored the King's command. With the help of one of the King's most important generals, this new man, Esteban, one by one, they impaled and burned the guards. When the King heard of her actions he became livid at her treason. He commanded her and Esteban to death and they fled into exile before they could be captured. All of this within twenty-four hours of Sarah's escape."

"I still do not understand how Mariska and this Esteban's exile aids our cause? And who is Esteban?"

"Quite simply told, actually. Esteban was the King's hand-picked general. He is relatively new to their coven. It seems DeMarco changed him for the express purpose of being the commander of his troops. He was a famous bullfighter known for his cruelty in and out of the bullring. DeMarco knows his crude vampires must be taught the finesse of evading an impaler. Apparently, he felt none could be better at finesse than a bullfighter., Even though he joined them only recently, he is a most powerful and charismatic leader and when he left with the Queen, almost half the army rallied to follow. The Spanish coven's forces are split; civil war begins between them."

"I see," Aris spoke, a slow smile of comprehension lighting his eyes. "Their internal conflict will give us more time to train our soldiers, more time to prepare while they do battle with one another."

"The Queen's army with Esteban in command retreats from the castle even now as we drive toward Barcelona."

"Did Simon have any idea what their destination might be?"

"Rumor in the coven is their ultimate objective is London. Now they travel through the Pyrenees Mountains to find a place suitable to train for war. Their way is difficult for in order for such a great number to stay out of the sight of humans they must travel the snow banked gorges of the mountains. Their progress is slow but they continue forward. The Queen is determined to murder Sarah and take over the Catacombs with or without the King beside her. Without him, her hope is Esteban.

Her troops are diminished by half and there are factions within factions. They are all ill-trained and undisciplined. Esteban must gain military control of the coven immediately. The exiled vampires must be brought into harmony before they can be taught to fight together against King DeMarco and then a war of extinction against the Immortals. The Spanish royal conflict is our windfall; we have a greater window of time before we must depart London for Spain."

"Richard, we must keep constant watch over Sarah. She must never be alone. Mariska took her once. She can do it again."

"Aris, she was taken from the hotel with Gabriela in the next room. Sarah has human needs, how can one of us be constantly in her presence?"

"I will not leave her alone. In London or Chicago or anywhere on this planet. Never again."

"But you cannot spend every moment with her. You are needed in the Catacombs. Without you, there is no leadership for the army. Without an army our society is doomed. You are the core of whatever becomes of our military. Aris, the Immortals need you if we are to survive."

They sat quietly listening to the hum of the tires against the paved road. Aris was deep in thought until at last, he broke the silence. "I will speak with the Council. Under the circumstances perhaps they will offer Sarah sanctuary in the Catacombs. I know she will be safe beneath the ground with our people."

"They will never agree. Never before in all of our history has a human visited the Catacombs and left without being changed into an Immortal." Richard shook his head. "Aris, they will never agree."

"Strange times breed strange acts. I will approach Bartholomew. As head of the Council, perhaps he will listen to reason. We shall soon see."

. . . .

A freezing wind blew the high drifts of snow in blinding swirls as Esteban drove the coven forward. Even with vampire vision it was a struggle to see more than just a few feet in front of him as Mariska trudged through the blizzard at his side.

"How much farther to the caves?" She could barely see him through the wall of white flakes.

"Not much farther if the trackers are correct."

"We must settle and feed on the herd of humans we have brought before they all die of exposure. We have already lost several."

"They were not lost." He smiled. "They made good fare and their blood will sustain us until we come to rest."

Turning to look behind them, Mariska could hardly see the herd being driven forward by her coven. Their own food was strapped to their backs as they staggered through the waist- high drifts.

"You were brilliant to collect them from the villages that we circumvented."

"And you, my Queen, were fast thinking to steal a supply of the blood taken from blood banks and stored in DeMarco's vault."

"Yes, without it we would not have the sustenance we need. It is tasteless and there are no death throes that are so delicious, but it will keep us strong and able to fight."

Stopping in his tracks, Esteban turned, raising his hand to halt the bedraggled army behind him. "There." He pointed to a huge sharp overhang of rock. "That is the cliff. Come, the caves are just below."

Far behind them, one of their captives fell to his knees. One of the guards swooped down upon the fallen human and began to feed. When he was satiated, he passed the dying man to his comrade. Once drained, the limp form was tossed aside as the vampires forged ahead through the blizzard.

. . . .

Thick fog surrounded the castle as DeMarco sat on the window ledge of the highest turret. Gazing out over the dense forest below, his thoughts were of Sarah. Raw feelings of love and hate filled what should have been an empty heart. A battle raged inside his head. Her denial of him drove him to the brink of murder. He dreamed of draining her to her death as a captive Aris watched, powerless to save her. His mouth watered as he imagined the smell of her throat, the taste of her blood. He remembered the look of fright in her beautiful blue eyes as he told her who he was and who he had been to her.

Memories of their life in a past century flooded his mind and his heart filled with sorrow that she was so unfaithful to their love. He knew his true wish was not for her to die. His true wish was to have her a vampire, ruling by his side, Queen to his King.

"Sire?" DeMarco turned to face the aid that had entered his chamber. He nodded to Julian to speak. "The plan is in place. I have chosen the two who will travel to London to kidnap the woman."

CHAPTER 3

Sitting in front of the fireplace in Aris' flat, the two Immortal men waited while Sarah bathed. Exhausted by the ordeal she had suffered, she slept most of the airline flight from Spain to England. Once their plane was on the ground, her first conscious thought was a hot shower. As their car sped through the night to Aris's apartment, all she could think of was a cascade of tiny drops of hot water pelting her skin, washing away the un-Godly experiences of the last few days.

Her legs quivered as they rode in the elevator of Aris's building. Wrapping his arm tightly around her, he steadied her as the door opened and they made their way down the hall.

Once inside, she kicked off her shoes, falling onto the soft sofa with a sigh. "At last." She spoke in a barely audible whisper. Overcome by exhaustion, her eyes closed as she began to drift into sleep. "No. I can't allow myself to sleep until I've washed that awful castle off my skin." She pushed her exhausted body off the couch, standing and stretching her arms toward the ceiling. "I'm going to take a shower, then I'll sit with you." She turned and left the room.

. . . .

Gabriela sat with her while Sarah scrubbed and put on fresh clothes.

As she entered the sitting room, she was dressed in comfortable gray sweats and her clean blond hair was still moist. Settling in on the sofa next to Aris, she felt truly safe for the first time since her kidnapping. He wrapped an Afghan around her as Richard handed her a China cup filled with her favorite Earl Gray tea. Smiling, she smelled the bergamot fragrance as she lifted it to her lips.

"Ummm, so good. I wasn't sure I'd survive to ever have another cup of tea."

"That is behind you. You are here with us now, safe and warm." Gabriela squeezed her human friend's hand, then brushed a damp blond curl off her forehead. "We are here to make sure you are safe. One of us will be constantly with you until this madness is settled once and for all."

Panic filled Sarah's blue eyes as memories of the dark King flooded her mind. "You must warn the Immortals. DeMarco wants the Infinity Diaries. He wants the power of the knowledge of life and death so he can rule over all the humans on earth." She shivered as she spoke, drawing the blanket more closely around her. "He wants to breed them for food and worse."

"We assumed as much, Sarah, however, your evidence will prove to all below ground that we must march on Spain. DeMarco must never get his hands on the Diaries. Knowing the past and the future of every being on the planet would enable him to control the whole human race. Through the Diaries he would be able to locate and recruit the vilest of the human species to aid him in his slaughter. He would know who was weak and frightened; who he could easily control. No, he must never possess them. We must stop him." His voice was confident as he spoke, but deep inside his soul the nagging doubt as to what the true outcome of the war would be reared its nasty head.

Determined to keep his eyes on winning the battle, he changed the subject of conversation. Aris reached for Sarah's cell phone, smiling as he handed it to her. "But before you do anything else, you must telephone Colleen. She phoned you on the second day of your abduction. I answered when the caller ID registered her name."

"Good grief, she must be worried to death." Sarah hadn't thought of her Chicago friends since her kidnapping. She had no idea what she would say to them. "What did you tell her?"

He grinned. "Your practice of yoga gave me an easy story." He refreshed her tea then leaned back, wrapping his arm around her, drawing her close.

"What story? Just what did you tell her?"

"I told her that you and Gabriela were on a yoga retreat for a few days. I said it was a cloistered affair and that you were not even allowed to have your cell phones with you. You were to have no contact with the outside world."

Sarah was amazed at how quickly he came up with such a plausible deception. "Did she buy it?"

"Luckily, she did. I told her you would call her when you returned so you had best decide what you are going to tell your best mortal friend before you telephone. We are just fortunate that we found you so quickly. Had it taken longer, I have no idea what would have been my next tale."

"It's almost four o'clock in the morning in Chicago right now. I'm sure she's sleeping. And I'm simply exhausted. I can't think straight, much less give a credible report about a fictitious yoga retreat." She yawned while leaning forward to place her empty cup on the coffee table. "I think I'll just go to sleep and call her when I wake up. It'll be afternoon for her and I'll be rested and able to make some semblance of sense when I speak with her."

"Excellent idea." Aris got to his feet. Taking her hands in his, he helped her to stand. Gently, he guided her through the bedroom door. Holding the comforter for her, he waited while she crawled between the clean, crisp, sweet-smelling white sheets. He covered her, kissing her gently before turning out the light and slipping silently from the room. She was fast asleep before he crossed the threshold. Leaving the door open, he positioned his arm chair so he could easily watch her as she rested.

Gabriela gave Richard a knowing nod. They both knew Aris had no intention of letting her out of his sight while she was above ground and the evil King and Queen still walked the earth.

. . . .

After Gabriela and Richard left the apartment, Aris watched Sarah as she slept. His sensitive ears could hear the soft whisper of her breath and the slow, quiet beat of her heart. Even in the dim light his Immortal eyes watched the rise and fall of her chest, the pulse of her blood just beneath the tender skin of her throat.

He was filled with a burning human desire and as he watched the steady throbbing of the artery in her neck, his vampire nature began to surface even through his measured restraint. He ached to hold her, to make love to her in time to the rhythm of her pounding heart. Yes, and to drink her blood as it pulsed through her beautiful throat. As he thought of their coupling, a deeper more beastly yearning raised its ugly head. He struggled to resist with all his Immortal strength, yet the same vile phrase haunted him over and over. *"Take her. Make her Immortal. Do not wait. Take her now. Take her while she sleeps. Take her now."*

He knew he could. He could make her his. For a moment, he was overwhelmed by his own dark vampire drive to taste her blood, to drink her, to possess her. As if in a trance, he rose from his chair and moved toward the bedroom door.

Reaching the threshold, he stopped abruptly as if an invisible wall stood between him and the trusting woman sleeping peacefully in his charge. *"What am I doing? What am I doing?"* Grasping either side of the doorway, he closed his eyes as he fought for control of his dark nature. A battle between love and evil raged within him-ripping at his very soul. His limbs quivered as he fought to silence the beast that demanded her human life. After what seemed to him an eternity, his blood rage subsided; he was able to open his eyes to gaze at the human he adored. She slept soundly, trusting him completely.

Devastated by the thought of what he might have done, his shoulders slumped as he buried his face in his hands. He could have taken the only human life that truly had value to him. He would have betrayed his Immortal Queen and his society. He would have broken the Blood Oath for the third time. He swore to Queen Akira he would never break it again. She would have turned from him for a last time.

Slowly he returned to the chair. He sank into it, his long legs stretching out in front of him. He knew in his deepest soul he could never have Sarah while she was in her human form. But eternity without her would be an eternity without meaning. Would she ever care enough to give up her human life for love of her own free will?

Hours or perhaps only moments passed while she slept, but to Aris it was all the same.

CHAPTER 4

The gray morning fog hung like heavy drapes pooling on the streets of London as Aris lit a fire in the fireplace for the still sleeping Sarah. After she was in bed the previous night and before Richard and Gabriela left the flat, the three Immortals devised a plan. The two women would spend the day together, freeing Aris and Richard to meet in the Catacombs with Bartholomew. A soft knock on the front door announced Gabriela's arrival. She laid her coat across the arm of the sofa, then busied herself in the kitchen. Catching her attention as she opened the refrigerator, Aris waved good-bye, before quietly closing the front door behind him.

Sarah woke as the fragrance of freshly brewed coffee permeated the air. She wrapped a soft robe around her as she walked into the sitting room and curled up in the brown wing-back chair in front of the fireplace. Leaning against the velvety upholstery, staring into the dancing flames, her mind floated in that sweet place between sleep and wakefulness. There were brief moments when she wasn't even sure where she was, London or her condo in Chicago.

Memories of her life in Illinois flooded her mind. She thought of Carlos Havarro, the handsome young Latino man who had changed her life. Without his hypnotherapy sessions with her as his facilitator she would never have met Aris. Carlos died to save his family from gang violence and there was still a deep ache in her heart for her lost friend.

Thoughts of Colleen Stevens-Drake, her best friend in the states, made her smile. Colleen's cocky attitude and her sensitive heart had helped Sarah through her messy divorce and without her suggestion, Carlos would have never begun his sessions with Sarah. As his parole officer, Colleen's recommendation of hypnosis for anger management brought him to Sarah and therapy.

She remembered all her friends and her life before Aris. She had found stability and contentment through her work. Her successful book added clients to her practice and rebuilt her confidence after her husband ended their marriage for another woman. Bonnie Petrillo, not only a dear friend, but her therapist, had been instrumental in helping her find herself once more.

Before Aris life had been predictable. Calm. When he first spoke through Carlos she thought he was a figment of her client's imagination. How could there be such a thing as he claimed to be. Vampires just didn't exist, not in her world anyway. But as their sessions progressed and she grew to know him, her disbelief turned into curiosity, then acceptance, and then something much more.

When Carlos died and Aris took over his body, her initial thought was to run away, but his kindness and understanding drew her to him. Her trust in him led to friendship and as she learned more and more about him, ultimately to love. With him life was magical, full of passion and adventure, a tight-rope that spanned fantasy and reality. She couldn't imagine being without him.

Returning to the safe life she had lived before him was simply out of the question. She was convinced he was her soul-mate and she would be safe with him no matter the circumstances. Yet try as she might, she couldn't see into the future with him. Vampire or human? A decision she knew she would one day be compelled to make. Even though she knew she wasn't ready to decide just yet, she also knew she would love him as long as she lived. Now here she sat in London after having been kidnapped by evil vampires and taken to Spain. How could it all be possible? And yet it was.

She had no idea how long she had been staring into the fire when a muted sound close to her startled her wide awake. Her eyes opened to see Gabriela was carefully placing a tray on the table in front of the fire. On it rested a steaming mug of black coffee, a sugar bowl, a spoon and Sarah's cell phone.

"Coffee to wake you up and the phone to call Colleen once you're awake." Gaby kissed her friend's cheek. "Take your time. I plan to sit in the corner to study Shakespeare as much as I can during 'Sarah Watch.' Frankly, this is the first quiet time I have had in days. I look forward to it."

"It appears I'm going to need a little while more to recover. I'm not always sure where I am." She spoke slowly. "I feel as if I'm still in a dream. It was pretty awful." She turned to Gabriela. "I was so worried about all of you and I didn't know how I was going to get out so that I could warn you." Sarah trembled, wrapped her robe a little closer around her, then smiled. "But I'm here now and I'm sure this coffee is going to be the best I've ever had."

Gabriela sat on the edge of the chair facing Sarah and leaned toward her, gazing directly into her blue eyes. "I want you to know I am here if you wish to discuss your ordeal and I am silent if you wish to be silent. I am your friend."

"I know that and I'm so grateful to have you in my life. To have all of you in my life."

"Now just rest." The tall dark woman rose from her chair, picking up a leather bound volume of Shakespeare from the coffee table. "I will not leave you. I will be right here on the other side of the room if you need anything."

Sarah sipped her coffee and felt greatly comforted by the genuine affection of her Immortal friend.

. . . .

Colleen laughed into the phone when she heard Sarah's voice from across the ocean. "You are the only person I know who would go to London and take off on a yoga retreat."

"I know; it seemed like a good idea at the time."

"Poor Gaby. How did she fare?"

"She was great." Sarah glanced at the Immortal curled in a chair across the room, the volume of Shakespeare resting on her lap. She appeared to be sleeping, but Sarah knew she was repeating the memorized lines of one of his plays to herself. "How are you and Bob? And how's that sweet baby girl of yours?"

"We're all fine. What is going on with Carlos and the art world of London?"

It had been days since Sarah heard anyone refer to Aris as 'Carlos'. It was only humans who called him by that name, the name of her dear dead friend who had become host to the essence of the bodiless vampire. For months she thought in vain of ways to have everyone call him by his true name. In conversation she caught herself time and again remembering to refer to him as 'Carlos' barely in the nick of time.

She answered her friend, "He's doing really well. He's being courted by an art agent who actually deals with members of the royal house."

"What's up with that? Is he going to stay over there?"

Sarah could hear her friend's baby laughing in the background. For just a brief moment she felt homesick. "No, not permanently. But he won't be able to come home as soon as we thought. He's going to be touring." She laughed at herself. Touring was a strange word for vampire war. She wondered what Colleen would say if she were told he was training an army of the undead to do hand-to-hand battle in the Pyrenees.

"When are you coming home?"

"That sort of depends on Bonnie. She said she could work with my therapy clients for a couple of weeks. I don't know what she has on her agenda, but I'd like to stay a bit longer, so, if she has the time, I'll be here until the end of the month. I'd like to travel with him for a while. I've never really seen much of England and it's a perfect season." Sarah was silently grateful she had a colleague such as Bonnie. She had gladly taken over Sarah's practice while she traveled and Sarah knew she could trust her friend to treat her clients well.

"Well, we miss you. I know you're having a ball but don't forget to come home."

"I won't. Miss you too. Take care of that handsome husband of yours and kiss the baby for me. I'll check in soon."

"We all love you. Don't forget that."

"Same here. Talk to you soon." She placed the telephone on the table and stared into the glowing embers of the dying fire. She pondered the dual life she was leading. *"How can I choose one over the other and yet, how can I continue to live in two completely separate worlds simultaneously."* She found no answers in the glowing coals.

CHAPTER 5

Shouting and the clash of metal against metal could be heard from the courtyard at the foot of the tower. DeMarco hurried to the window. In the rubble below, he could see two vampires battling to the death. A huge crowd surrounded them laughing and shouting and pushing one another. Before his eyes and without cause, another fight broke out and, within a minute, all of the spectators had become combatants. Knives were drawn and vampires fell dead in the dust.

"Guard!" He rushed to the door. In an instant five of his personal bodyguards stood at his bidding. "Go to the courtyard, stop the fighting and get rid of the bodies. Go. Now."

"My Lord?" Julian stepped into the room. "I have news from London."

DeMarco pulled a chair close to the window and sat, watching his men clean up the mess left from the conflict. "Yes, what have you to tell me?"

Julian was a young vampire, changed against his will to fight for Spain. Weak and frightened as a human, once bitten, he surrendered completely to his new powerful and wicked undead nature and fell easily into the vampire life. He had become DeMarco's aide and confidant since the Queen's treachery.

"The woman is living in a flat with one of the Immortals. She is surrounded by them night and day. It has been impossible to find access to her." It was obvious by his tone Julian feared the reaction of his King.

Leaping to his feet, DeMarco flew across the room and grabbed Julian by the shirt, shouting in the face of his servant, "Impossible? What do you mean impossible?"

His voice shaking, he replied. "If any of our people are seen by the Immortals, they will know what we are. We don't want them to find us out. Who knows where they will take her if they know we are coming for her."

"I see." Releasing his grip on the young vampire, the King walked to the window and stared out in silence. Julian waited to be dismissed.

DeMarco's words were thoughtful. "Then we will send a human. They would never suspect a human. Find the general. Tell him to find a corrupt man being held for food in one of our prisons. Offer him eternal life rather than being dinner if he completes the task. I want Sarah Hagan brought here to me, no excuses." Menacingly he walked slowly toward Julian. "Do you understand?"

"Yes, Sire. I do. But what of the war? What of the Queen?"

"Be damned the war! Be damned the Queen!" His face turning crimson, he shouted, "Do you dare question me? Do as I say or be thrown into the fire."

"Yes Sire," he whispered as he fled from the room, quickly shutting the door behind him.

CHAPTER 6

Aris paced the floor outside the closed chamber doors. Bartholomew had agreed to see him as soon as the twelve members of the Council were assembled. Sounds of heavy chairs scraping against the stone floor escaped through the door as the appointed leaders of the Catacombs took their places. At last, when all was silent, the huge doors swung open. Richard stepped forward to lead his friend into the chamber.

"So Aris, what news do you bring us from Spain?" Bartholomew, Head Council, was the only one standing, his long black councilor's robe hung open over his expensive modern business suit and tie.

"As you know," Aris replied to the question, "there is now civil war between the King and Queen. This gives us precious additional time to make ready to attack. They both want the Infinity Diaries and they will stop at nothing until they possess them or they are all extinguished. While they battle one another, we must step up our training. The weapons are at the ready. I have spoken to the commanders and the troops are coming along, but we must escalate our labors. The Spanish coven's civil war does give us some extra days, yet time is still of the essence. We must hasten to Spain. There can be no battles in England. If there is, the humans will know of us and our world will be destroyed. Without our existence, the human race will become food for DeMarco's minions. There must be no battles in England."

Silence hung heavy as Bartholomew glanced from one Council member to another. At last he spoke. "And what of this human, this Sarah Hagan? Where is she?"

"She is above ground and safe at the moment."

One of the female members stood. Her voice was soft and clear and all turned to look toward her when she spoke. "This Sarah was in the presence of the King and Queen in Spain?"

"Yes."

"Why did they capture this human?"

"They wish to kill her for her actions when they were all human together in a century long ago. They hate her for her past and fear her for her knowledge of them in the present. She knows much."

"And what has she to tell?"

"All that she saw and heard; the lay of the castle, the thoughts of our enemies. She was among them and knows their treachery has no bounds."

Another Councilor spoke up. "Aris, what did she tell you of them?"

"I believe no one can speak for Sarah. She must speak for herself if we can keep her safe. I request that she be brought to the Catacombs for sanctuary. When she is here, you may question her your honorable selves. She needs our protection due to what she has seen and for her loyalty to the Immortals."

Everyone was still, waiting. Bartholomew broke the silence at last. "Bring a human to the Catacombs? Do you have any idea what you ask? It is against the basic law of our society to bring a human into our world."

"Her willingness to tell us all she learned has put her life at great risk. We are unable to protect her in her world. She was kidnapped from our safekeeping once and it can happen again. Only here, beneath ground, will she be safe. Only under our protection will she be free to share what she knows and help us defeat the Spanish."

Bartholomew remembered the trial of Aris. He remembered the tale told of the modern woman who was the reincarnation of the sixteenth century soul-mate of the tortured vampire. The Head Councilor knew without asking the true reason Aris petitioned for the human to come below ground. He could not bear to lose her again. And Bartholomew understood.

He spoke. "I will ask for an audience with Queen Akira. She must make the final decision." The other members of the Council murmured among themselves, disconcerted by the thought of a human among them, a human without desire to become Immortal. "When our business is complete, I will seek a discussion with the Queen."

"There is more to discuss?"

"Yes, Aris. Sebastian has a new member of the training corps to introduce to you. She arrived while you were in Spain." Bartholomew beckoned the guard to open the great doors and Sebastian entered followed by the newcomer.

"Sebastian, brother." Aris embraced his friend. "And who is this warrior?" He smiled as he extended his hand in friendship to the woman who stood before him.

"Kitsuko." The petite young Asian woman tilted her head and placed the palms of her small hands together in front of her chest in greeting.

"Kitsuko is a jujitsu master and will train the troops in evasion and techniques to turn the enemy's strength against themselves. She was made in ancient Japan." The young woman tilted her head forward and lowered her gaze to the floor, appearing to be embarrassed to be the subject of conversation.

When he realized the female was not going to speak, Sebastian continued, "As a child, a traveling monk came to her village. He told fascinating stories of the first fighting monks to be trained at his monastery. He told tales of their great physical prowess and high spiritual powers. It was from that day forth, that her wish above all things was to become one with that unique order. In her twelfth year, she ran away from her village, traveling in disguise as a young boy. Females were not allowed at the monastery and she was determined to find a way to be accepted."

Aris caught her eye and smiled. The corners of her red lips turned up and she closed her eyes as she tilted her head toward him. He couldn't imagine anyone so small and delicate in a battle.

Sebastian continued. "Kitsuko began as a servant to the monks and as time passed, she pleaded to be accepted into the order. Because of her diminutive size, the trials and tests presented her could have been overwhelming, yet her amazing speed was the great equalizer with her opponents. Taken in and trained at last, her skills were so exceptional that, soon, her fame began to spread.

"The young monk came to the attention of a small coven of Immortals living near the monastery. Their leader began to hear new stories of a great warrior in training. She decided to visit the cloister to see for herself if all the tales she heard were true. Spending but a short time with the legendary fighter, the coven leader realized that this powerful force was, in fact, a female. Intrigued, she had the young monk watched closely by members of the coven and was soon even more impressed by the reports, not just with Kitsuko's physical ability, but also with her honor and integrity. Eventually, Kitsuko was approached and courted to join the Immortals. When she was offered eternal life, she agreed and it was there she was changed. Her fighting skill is unique and powerful. She is brave and loyal, coming to us the moment she found the Catacombs had need of recruits."

Aris placed his hands together and, responding in kind, tipped his head toward the woman, returning her respect and honor.

"We welcome you," Aris spoke. "We are grateful for your assistance. Will you join us on the training floor tomorrow?"

Kitsuko nodded her head in agreement. Sebastian smiled at his friend before turning to lead the new captain from the Council meeting.

The sound of the great doors once again being opened signaled Aris it was also time for him to leave. He bowed his head toward the assembly who held his and Sarah's fate in their hands as he slowly backed out of the chamber.

· · · · · · · · · · · · · · · · · · ·

Sarah circled her traveling bag much the same way a lioness surveys her prey. Chuckling, Gabriela sat on the edge of the bed.

"It is not as if you are traveling to another planet. Anything you need, we are able to provide." She noticed her friend's hands tremble as she folded a blouse to pack in the open suitcase. "Sarah, are you frightened to go to the Catacombs? You know you are in no danger from any of us."

"I know. It isn't that." She sat next to her friend.

"Well?"

"It's just being below the ground. I'm not really fond of caves and pitch dark and rocks and cold."

"Your mental image of the Catacombs is simply an image, not as it truly is. It is warm and bright. The surroundings are marvelous, a perfect blend of modern and ancient. You are to be welcomed by all who live there."

"I know. But meeting the Council? That is a little bit scary. You have to admit that. I'm used to being with you and Richard and Aris, just the three of you. I know you. I'm comfortable with you. I can't imagine what it's going to feel like to be surrounded by nothing but Immortals, to be the only human on the block." Her chin trembled as she tried to grin.

"One of we three will be with you any time you need us. If you wish human companionship, we will bring you above ground. But you must be kept safe until we march on Spain. Once the Spanish coven is no more, you will no longer be in any danger. Your life can return to normal. You see, Sarah, Aris will not leave you and without him, our cause is lost. Only with you safe in the Catacombs will he take his position as commander of the army."

"I understand." Sarah rose and resumed her packing knowing her life would never be what Gaby called normal again. After a moment she spoke. "I really have stepped through the looking glass and now I'm on my way to Wonderland. Who would have ever thought?"

CHAPTER 7

"I am so sorry, sweeting, but I must bind your eyes." Richard drove while Gabriela sat by his side. Aris and Sarah rode in the back seat as the car made its way through the crowded early evening London traffic. "No human may ever know the entrance to the Catacombs." He tied a black silk scarf over her eyes then took her hand in his.

"I understand." Her voice was shaking as she answered.

Gabriela turned at the sound. "Sarah, do not be afraid. All is well."

A nervous laugh escaped Sarah's throat as she tried to speak. "Easy for you to say."

Gabriela reached into the back of the car to pat her friend on the hand. "No fears. Aris has worked like a madman to create a place for you that will be comfortable for you. We are all here to stand by you. Your stay will be made as pleasant as those of us who love you can make it. And you will be safe from harm. Soon we travel to Spain and this will all be behind you. You will no longer be in danger and can return to your human world."

Her human world. Sarah thought about her friends in Chicago. Colleen, Bob and their daughter, Collette, her godchild. Bonnie, her therapist and friend. Maggie, her assistant who always made her laugh. When she telephoned them, they had all readily accepted her story that she was going to stay in England a few additional weeks to travel. Bonnie had been more than willing to help by taking over her practice while she was gone. Maggie would step in whenever she was needed. She was happy to have some free time to spend with her new boyfriend.

Sarah loved her human friends. She missed them. She longed to share her other life with them. Her secret caused a deep gap in their relationships only Sarah felt. Her mind raced between her two worlds as the car drew to a halt.

"We have arrived." Aris spoke softly. "Here, take my hand. I will lead you."

She felt the warmth of his hand on hers as the car door opened. Carefully, she stepped out. The atmosphere around her was close and moist. There was no light shining through the black silk that bound her eyes. She knew there was no turning back. Aris squeezed her hand, wrapping his free arm around her waist to guide her into the deep cavern of his world.

. . . .

A gentle breeze touched Sarah's hair and the air she breathed was warm and sweet. The four friends had walked for what seemed an eternity to her. They maneuvered stairs and countless corridors speaking only when necessary, Aris guiding her confidently forward. The floor beneath her feet changed from hard stone to soft carpet. Their movements no longer echoed on the walls.

"We are here." He untied the silk binding her eyes. "Here are your rooms."

Even though the light in the room was soft, her eyes had been bound for such a long time, she blinked furiously. As she became accustomed to the light, she saw the wondrous room that surrounded her. Aris had created a palace for her.

The walls were covered in pale blue silk brocade. An over-stuffed sofa and chair upholstered in the softest pink velvet sat before a fireplace blazing in welcome. The white marble mantle held an antique porcelain clock flanked by blond cherubs on both sides. Pink and white roses rested on the table before the fireplace. Perfect white marble lamps with pale, pale pink silk shades sat on the side tables.

"It's beautiful." She wrapped her arms around Aris and buried her face in his shoulder, taking in the intoxicating fragrance of his skin.

"Come." He took her hand. "See your bed chamber." He led her from the room as Richard and Gabriela sat quietly gazing into the fire.

A four poster bed large enough for a whole family waited for her. The bed hangings and spread were white satin; the walls were covered by tapestries. Thick silk Persian carpets adorned the floor. Sconces mounted on either side of the bed radiated the soft light of a perfect sunset.

The bathroom was appointed with a huge claw foot tub and pedestal sink as well as all the necessities to fulfill her human needs.

He watched her closely as she examined every inch of the beautifully decorated room before her. "Will you be comfortable here?"

Turning to him, she smiled. "Aris, how can I ever express my gratitude? You have given me a haven of safety that looks like Versailles. How in the world did you do this so quickly?"

He laughed. "Super powers, remember?"

"How could I ever forget?"

"Are you hungry?"

"There's a kitchen too?"

"Not a full kitchen. You have a small pantry and a place to brew coffee and tea. Your meals will be delivered to you. There is a call button in the pantry. If you desire anything at any time, simply press the button. One of our women has been assigned to assist you with anything you might need. She will bring your food and keep your quarters for you. If you like, we can summon her now so that you may meet her this evening."

"At the moment, I don't know what I would like. I'm amazed at this home you've created for me. It is so beautiful, so royal." She gazed at the lights. "Even below ground without windows or sunlight, the room is warm and bright and welcoming."

"See here?" Lightly touching one of the wall sconces, he changed the brilliance of the globes. "You are able to change the light to match whatever time of day you choose. Watch as the light changes from sunset to sunrise with the touch of a finger." Again he reached toward the sconce. "And now, mid-day."

"How did you do that? What are those globes made of?"

"Immortal light. There are many wonders in the Catacombs. Tomorrow we will begin to show you, but for now, rest. I will wait with the others while you dress for bed. Tomorrow morning you meet with the Council and Queen Akira."

Sarah stiffened at his words.

"Have no fear. You are safe here. All who live underground know of your visit. They all are grateful you chose to come among us to aid in the planning of the battle to come."

"I'm not afraid, just a little anxious."

"I understand. Now take your time to bathe and dress for sleep. I will be waiting." He stepped from the room, closing the tall white door behind him. Sarah stood in the center of the chamber, her eyes drinking in the opulence that surrounded her.

"*It truly is Wonderland and tomorrow, I meet the Queen.*"

. . . .

Lying in the warm bed covered with a thick down comforter, Sarah drifted in and out of slumber. After her bath, Aris had called for Jane Howard, her attendant. Her attendant? How strange it was to her to have someone to meet her needs. She had taken care of herself since she was sixteen and now, once again, she was in the charge of another being.

Jane was young and beautiful. She was shy and cast her eyes down when they met. Sarah liked her immediately yet she wasn't sure she liked the white wolf that entered the room with Jane. He sat rock still by the door as the human and the Immortal exchanged greetings. Sarah was glad Aris, Gabriela and Richard were with her. A wild animal sitting in her living space staring at her was yet another new and strange experience. Since Aris entered her life it seemed every day had been filled with nothing but new and strange experiences.

The soft texture of the sheets brought memories of nights in her bed in her Chicago apartment. She remembered the sensual dreams she had had of Aris. He made love to her over and over in her night-time fantasies, yet kisses were all they shared in the real world. There were times when she wanted him so deeply it became the sweetest of pain. She wrapped her arms across her chest, curling up on her side as she put her craving for him out of her mind.

At last Sarah drifted into a sweet, deep sleep while Aris watched over her during her first night in the Catacombs. He knew he would not be able to stay with her as he wished. His duties to the army would take most of his time until the Immortals left to fight in Spain so he relished this night watching her sleep. He valiantly overcame his desire to hold her and caress her, to make her truly his body and soul.

CHAPTER 8

The fragrance of coffee brewing roused Sarah from a deep sleep. She opened her eyes to the white bed canopy floating above her. She adjusted the wall lamps to mid-morning light and threw back the covers.

"Sarah?" Gabriela's voice was soft as she called from the next room so as not to awake her in case she was still asleep.

"Come in." She slipped on her robe and slippers as Gaby entered. "I have coffee for you and Jane will bring your breakfast when you are ready."

"Coffee will do just fine." She reached for the mug held out to her then sat cross-legged on her bed. "Where is Aris?"

"He had a meeting with the commanders this morning. Did you sleep well?"

Sarah laughed as she replied. "Like the dead. Really, I haven't had such a wonderful night's sleep in such a long time. Thank you all so much for taking such good care."

"We are pleased to make you comfortable. Take your time to dress. Let me know when you wish your breakfast. Your usual scrambled eggs this morning?"

"That sounds great. I think I'll just snuggle down for a bit and drink my coffee before I dress. Would you mind?"

"Not at all. I will wait in the sitting room until you are ready." Gabriela closed the door behind her as Sarah plumped her pillows, then leaned back to enjoy her morning coffee.

Although she felt disoriented in these strange surroundings, all of her fear had faded with her sleep. She somehow felt comfortable. It was as if she belonged there. She didn't even mind that there were no windows in her rooms. The Immortal light made up for the lack of sun and she knew that anytime she wanted to return to the surface, Aris would see that it was done. When she thought about her appearance before the Council, her heart began to race. She wondered how she would be able to help them.

As she took her last sip from the cup a strange electronic beeping sounded from the other room. It lasted but a moment and then was silenced. Gaby rapped on the closed door. "Sarah, Aris wishes to speak with you. May I come in?"

"Of course."

The device Gabriela handed to Sarah resembled a cell phone in many ways, yet there were no numbers and no display. It was small enough to fit in the palm of her hand. "Where do I speak into it?"

"Just place it anywhere in the room and talk as if he were standing next to you. It is the communication device we use below ground. It operates on the same power source as the lighting. The technology was developed by Queen Akira when she built the Catacombs." She laughed. "We had an Immortal version of your human cell phone centuries ago."

"Sarah." Aris' voice was crisp and clear.

"Good morning Aris. If it is morning. I have no idea what time it is."

"Shortly after eight AM. I wanted to make sure you slept well and that all your needs are being met."

"I slept wonderfully."

"Good. Gabriela will show you how to use the communication

device. Carry it with you at all times."

"When will I see you?"

"I have a weapons session this morning with Sebastian and the new captain. As soon as I am free I will come to you. When you feel hungry for breakfast, call Jane. She is looking forward to knowing you. You are the first human she has seen since she came to the Catacombs hundreds of years ago."

"Aris, when will I go before the Council? I have no idea what to expect and I get flushed whenever I think about it."

"Do not fret. They all look forward to speaking with you and are very grateful that you agreed to come below to meet with them. After the interview, if you like, I will be pleased to show you a little bit of our Catacombs."

"That sounds wonderful."

"I will contact you later. If there is an opportunity, it is my wish we spend some leisure time together before your audience. I know you must be full of questions. Now, I must rush off or I will keep the troops waiting."

"Alright, talk to you soon."

"Goodbye, sweet Sarah. I am glad you slept well."

Sarah turned to speak to Gabriela only to find she had stepped from the room. Then, as if it were a normal morning, the mortal woman made her bed, dressing for the day in a dark gray business suit and heels.

• • • • • • • • • • • • • • • • • •

"Your breakfast has been ordered and it will be here soon." Gaby had just finished calling Jane when Sarah entered the room. "If you do not mind, I will leave you to her care while I go to Richard. He meets with the other commanders and wishes for me to join them."

"No, I'm fine." Sarah was amazed that her words matched her

emotions. She was below the ground surrounded by the undead and had no idea how to get out if she wanted to. She was dependent on the Immortals for her every need. There was no natural light or ventilation. No one knew where she was or would believe it if she told them. She was set to go before the lawmakers and rulers of a society that could extinguish her at a moment's notice, yet she was hungry and looking forward to her breakfast. She wondered at her sanity. Perhaps it had finally given way. Everything that was happening to her seemed perfectly natural and normal. Yes, she was quite sure she was mad. And she didn't mind. That was the only thing that truly frightened her. That she wasn't the least bit frightened.

"We will be with you when you meet with the Council. Richard, Aris and I, all of us, will be there if you need us. There is nothing to fear."

"I'm not frightened anymore. It's so strange. I feel I belong here, although I can't say how I'd feel if I didn't have the three of you."

"Well, you have us." A soft knock on the entrance door brought their conversation to a close. Gabriela opened it and Jane stepped into the room. She carried a covered tray, which she placed on the coffee table.

"Did you sleep well, Dr. Hagan?"

"Please call me Sarah."

"Sarah then, would you like me to light the fireplace?"

"Gaby, how in the world can a fire burn here? How is the air down here so clean and fresh?"

"Jane will answer all your questions. I will leave the two of you to become acquainted." Gabriela brushed her lips against the human's cheek. "Richard and I will join you and Aris later today. We three will accompany you to your meeting."

"Bye Gaby, thank you." The door closed silently as Gabriela left Sarah's rooms.

"Here Jane, sit down. The fire can wait." Sarah patted the sofa, indicating a spot for the young woman to sit next to her. "Where is your wolf this morning?"

"He waits for me outside the door. I could see he frightened you last night and I most certainly do not wish to add to your discomfort."

"I'm not uncomfortable. Please, bring him inside." As she spoke, she lifted the cover from the tray. A perfect breakfast waited there for her. Jane brought the wolf into the chamber and motioned for him to sit near the door. He waited so patiently, so quietly.

"You may bring him closer."

The vampire motioned to the huge animal to come. He rose gracefully from his haunches moving slowly to sit near his mistress.

Sarah reached her hand tentatively toward his broad white muzzle. "He is so beautiful. Do you think I might touch him?"

"Hawke, be very still." The wolf responded instantly to the soft command issued by Jane Howard. "There Sarah, you may stroke his nose. He will not move until I grant it."

Surprised at the texture of his coat, Sarah spoke quietly as if she thought she might frighten him. "He's so soft. I don't know when I've ever felt such soft, thick fur. Wherever did you find him?"

"I did not find him. He found me. It was he that brought me here to the Catacombs."

"May I ask why you wanted to come underground?"

"It was not my wish. I know not why he brought me here. I was tattered and torn and close to death when I opened my eyes surrounded by Immortals and guarded by Hawke." Jane scratched his ears and the great animal made a resonant rumbling sound deep in his throat. "He has not left my side since that day."

"Jane, I don't mean to pry, but how long have you been an Immortal?"

"You do not pry. Please feel free to ask anything. I will be more than happy to answer all of your questions that I am able to answer. I was brought here in the sixteenth century from the court of

Queen Elizabeth I."

"Are there many Immortals from the Tudor reign?"

"A few. There are few humans who have changed. Through all of the millennia of our history there are only a few thousand of us."

"Do you all live in the Catacombs?"

"Oh no, many live human lives above ground. It is mainly the royal court and the scientists who live below."

Sarah ate slowly, yet the food stayed as warm as it was when it was brought to her. "Why doesn't my breakfast get cold?"

"The tray keeps it warm. There are some of those who live here who still enjoy human food so we have developed ways to keep things fresh until cooked and warm until eaten. It all must seem so strange to you."

"Strange, yes, but so very intriguing." She poured more coffee from the silver pot sitting on the tray. "Will you tell me more about your way of life?" Sarah settled back into the cushions of the sofa as she spoke. "The air? It's so pure down here. How do you manage that?"

"Our entire atmosphere is controlled by Immortal alchemical energy. When our Queen came to earth, she brought great knowledge as a scientist but she had no idea how to adapt earthly elements for Immortal use. Then the day came when the Master Keeper of Records joined the Catacombs. He had lived a mortal life as a scientist before he joined us. With his help, she was able to adapt the formulas from her home planet to the earth's atmosphere and components. The two fashioned the ancient science of alchemy."

"But no one practices alchemy any more, Jane."

"It is true. Only a few of the ancients were taught by the Queen. There are no humans who have the formulas in your present time. Only Queen Akira and the Master Keeper. And only our society today uses an energy that is in harmony with this planet. Our life leaves no scars on the earth or its inhabitants."

"But what of your vampire nature? You drink human blood. You take human life. Isn't that leaving a scar on humanity?"

"May I ask you whether a lioness leaves a scar on nature when she eats a zebra? Does a man leave a scar on nature when he eats a fish? We do what we must to survive. Immortals can live as humans and subsist on human food most of the time if they wish, but there are instances in the existence of an Immortal when they are driven by the desire for human blood. In the past, nothing less than taking human life could satisfy a fire that seared our veins without ceasing.

"In long ago centuries before written human history, Immortals were forced by the demand of their physical nature to drink until a living body was empty. Humans were sacrificed for our survival, but even then we were taught to be discerning in our feeding; only evil humans were to be taken. The blood lust is rare for a mature Immortal, perhaps once in a century or two. In more modern times your blood banks acted as our feeding grounds. Now we have synthetic blood created through alchemy and no more is human life, good or evil, spent for our survival. We now are able to drink not just for survival, but for pleasure without any harm to your race."

Sarah didn't speak. She sat staring into space, processing all she had just heard. After a few moments Jane broke the silence. "What else would you like to know?"

"Do you have places where you gather with your friends besides your home?" Jane looked bewildered. "Shops? Restaurants? I know it may sound silly to you, but I have no idea of what life below ground would be like."

"There are places where we congregate, public houses you might call them. Our world is much like the royal world of early England although, as you can see, we have made quite a few improvements." She laughed. "Of course, those who live above ground live a very modern human life, but when they enter the Catacombs, they leave that world behind.

"For those of our kind who enjoy human food there are restaurants where they may eat. There are Sanguinarias where those who wish to drink the alchemical drink at any time may do so. As I told you, even those Immortals who choose to live human lives and eat human food must drink blood at intervals. If you wish, I will take you on a tour of the main district."

"I would like it very much. I want to learn everything about how you live."

"I am pleased to help you. I have not seen or spoken to a human since I was brought here. I wish to learn about you as well."

"It looks as if we're well suited to one another." Sarah's hand still rested on the animal sitting next to her. She stroked his head as she spoke. "Hawke is such a strange name for a wolf. How did you find that name?"

"When I was changed, he never left my side. Bartholomew as head if the Council was the one who changed me and he told me the wolf watched me throughout the metamorphosis with the eye of a hawk. I wanted a name to call my savior, so Hawke it became."

"Will you tell me that story?"

The communication device began its beeping to announce a call. Sarah looked at it dumbly then smiled. "How do I activate this?"

Jane slid her fingers over a bar that had gone unnoticed by her new friend. "Here, just like this. To shut it down, reverse the pattern."

"Sarah? Have you eaten yet?" Aris' voice always made her heart smile and her flesh tingle.

"Yes, Jane is here now."

"Good, I will be with you shortly."

"I'm looking forward to that." Her eyes lit with excitement.

"Soon my love. Farewell until then."

Sarah closed the circuit as Jane gathered the empty dishes and tray. "Jane, when will I get to see you again? I have enjoyed talking with you so much. I look forward to more conversation."

"I have been assigned to you for your stay. Just use the buzzer to summon me or use the device. Turn it on and speak my name, Jane Howard. I, too, look forward to seeing you." Her voice grew very soft. "I have been quite alone in the Catacombs except for Hawke. I have few friends. As you know, I did not choose this life. At times, I resent it. I would rather have died. To this very day, I miss my humanity. I hope you understand what it means to me to come to know you, to remember my life as it was."

"Thank you, Jane. You will always be welcome here."

"Good day, Sarah." As Jane moved toward the door, the great white animal rose, stretched and trotted along at her side.

. . . .

When Aris stepped through Sarah's door he was surprised to see Richard and Gabriela already sitting comfortably on her sofa. He had hoped for some private time with her before her interview with the Council. He hadn't had a moment truly alone with her since her rescue. He longed to simply hold her in his arms, to kiss her.

"Brother." Richard stood to embrace him. Aris stooped to kiss Gabriela on her cheek. "Sarah will join us in a moment. She spent the early morning with Jane Howard and she wanted to freshen up before she saw you."

Aris paced in front of the fireplace. "She must be frightened to meet with the Council."

"Relax and sit down. She is fine. She is actually looking forward to it. She and Jane have made such a hit, she wants to meet as many Immortals as she can. She is an amazing woman, Aris."

"I know." He sat next to Gabriela on the sofa. Leaning forward, his elbows resting on his knees, he turned to face Richard as he spoke. "But how can she not be afraid? Landing in a city made solely of blood drinkers. Attending a meeting of the Grand Council without any of us with her. Standing alone before thirteen Immortals she has never seen before. She is amazing, but she is not a super woman. How can she not be afraid?"

Gabriela responded. "I asked her just that when we arrived. She said she feels more safe here than she felt on the streets of Chicago. I really have no understanding of it yet she seems to fit here. And she knows it too."

"She fits in her world above ground. She is a human taking a vacation in a different reality. To live here permanently, to become one of us? Sarah is not ready and probably never will be." There was sadness in Aris' voice as he spoke.

As Richard stood to respond, the bedroom door opened. Sarah joined them smiling. "I feel like I've got bats in my stomach, I'm so excited." She recognized her friends' concern. "Please, don't worry about me. I don't even need you to sit in the meeting with me. I'll be fine alone. In fact, I prefer meeting the Council alone." She turned toward the door, leading the other three, who followed just steps behind her. "Let's get going."

They left her rooms, walking silently through the corridors. The Immortals were silent out of concern. Sarah was silent to keep from babbling maniacally about nothing. When they reached the tall carved double doors leading into the Audience Chamber, the three vampires embraced her, then watched as the guards swung open the huge doors and their human friend stepped inside.

Aris stood silent for a moment before he turned to his friends. Gabriela could see the concern in his eyes and she reached to embrace him. "Come, let us go to the Sanquinaria for a drink. She will be fine."

"I know, I know. I just am concerned for her in there alone."

"That is how she wished it to be. Come. Standing here is no help to either Sarah or to you."

Aris nodded in agreement and the three Immortals walked slowly down the corridor toward the blood bar.

CHAPTER 9

She entered the huge room barren except for a tapestry hanging on the wall and a long table with thirteen chairs gathered around it; the largest situated at one end, the other twelve spaced six to a side. The men and women seated around the table all wore long black robes over their modern clothing. All thirteen in the room were very aware of Sarah's mortality and very careful to sit quietly, not wanting to frighten her.

A tall Immortal rose from the end chair and extended his hand in greeting. "Hello Sarah, I am Bartholomew." He motioned to a guard to bring another seat to be placed beside his. "Please, be comfortable. We are very grateful you have come to us and we understand how difficult all this must be for you."

As she sat, the guard placed a water carafe and glass on the table in front of her. She smiled. "It's not so difficult as it is unnerving, but I am glad to help in any way that I can."

He introduced each of the members of the Council to their guest. Larence was a scientist aiding the Master Keeper of Records, Chanelle was a perfect Snow White look-alike with pure alabaster skin and raven black hair. Brilliant red curls cascading down her back and one long earring dangling to her collar bone gave the one named Adelaide the appearance of a free-spirited artist, yet she was second in command of the Council. Bartholomew continued introductions around the table until each member was presented and welcomed Sarah.

At last he sat next to her. "If it pleases you, Sarah, what can you tell us of the Spanish coven and its rulers?"

Sarah explained all she knew about the Spanish castle and the surrounding terrain. They asked questions about the Spanish army and their weapons. She had no information about the troops, but she shared all she had heard of the conversation between King DeMarco and Queen Mariska and anything else she could remember she thought might help the Immortals. When the interview was finished, she wished she could have told them more, yet they thanked her, telling her she had been a great service to them.

Bartholomew rose and told the guard to show Sarah to Queen Akira's chambers. Sarah's heart began to race. Even though her interview with the Council had been comfortable and without incident, she became anxious as she anticipated standing before the Queen of the Immortals.

CHAPTER 10

The guard ushered Sarah down a long hall and into a magnificent antechamber where she waited to meet Queen Akira. The walls were covered in cream-colored velvet and there were many high-backed comfortable leather chairs scattered around the room. The lighting globes glowed softly, casting a warm light on the silver tea service resting on the table near her chair. Her meeting with the High Council had gone smoothly, yet she couldn't control her uneasy feeling as she anticipated her audience with the Queen.

She had been nervous before meeting the Council, however, she had no fear of them. As she waited for their monarch it was quite a different story. An alien. An ancient being from another planet. As she entered the ante-chamber, the guard spoke softly as he showed her to a seat. "Fear not, the Queen is kind and fair-minded." Sarah smiled a tentative smile at him as he left the room. Yet as she waited alone to meet the Queen her stomach was tied in knots and the palms of her hands were wet with perspiration.

The sound of an opening door startled her as Sebastian entered the chamber. He greeted her warmly and she was grateful to see a friendly face.

"Her Majesty is ready to see you now."

Sarah rose; she felt light-headed and dizzy. Smoothing her suit skirt, she took just a moment to compose herself before she followed him into the royal audience chamber.

No Immortal light illuminated this room. Instead, candles by the hundreds cast dancing shadows on the strange being seated on the majestic throne before her. A second unoccupied seat was positioned near the alien monarch.

"Welcome." The voice of the Queen was soft yet commanding as she rose from her chair and glided across the floor toward the human woman. Sarah could see her legs bend and stretch as she stepped forward, but her gait was so smooth, she appeared to roll across the marble on wheels. Sarah had been afraid of what an alien would look like, but Akira was not frightening; she was beautiful. Her long silver hair reached almost to her knees, glistening as the candle light shimmered on its thick strands. She was tall and lean and her rich purple velvet robes rippled softly as she reached to touch Sarah's shoulder. Her touch was light, but without warmth or chill, as if she were an inanimate object moving through her inhuman world.

"And so you have come to our kingdom." Sarah was captivated by her strange unblinking eyes. "You are the first human to see our way of life who has no desire to become an Immortal." Her voice was as melodious as the voices of all who lived in the Catacombs, yet her demeanor was cool, aloof as would be expected of any Queen. "We appreciate the courage you show in coming below ground."

"I am grateful that you have allowed me to be here, your Majesty."

"You are here and under our protection for as long as necessary to keep you safe from harm. You are free to move about the Catacombs as you wish. I understand Jane will be attending to your needs. Ask for her guidance at any time."

Sarah wasn't sure what to expect of her audience, but she didn't think it would end so abruptly. She was startled by the sound of the great door opening as Sebastian entered the chamber.

The Queen spoke her last words. "Sarah, please enjoy the delights of the Catacombs and I know I need not caution you about revealing our presence to those above ground." Her beautiful mouth was stern as the alien female lowered herself silently onto her throne and watched as Sebastian ushered Sarah from the chamber.

CHAPTER 11

Sitting on a cold rock ledge in the heart of a frozen cave, Mariska and Esteban spoke in soft whispers so as not to be heard by the others who were standing nearby.

"The troops are coming along although the training is slow and treacherous in this deep snow."

Her forehead wrinkling in a scowl and her lips pulled tightly across her teeth, Mariska spoke angrily to her general. "I do not want to hear of your problems. We must pull this army together to march on London. It was your choice to bring them to this hell hole, now handle it."

"My Queen, it is not an easy task to hide a thousand soldiers." He was silent, looking for the words to tell the furious woman beside him his true thoughts.

"Well, what is it? Speak up."

"We know there are over two thousand Immortals. Our thousand soldiers will not be enough to defeat them even if we could surprise them. A thousand undead marching on London would be a death sentence to our cause."

Jumping to her feet, she stooped so her face was directly in front of his. Menacingly she asked, "What are you saying?"

"Within days DeMarco will leave for London. His troops are loyal to him and will fight to extinction. I have heard dissension among our people. My fear is some will flee. There are even rumors of some wishing to return to the King. Can you not put your anger aside and rejoin him in order to complete our task? To win this war?"

The sound of her hand slapping his face echoed throughout the cave. "How dare you. Now get back to work. Do your job or you will be the one who is made extinct." She spun on her heel and walked away.

CHAPTER 12

Sarah and Jane sat before the dancing fire as she waited for Aris to call for her. He was taking her on her first excursion into the center of the Immortal's underground city. Hawke lay sleeping, curled on a Persian rug close to the warmth of the blaze. At intervals he would raise his head as if he were checking on Jane to make sure she was safe with the human woman.

"You must have so many questions about our society." Jane smiled sweetly as she spoke. "Please ask anything. I will do my best to help you understand our way of life."

"Really, I'm so overwhelmed right now I don't even know what I don't know. I'm not sure where to begin." Sarah laughed at her own confused answer. "Why don't you tell me more about you? I am fascinated by your human life in the court of Elizabeth I."

The Immortal vampire sat silently gazing into her distant past.

After a moment, Sarah spoke again. "Does it pain you to speak of it?"

Brought back into the present, Jane answered. "No. My life at the royal court brought me a great deal of joy as well as a garden of sorrow. I am just not sure where to begin."

"Were you born into court life?"

"Most of my family held positions at the royal court throughout the reign of all the Tudor kings and queens. I was born in the year 1571 twelve years after Elizabeth came to the throne."

"Will you tell me about your life in the palace?"

"As a child, I was raised as all females were. I was schooled in language, music, embroidery and dance, destined to be a perfect courtier." She was silent for a moment, pensive, thinking of what might have been. Sarah waited without question.

"I was twelve years of age before I was ever brought before the Queen. I remember the awe I felt at seeing her glorious jeweled golden gown. Bright copper curls were piled high on her head and her fingers were heavy with precious stones. She absolutely glowed in the light of the candles.

"When it was time for me to be presented, I could hardly breathe. I made my very best curtsy and she laughed as she took my hand to raise me. When I lifted my gaze to hers, her eyes were such a dark brown they appeared black and they danced with delight. I remember distinctly, she said I was a lovely child. She promised when I was of a more suitable age, she would call me to be one of her maids-in-waiting.

"I could barely contain myself. It was the sole desire of every maiden in the royal house to wait on the Queen. And I had been chosen. I have no memory of the rest of that evening, my mind so lost in the great opportunity that was laid before me. My family was infinitely proud of my achievement. I was granted a new wardrobe and the very first horse I was to ever own. He was snow white with a mane thicker and a tail longer than any stallion I had ever seen. He became my constant companion when I was able to escape my lessons." Jane laughed as she remembered her human life.

A quiet rap on the door interrupted the two women.

"Come in." Sarah rose as Aris stepped into the room. Without thinking, she moved into his open arms, his soft lips covering hers, her body pressing hungrily into his. Jane rose, motioning Hawke from his sleeping place. She moved as silently as she could, but they still heard her. Sarah turned toward her smiling shyly.

"I'm sorry Jane. It seems an eternity since Aris and I have seen each other."

"Please, no apologies. I will show myself out. We will speak again soon." She cast her eyes toward the carpet as she and the white wolf passed through the door leaving the couple alone.

· · · · · · · · · · · · · · · · · · · ·

"I hope I didn't embarrass Jane by flinging myself at you. I couldn't help it. Everyone has been very kind, still I've missed you so much today."

Aris led her to the sofa. He sat, pulling her down on his lap. "I, too, have missed you." His words were put to an end as she, once again, kissed his thick tender mouth.

Desire rose in her like a hungry eagle stalking prey. She twined her fingers in his thick black hair, her kiss becoming more demanding. His body responded to her demand as arousal coursed in his vampire veins. Still sitting on his lap, she felt the power of his manhood hard against her. Melting into him she longed for him to take her. Gasping for breath, she spoke. "Please Aris, make love to me. I've never wanted anyone or anything as I want you."

Her plea brought him to his senses. "No, my sweeting." He shook his head to clear his mind then gently he took her hands in his. "Wanting you this way is torture because it is impossible as things are." He stood, lifting her to her feet. "I am in torment as you are, yet we cannot make love as human men and women can. I am not a man. It is impossible."

She wanted to weep. Her body cried out for him, yet she knew if he could control his desire so must she. Closing her eyes, she took several deep breaths to compose herself then carefully smoothed her skirt.

He held out his hand to her. "Come. There is much to do before we leave for Spain. I must stay focused." He wanted to take her in his arms once again, but knew he couldn't trust himself. "Our friends are waiting. Shall we go?"

Placing her hand in his, she spoke. "Alright, I understand." Her lips curled in a playful smile and her voice was a suggestive whisper. "But there are many other things I would rather do right now." He stared into her eyes, the back of his mouth dry with desire; the silence of the room broken only by the rasping of her breath.

A soft rap on the door jolted them from their trance. "Sarah, may I take your tray?" Jane's question was muffled by the thick wooden door that stood between them.

"Yes." Sarah opened the door for her friend. "Please come in. We were just leaving." For just a moment, her eyes brimmed with unshed tears of frustration as she moved into the corridor. "Let's go; our friends are waiting."

. . . .

Aris still held Sarah's hand as they walked the length of the corridor. She felt she was in a labyrinth, twisting and turning corner after corner. Richard and Gabriela were to meet them at a dining hall in the center of their Immortal village. Sarah nervously wondered what her companions would be eating, but Aris assured her they were visiting a restaurant that catered to those who lived above ground. She was relieved. She wasn't sure she was quite ready to see her friends drink blood from goblets as she had seen DeMarco and Mariska do when she was held prisoner in their castle in Spain.

Their footsteps echoed as the corridor turned into a narrow rocky tunnel with an incredibly high ceiling. The tunnel turned at ever tighter intervals until, quite suddenly, they stepped into an enormous cavern larger than an American football field. Sarah knew they were still underground, but it appeared as if the cavern opened straight up to the sky. Late afternoon light fell from above as if a perfect sun shown down onto the cobblestone road leading through the town center. Shops, taverns and restaurants lined the street.

Sarah's eyes found no rest as they darted from one amazing sight to another. She noticed two distinctive modes of dress. One, clothes worn by those Immortals who led human lives above ground and the other, more simple. Softer fabric. Flowing lines. Similar to Queen Akira's beautiful robe.

All of the inhabitants of the Catacombs had one thing in common. An unearthly physical beauty, ageless, timeless. Sarah felt out of place in her human skin with her human flaws, yet everyone smiled and greeted her as they passed. She was a celebrity, the first human freely allowed below ground. One who came below of her own choice to assist in a battle that had little to do with her. She was known and respected in the Immortal world.

"Aris." A soft feminine voice spoke from just behind them. Turning, they stood face-to-face with Kitsuko. "Hello."

Aris smiled, returning the slight bow given by his newest commander. He had watched her a few times on the training field and was impressed by her skill and leadership. His respect was apparent when he spoke. "Kitsuko, I would like you to meet Sarah."

Kitsuko watched as the blond woman released Aris' hand in order to shake hers. A tide of jealousy washed over her at the human touching her general with such propriety. The powerful Immortal warrior had no business being with a human. Especially when Kitsuko grew weak every time she thought of him. When she worked with her troops and he was present, it took all of her control to keep from telling him her feelings. Feelings that were present from the first moment she saw him. Sweet passions that as a warrior she had never believed it possible for her to feel and she didn't know how to deny.

Sarah sensed the animosity brewing in the air between herself and the martial artist, but didn't understand why it was there. Aris told her about his amazing new warrior, about her speed and authority. He praised her abilities to teach. Sarah had been glad he had someone so accomplished to help him. She assumed such a woman would be powerfully built to have such prowess at battle and was surprised at the diminutive size of the soldier standing in front of her. She hadn't thought she would be so feminine, so beautiful.

The two females acknowledged each other, but the greeting was without warmth or welcome. Turning to face Aris, Kitsuko smiled. "I look forward to seeing you on the training floor."

Aris lifted his hand in farewell as she continued on her way.

Sarah reached for Aris's hand once more, "Very attractive."

"Who?" Sarah motioned behind her at the retreating figure. "Oh, Kitsuko? I had not noticed, but I will be more aware the next time I see her." He laughed and kissed her softly then continued toward the restaurant.

Café tables lined the walk-way. They chose one situated beneath an awning. Filtered light shining through the soft golden fabric created interesting shadows on their faces.

"Richard and Gabriela are going to meet us here. As well as someone else who is looking forward to meeting you."

"And who is that?"

"Henry."

"Henry?"

"Yes, the Master Keeper of Records."

"Isn't he in charge of the Infinity Diaries?"

"He is."

"Aris, you've never explained, why do the Immortals keep the Diaries?"

"It is a part of our science. The Master Keeper is deeply involved in the process of human evolution and evolution of the spirit. Queen Akira came to earth originally to study the behavior of its' inhabitants and has been collecting information since her arrival. When the Keeper joined the Catacombs, he joined in her research and devised the Diaries. The Queen finds humans baffling in their habits and their emotions, how they continue to destroy their own kind for power and for pleasure. No other mammal on the planet does that. She has spent millennia striving to understand your species. In his human form, the Keeper was equally interested in humanity and was grateful as an Immortal to join in Akira's research. It was his scientific knowledge learned as a human combined with the alchemy Akira shared that made it possible to find a way to collect the information. It never occurred to either of them the Diaries would be used for other than science—to be used for evil purposes."

Sarah stopped mid-step. "Wait, I don't understand. If the Master Keeper of Records is so important, why would he want to meet me?"

"He is intrigued by your soul-chart. Remember, he had to reconstruct it after DeMarco stole it? He finds you intriguing."

"I'm not sure if I should be flattered or nervous." Sarah thought about her past life and wondered if she liked sharing it with an unknown undead.

"Flattered would suit the situation." Aris took her hand while they waited for the rest of their party.

"Aris, as I understand it, the Diaries contain the soul-chart of each human from its inception to its culmination, the journey from one incarnation to the next. But where does the soul come from and where does it go?"

"Ah, Sarah." He smiled. "The eternal question and the basis of our research and of the Diaries. What is before and what is after human life?"

They sat silently as her mind worked to absorb everything he had just told her. A gentle wind ruffled the blond curls around her face, bringing her back to the material world of the Catacombs.

"Did you feel that breeze? The temperature here is perfect. Is it like this in all the Catacombs?"

"No. Some areas are covered in snow and others are desert sand. We have created different environments to suit our moods."

"And it's all here? Underground?"

He nodded his head yes just as Richard and Gabriela reached their table. They greeted their friends warmly.

"Sarah, how do you like our Catacombs?" Gabriela gestured with her hand indicating all that surrounded them.

"I am awed by what I've seen. I want to learn everything I can about the science that runs this place."

"Well," Richard grinned as he spoke. "Here comes the one who can help you with that." He stood as a tall, white-haired man approached them. He was dressed in a dark business suit and wore an old fashioned black Homburg hat on his thick shoulder length hair. Dark green, round glasses covered his eyes.

Removing his hat, he greeted everyone at the table. When it was time to meet Sarah, he removed his dark glasses as well. She was stunned by the strange color of his eyes (neither green nor brown but something in-between) and the tenderness of his gaze.

"So, at last, I meet Sarah Hagan." He stared at her a moment before he spoke again. "I must say, you are quite what I thought you would be from your description in the Diaries."

Sarah flushed at his knowledge of her past with Diego. But his reassuring way and gentle tone soon put her at ease. She realized Richard was telling Henry how interested she was in their way of life.

The Master Keeper of Records leaned toward her as he spoke. "Sarah, please come to visit me in the Hall of Records any time. I would be honored to answer any questions that you have."

"I wonder," she thought, "if you can answer the ultimate question–why I feel so at home here beneath the earth with a city full of the undead? I wonder if there is anyone anywhere who can answer that question."

CHAPTER 13

The four vampires sat around the heavy wooden table, full goblets of rich red blood in front of each place. "What are you saying, Ricardo?" DeMarco stood, leaning menacingly toward his general as he spoke.

His voice held an unspoken challenge. "I am saying you need the Queen and her soldiers if we are to win this war."

DeMarco leaped to his feet, sweeping the goblet from the table with his arm. He shouted, "Do you dare to tell me you have not been doing your duty?"

Subdued by his Sovereign's fury, Ricardo stared at the floor as he spoke. "We have all been doing our duty. We are an army of less than one thousand. You ask us to travel to London unseen and attack the fortress of the Catacombs. You have well versed us on the lay of the land beneath the ground, yet we will be fighting on their turf. That is their first advantage. Their numbers are greater than ours. Our spies in London have reported their numbers have been increasing steadily as more and more Immortals arrive to join their forces. We need all of our people." His voice was just above a whisper as he said, "We need Esteban."

"Esteban? That traitor? I saved him from execution after he murdered his lover and how does he repay me? With treachery. Never. Now, get out of here and get to work." He turned his back as his four captains rose and left the room. Silently he stood by the window gazing over the forest that surrounded the castle. His thoughts returned to Sarah. He vowed to defeat the Immortals without Mariska, to kill Aris and to take Sarah for his own.

CHAPTER 14

"I want to make sure I call Colleen while we're above ground."
Aris and Sarah hurried down the street toward the gallery showing
his latest artwork.

"Would you like to stop now to phone her?" Aris looked around
as he spoke, always concerned for her safety when she was above
ground. She was fully confident he could protect her, but he was
not as sure. He would fight to extinction if need be, yet how many
of DeMarco's men could he defeat if set upon in numbers?

"No, I'll take a break from the show to call. We have to rush or
we'll be late and the artist should never arrive after his patrons." He
smiled at her words.

It was Aris' second art show at the London gallery and Reginald
told him earlier in the day Beatrix Sloan, one of the most prominent
agents in London, had decided to speak with him about representing
him in the London art world. It was a decision that could not be
easily made. Did he want to continue as a human? Or did he want
to return to the cloistered world of the Catacombs? And what was
to become of Sarah and him.

As they entered the gallery, which was already jammed full of
people, everyone turned toward them applauding. John Marshall,
the gallery owner from Chicago, and the London gallery owner,

Reginald Clinton, hurried forward. Reginald shook Aris' hand and led him toward a circle of very rich looking, very interested ladies, their wealthy husbands close in tow. John Marshall took Sarah's arm, leading her toward the refreshment table. Crystal champagne glasses glistened in the light from the chandelier. He handed her a glass then excused himself as he waved to another new arrival.

Sitting in a chair in a quiet corner, she marveled at Aris' amazing artwork. She remembered his first meeting with John Marshall at her mother's house during their last Christmas dinner. When John offered to look at his work, neither of them ever imagined he would so quickly become so well known in the art world. His first show in the states sold out. His paintings of ancient kingdoms and monarchs were so alive, so warm and vibrant, he was recognized as a modern master by every critic. She smiled when she thought it was only natural since he was taught by the ancient ones. His forté was painting England and its people so it was merely a matter of course that he was welcomed with open arms by the British.

She took a sip of her champagne just as she saw a tall, sleek redhead approach the group where Aris stood. She watched, grinning broadly as he mesmerized the poor woman with his smile. Sarah knew, if he wanted it, before the night was over he would have a contract with whatever terms he requested. The question was what would be his decision? Would he choose to live above ground or would he leave her and her human life to live below. Of course, there was always the ultimate solution, become Immortal like him, be with him wherever he chose. As she watched her only true love, the answer to her quandary was becoming more and more apparent.

. . . .

The cushions on the sofa in the gallery lounge were soft and comfortable. The lounge was the farthest Aris would allow Sarah to stray from him above ground. He could still see her where she sat and he made sure she was always within his line of sight. Sarah leaned back as she dialed her best friend in Chicago on her cell phone. She heard two rings then another before Colleen answered. "Hello?"

"Hi hon, it's Sarah."

She could hear her friend's baby cooing in the background. "I'm at the gallery for a showing and I thought I'd give you a ring."

"You're lucky I'm up. Collette has been fussy this week and hasn't been sleeping very well." She yawned into the phone and Sarah could hear the sound of coffee being poured on the other side of the Atlantic Ocean. It was comforting.

"I'm sorry, I didn't realize it was so early. I miss you and wanted to hear your voice."

"Yeah, you miss me alright. You're over there with Mr. Wonderful and you haven't thought of us for a minute." She laughed. "If you did, you'd be nuts. How is he? How are you for that matter?"

"We're great. He's been welcomed in an unbelievable way. I think he's going to take on an agent here."

"Yeah? What does that mean?"

"It means he'll be in England a lot more than we anticipated."

"What about you? What're you going to do about your clients, Sarah? And us? We miss you too. We don't want to lose you to the other side of the planet."

"Calm down, C. You aren't going to lose me."

"So, when are you coming home? You've already stayed longer than you thought you would and Bonnie's still holding down your fort."

"I know. Quit trying to make me feel guilty. I'll be home in a couple of weeks. By then we'll be able to sort things out. Don't worry. I'm not deserting you."

The baby started to fuss in the background. "Sorry hon, Collette is about ready to blast. She hasn't had her breakfast yet and I've got to go before she starts to wail. Love you."

"Love you, C. Talk to you soon." There was silence on the other side of the line.

. . . .

The lounge was still empty as Sarah relaxed into the sofa cushions. She was constantly astonished and in an honest state of disbelief whenever she thought about the two distinctly different worlds she inhabited.

Her life above ground. Her old friends in Chicago. The new friends she was making in the art world in London. Her business. Her home. The life she had worked so hard to build. The life that seemed to be fading into the background, becoming nothing more than a shadow of her true existence.

What was taking its place? How can you describe something completely unknown. No life. No death. Undead. Vampire. Immortal. Eternal life. Eternal love. No turning back. Eternity in a Utopian underground kingdom. A fairy tale.

Sarah's heart was racing as she imagined a future as an Immortal when two women entered the lounge laughing and chatting about the handsome genius young artist on display.

Sarah took a deep breath. Sighing, she rose from the sofa, and glanced in the mirror. She ran her fingers through her short wavy blond hair before leaving the room to join the fans of the newest (and oldest) art sensation of the decade.

As she stepped from the room she noticed an incredibly handsome tall well-dressed man lounging near the entrance to the gallery. His dark eyes followed her as she joined John Marshall and a group of people admiring one of the paintings on display.

CHAPTER 15

"Are you sure these are the latest topographical maps?" Because time mattered little, there were a few other Immortals in the Catacombs library even though it was late in the evening. Aris leaned closer to Sebastian and Richard so he didn't have to raise his voice for them to hear.

Gabriela entered the room silently, easing between the two men. She answered his question. "Yes, I checked with Henry. This is the latest satellite map. You see the pinpoint of the castle here, at the base of this mountain?" Leaning across the table, she pointed to a small speck at the base of the Pyrenees mountain range.

"And see here?" She traced a line drawn over a deep canyon between two massive peaks. "Mariska followed this route and camped here." Her finger stopped moving, tapping a large flat plane at the end of the gorge. "We have spies in her camp, but because of their location between two mountains it is difficult for them to send information. Bartholomew had news just this morning there is great unrest among her troops.

"It seems Esteban takes his role as commander very seriously and is determined to build an army that can take the Catacombs; he sees himself as the new King ruling by Mariska's side. Through our contacts, we have learned a great deal more about him.

"As a man he was cruel, without scruples. He trussed and carved the woman who was his lover because he had been told by one of her enemies she might have an interest in another. He bled her to death slowly, methodically to cause her the most lingering death, the greatest physical pain.

"As a bull fighter, he gave no sport. He was without mercy. The more agony felt by the bull, the more blood covering the ground, the greater was his foul triumph.

"As a vampire, he is evil incarnate. He rules his troops with the same blind driven vengeance he ruled his human world. His warriors have progressed; there is some cohesion, some semblance of an army working together even though it is based on fear of extinction. Still, the army is made up of renegades. They run wild from time to time and swerve out of control. Esteban always regains domination and demands obedience. He then makes sure he gets it, at least for a while, by exterminating any vampire that is unruly. It only takes a few burnings for the rabble to realize the harsh consequences of insubordination, to develop a deeper hatred and fear of their new leader.

"Needless to say, these vampires have no loyalty and inflamed by their loathing of Esteban, one by one, steal away to re-join DeMarco. It is becoming evident to all save Mariska that they must rejoin the King in order to wipe out the Immortals and take the Catacombs. We still have some time but we must move forward with all haste."

The silence was heavy as they waited for Aris to respond. His mind was flooded with visions of war and the loss of those he loved. He remembered the anguish in the aftermath of the battles in his long-ago past; he felt once again the emptiness of heartache. He feared for the Immortals and their peaceful ways, yet knew there was no way out. The responsibility for the safety of his society and his species lay directly in his hands.

His words were spoken softly. "We begin our movement to Spain very soon. We will travel in small groups and rendezvous just outside Barcelona."

"Getting us there will be no problem. Getting the weapons there is a whole other story." Richard sat, motioning his companions to do the same. "Is there any plan to ship them from England to Spain? We will never pass airline security with two thousand impalers and stilettoes."

His attention fully in the moment, Aris smiled, "My plan at the moment is to ship by couriers. Our fastest and most powerful soldiers will do a smuggling run of crates carrying our weapons over water to France and then over land to Spain. They will run through forests and on rarely travelled back roads. Immortals run faster than bullet trains and are stronger than elephants. I calculate they can transport all our weaponry in one twenty-four-hour period. They can hide the crates in the forest that surrounds the Spanish castle."

"An excellent plan." Sebastian nodded his head in agreement with Richard and Gabriela.

"So that is settled. Richard, we need fifty of our most well trained for this mission. I want them chosen by tomorrow morning."

"Aris, we know there will be those of us who will be lost. We go into battle with that thought, yet what do we do with the bodies of our fallen comrades? Do we burn them and end their existence or do we simply bury the dead, leaving their essence to float until they are able to enter another body?"

"A question that must be addressed. Of course we hope the casualties are few or better yet, none. However, we know that will not be the case."

Richard began to pace. "How can we decide what should be done. I surely do not want the responsibility of deciding their ultimate fate."

"Nor do I, Richard." Aris sat silent for a moment. "We will allow each warrior to decide what should be done with their lifeless bodies if their Immortal light is extinguished." He turned to Gabriela. "Do you agree?" He looked at each one of his comrades. "Each Immortal chooses their own destiny."

With one voice, they answered. "Yes, each Immortal chooses before we leave for Spain. They must know there is a grave chance they will never see the Catacombs again. They must prepare if that is to be their fate."

"And the evil ones? We burn them?"

"Everyone who is impaled is burned. We must give them no chance to return to attempt to steal the Diaries again."

"Aris," Gabriela spoke, "what if there are those who seek clemency, who lay down their weapons in surrender?"

"That is an issue I have been contemplating for several days. I propose to put it before the Council that any who ask for clemency be spared if they return to the Catacombs and take the Blood Oath."

"What if they lie to save themselves? What if they have no intention of living an Immortal life?"

"We will watch them carefully. They will never be given a position of any power. The Council learned well from the experience with DeMarco. I believe we will not be so trusting again of those who come from outside our society." Aris rose, pushing his chair under the table.

Seeing the meeting was at an end, they gathered their things to leave. Sebastian broke the silence. "Have any of you seen King Khansu? I do not remember the last time he was seen in public."

"No, even with the threat of war I have not seen him. Not since I was condemned during my trial for the murder of Cardinal Woolsey and Queen Katherine in the Boleyn affair and that was hundreds of years ago." Aris turned to Richard and Gabriela. "Have either of you seen him? The Queen has been present several times, but she is always alone."

The couple shook their heads 'no.' Richard answered for them both. "Not since the trial is true for us as well. It seems he has completely withdrawn from public life. I have heard it told that he is retreating into a trance of seclusion, perhaps never to return. They say his melancholy is so great because he longs for his own planet and his own society, so he withdraws from this one. We know so little of their way of life and he has been on earth for so many millennia. Is it any wonder he longs for his home?

"But what for us? Since our kind came into being there has always been a Queen and a King. What now for the Catacombs?"

Aris stood. "What now for the Catacombs is war. We must prepare for the future, but live in the present. Presently, my friends, there is a coven of evil, twisted vampires that want to wipe us off the face of the earth. I suggest we look at the weapons at our disposal for the coming battle and worry about our King when we are assured of continuing to have a kingdom."

Richard nodded in agreement. "So we meet at dawn to survey the arsenal."

The four friends quietly moved toward the door and out into the corridor.

. . . .

Jane brought Sarah's breakfast and chatted pleasantly with her while she ate. The Immortal spent time with Sarah whenever she could. It gave her a great deal of pleasure to be in the company of a human. Sarah was the first human Jane had known since her changing and she waited patiently as her new friend showered and dressed for her day above ground with Aris.

It had not been Jane's choice to be made Immortal. It was not a choice she would have made. She would rather have died a human death when the time was upon her, but she had been unconscious and the Council made the decision for her. Her only memory of any of the events of the day of her changing was the early morning. She remembered preparing to ride out with the Queen for a hunt at dawn. She mounted her beautiful white stallion and sipped from the warmed wine in the stirrup cup to take the chill from her bones. The spices in the wine had a strong flavor, but she recalled it was warm and welcome in the early morning fog.

She recollected the sound of the trumpets as the Queen arrived and all the courtiers mounted their horses. Essex, the Queen's young favorite, had maneuvered his huge black stallion next to hers in an attempt to join her in conversation. It was then her head began to swim and her vision blurred. She wondered if there had been something added to the wine she drank. That was her last rational thought as a human.

The rest of the day was lived as if in a dream. She knew Essex was involved. She could remember him tearing at her clothes, the smell of wine on his breath and the stink of his sweat as he wrestled with her. She had no recall of why they fought or what the outcome had been. She could remember she felt as if she moved in a heavy black shadow as she tried to run.

Her next memory was the agony and the ecstasy of the changing, her heightened awareness as she gazed around the room at her first sight of the members of the Council, her first sight as an Immortal. Her new eyes saw a different world. She could see the individual hairs on the head of Bartholomew as he stood above her. His long eyelashes shaded his eyes and cast shadows on his cheekbones. She marveled at his thick lips, his perfect skin without flaw or wrinkle. His first words to her sounded like music to her ears. "You are safe with us in the Catacombs. No one will ever harm you again." For the moment she was glad to be alive and out of pain. But those feelings of joy were only momentary. As she became more aware of what she had become, she longed for her human life, for human death.

"Jane?" Sarah entered the sitting room to find her friend deep in thought. "What shall we do this morning while Aris is with the commanders?"

"Whatever is your pleasure. When will he be joining us?"

"We have a lunch appointment with the owner of the gallery showing his paintings. At the moment he is with Richard and Sebastian. They're doing a weapons check and preparing to send them to Spain so I would think we have an hour or so of girl time."

Puzzled, Jane asked, "Girl time?"

Laughing, Sarah explained. "Time for just the ladies to be alone and talk of lady things."

"I understand." Jane stared at her new friend for a silent moment then spoke. "Sarah, may I share something with you?" Jane stood, moving closer to the human.

"Of course." Sarah took her hands, leading her back to sit once again on the sofa. "What is it?"

"I have never spoken of my feelings to anyone, not since being brought to the Catacombs. I know the Immortals here love their society. I know it is an honor to be a part of it. In recent centuries, all of them have been changed at their own desire; my case is very different."

"Yes?"

"I was torn and dying when my wolf brought me here. I have no memory of the journey or even where the wolf came from. That time is all a blur somewhere inside my mind. I have tried desperately for centuries to remember, yet I cannot. I know the story of you and Aris, how he came to you through someone who you had placed in a hypnotic state.

"Sarah, do you think you could hypnotize me? Do you think it would help me to remember?"

"I don't know, Jane, but I am more than willing to try." She hesitated. "I've never hypnotized an Immortal vampire before, but you're still half human so I don't see why it wouldn't work."

Sarah glanced at her watch. "Aris will be here before long; we really don't have a lot of time left alone together right now. Let's plan for tomorrow rather than just an hour today. How about we do a session in the morning right after breakfast?"

"Thank you." Jane was silent for a moment, deep in thought. "I feel nervous, but I must know what happened. I am willing to do whatever is necessary to find out."

"Alright, tomorrow then."

Jane rose and left the chambers, the white wolf following at her heels.

. . . .

The huge room was empty except for the three Immortals and several narrow wooden crates containing weaponry. Richard held a perfectly crafted stiletto in his hands, checking its balance and weight. Aris watched his friends as they practiced with the unfamiliar weapons of destruction.

Light bounced from the shining blade as Richard made tentative thrusts at an invisible enemy. He noticed ancient runes carved into the metal. "Aris, what are these symbols?" He handed the knife to his commander.

"These are the runes Queen Akira etched into every blade." He ran his fingers over the delicate carving. "They are engraved through a process only the Queen knows."

"What power do the runes give?"

"The runes cause the weapon to release quickly and easily from the heart of the enemy. When impaled, the vampire heart locks onto the stake and it is nearly impossible to remove. Akira used the ancient science so the blade will slide out easily, saving time and hopefully the lives of our soldiers."

Richard took the weapon back from Aris and gingerly ran his

finger over the edge of the blade. "The edge is not sharp."

"Only the point. A direct hit to the heart is the only way to make a kill. There is no reason for the edges to be sharpened." Motioning his friend to place it back in its carrying chest, he nodded. "All is as it should be."

"As it should be? The thought of impaling one of our own kind, eliminating them for all time, is that as it should be?"

"Richard, I understand. To kill when we have spent centuries finding ways to live without taking life. To wittingly kill when we have fought the beast that lives within each one of us and won. To become less than what we have strived to become. War. You question how we are able turn our backs on our own integrity, our honor. How can we become like human beings who kill without mercy? But remember, our war is not a human battle. Humans fight wars for power. It is greed that drives them. Greed for money, for material goods, for land that belongs only to the earth, not to any man. The battle in Spain is for our society and for the society of humans that lives above ground. Without this fight, both ways of life will be lost forever."

A sound behind them caused the three to turn quickly. Gabriela joined them with fresh information from their spies in Spain. "Bartholomew received additional news from Alexi late last night. It is most certain that the Spanish King and Queen must reconcile to have any chance of victory. She is unable to control her faction at all; Esteban keeps killing and burning his own soldiers and DeMarco is left without enough vampires to win a war with us alone without having to fight Mariska as well. The Council believes the royal couple's mutual desire to rule the Catacombs will bring them back together. We must move as quickly as possible. If Queen Mariska returns to DeMarco, we will have them all in a single location. If we strike before her army is settled, we will have surprise as well as distraction on our side."

"We will soon be ready." Aris closed the open containers. "Our

Immortals are now well trained and prepared to travel. A few more weapons drills and they will be expert."

"Aris?" Gabriela spoke. "What about Sarah? What will happen to her while we are away." She hesitated. "What will happen to her if we are defeated?"

"She will stay in the protection of the Catacombs while we travel. And never fear, we will not be defeated." He spoke with great conviction even though a heavy seed of doubt lay hidden deep in his heart.

"*I only hope he is right,*" thought a concerned Gabriela as she turned with her comrades to leave the room.

. . . .

"Aris, may I have a word?" Kitsuko hurried from behind to join the three commanders as they walked down the corridor.

"Yes, of course." He motioned to Gabriela and Richard to continue on to the Sanguinaria. "I will meet with you in a bit." He waved then turned his attention to the small woman standing at his side.

Kitsuko was truly lovely, her long black hair pulled tightly off her face and braided into a thick plait hanging to her waist. She was dressed in a soft white shirt tied at the waist with a black belt and tight white pants. Her features were refined, her flashing black eyes demanding total attention of any who spoke with her.

"How can I help you?"

"If you have a moment, I would like to show you a few new defensive movements that I have developed for your troops. Sebastian suggested that we spend some time together on the training floor." Kitsuko had not been able to get Aris out of her thoughts. She longed to spend time with him alone and Sebastian's recommendation gave her the perfect opportunity.

"Now would be the perfect time. Let me contact my friends to tell them I will not be joining them. I will meet you in the training pavilion in just a few moments."

"Splendid." Kitsuko smiled to herself as she walked away.

· · · · · · · · · · · · · · · · · · · ·

The pavilion was empty except for Kitsuko working out and the sound of Aris' boots echoing off the wooden floor as he entered. Thoroughly focusing she moved rapidly through a fighting form. As he watched her work, he was still amazed by her speed. Even with his Immortal vision, it was difficult to fully recognize what she was doing as she spun and twisted to evade an imaginary opponent. Impressed, he watched her silently.

Coming to rest, she noticed him and laughed at the look of surprise on his face. "Aris. How long have you been standing there?"

"Just long enough to be grateful you are helping in training our soldiers. How did you become so accomplished in martial arts?"

Laughing, she answered. "I have been practicing for many centuries. I was taught the skill from monks in the Himalayas many hundreds of years ago. My small size added to my speed and agility and rapidly I became a master."

"Were you human or Immortal?"

"At that time, I was human. My skill was so great that I was honored and asked to join a cult of fighting monks of the highest caliber. I was told these warriors had the amazing ability to defy gravity and to live eternally. They were a group of the earliest Immortals. I joyfully agreed and was changed."

"Defy gravity? I am an Immortal and I cannot defy gravity?"

"Watch." Backing away from him a short distance, she closed her eyes, took a deep breath and as she jumped over him as if he were a blade of grass, uttered a strange guttural incantation. Landing lightly on her feet, she leaped again this time to a height of more than fifty feet to reclaim the spot from which she began.

Astonished, he stood with his mouth gaping open. "Amazing. Your skills are most useful."

Her eyes locked on his as she smiled a slow seductive smile. "Ah Aris," she stepped closer to him. He could smell the fragrance of Jasmine that surrounded her. "I have many skills." She laid her small hand on his arm and he was shocked at the desire that swelled inside of him. She knew her touch had stirred him and she waited for him to reply.

"I must, I must go," he stammered shocked at his physical response to her. "I must meet my friends." He turned, hurrying from her presence.

She laughed out loud as he left the pavilion.

. . . .

Walking toward the Sanquinaria, Aris held a silent dialog inside his head. *"What was that? I love Sarah and only Sarah. I have not desired a woman for centuries, not since I knew my Elizabeth. How could I have been so stirred by another?"* He shook his head to clear his mind. He cautioned himself out loud. "How is not important, my man. You must stay far away from that small piece of dynamite." His thoughts were determined. *"I will never stray from my beloved and I have no intention of allowing myself to be tempted."* He quickened his pace, yet he couldn't rid himself of the vision of her black, erotic eyes.

. . . .

"How did it go?" Sebastian spoke as he filled an empty goblet from the pitcher resting on the table.

Aris sat and before speaking, lifted the goblet to drink all of the liquid in it. Feeling refreshed and once again in control of himself, he spoke. "It went well. She is blindingly fast and greatly skilled. She will prove to be a pronounced asset to our army."

"I felt the same. Richard worked with her earlier today and he, too, was impressed."

"Yes, both Gabriela and I have spent time with her on the training floor. She is not only accomplished, she has an ability to teach that is rare. In a very short time both Gabriela and I were able to jump to great heights and spin like tops to avoid contact with the enemy. Kitsuko can teach us skills we do not now possess to avoid the impalers of the enemy."

"We will need all the skill she can share and more." A look of concern spread over Aris' face. "Unfortunately, right now the Spanish army and our army are evenly matched in numbers. At this point, our only advantage is our connected society. I believe we will win, but at what cost? With these new fighting skills, perhaps many more of our peace-loving Immortals will walk away unscathed."

"To victory." Richard spoke as he raised his goblet.

Joining him, his comrades spoke with one voice. "To victory."

CHAPTER 16

The taxi stopped in the circular driveway in front of an enormous home just outside London. Aris scanned the area carefully before they left the taxi and he took Sarah's arm as they walked toward the large brass-plated door. He tapped the knocker several times. They waited patiently until, at last, the door opened.

A very lean, well-dressed butler stood before them. He stepped aside to welcome them into a huge foyer with a pristine white marble floor and an elegant, curved staircase leading to an upstairs gallery. A long oak side table filled the wall opposite the doorway. On it rested a vase half as tall as Sarah. The fragrance of the colorful flowers in the vase greeted them as they stepped inside.

"Please, this way." He gestured toward two ornately carved double doors with brass knobs. "Sir Reginald will be with you in just a moment." He turned to lead them into a lovely sitting room. Towering narrow windows opening onto a perfect green lawn filled one entire wall. An even higher ceiling topped a dark wooden floor covered in hand-crafted silk carpets in floral patterns of soft muted colors. The furniture was French and expensive.

"May I pour you tea?" Aris nodded yes. The servant tipped the blue and white teapot and steaming dark liquid spilled into two matching China cups. "Cream?"

"No, thank you." The attendant raised one eyebrow at the uncivilized way the Americans chose to drink their tea. Handing the cups to the guests, he spoke. "May I bring you anything else?"

"No, thank you." Aris, sipped his tea as the butler left the room and shut the double doors behind him.

"An actual British drawing room." Sarah laughed. "I would never have imagined I'd be invited to lunch in a house such as this. And served by an authentic, disdainful butler."

"Yes, he did seem quite put out."

"Aris, I didn't know Reginald Clinton was a 'Sir.'"

"That he is. I doubt if I would have gotten the notice of the royal house if he were not."

The doors opened again and John Marshal, their friend and patron from the states, was led into the room. He spoke with the authority of someone who felt at home in this great house. "That will be all Geofrey." The servant tipped his head as he left the room, once more closing the doors behind him.

"So, how are you two enjoying your visit to the British Empire?" John's blue eyes sparkled as he spoke.

"It's been enlightening, to say the least." Sarah glanced at Aris with a wink and a knowing smile.

"Well, I must say, Aris, your art certainly has taken the Brits by storm."

The doors burst open and Reginald Clinton entered laughing. "I hear you have sent my man into a tailspin by drinking your tea black. He is such a traditionalist that he can become unbearable. Please forgive his churlish attitude. It goes with the post." He hugged John, kissing his cheek then moving away.

"Not to worry, we found it charming." Aris stood to shake hands with the two men.

The four sat comfortably chatting as they waited for luncheon to be called. It was served on a covered veranda facing the lush green lawn of Sir Reginald's estate. The food tasted delicious and the white wine was chilled to a perfect temperature. They ate slowly, enjoying the fare spread before them as well as their lively conversation and each other's company.

At last, coffee served, the two gallery owners broached the conversation of Aris' next showing.

"Before we begin to discuss the next presentation, I would like to speak with you about something that is dear to my heart." Aris directed his words to the two men. "First, I must say that you two gentlemen have changed my life. You, John, by your faith in my work. You, Reginald, by giving me the chance to expand my horizons to both sides of the ocean. I am forever grateful to both of you."

Sarah sat silently, waiting to see the reaction of the two men to what she knew Aris was going to present to them.

"In my past, I lived in Chicago in a world of ugliness and despair. I lived a life as Carlos Havarro, full of pain and hopelessness. That life is behind me now. The ugliness transformed into beauty. The despair changed to faith. I live a new life. I am a new man. I wish to put my past to rest, to put Carlos Havarro to sleep for the last time." The group at the table sat silently, waiting. "Gentlemen, I desire a new name."

John leaned forward in his chair. "A new name?"

Reginald continued. "But you are just becoming known. Your name is only beginning to be spoken in the art world."

"Yes," Aris replied. "Yes, and so it is a perfect time to change. You see, when I was still very young, I was nurtured and guided by a man who saw something special in me. He led me on a path of beauty and fulfillment. But I lost him. He is no longer. The world lost his talent for seeing and transferring a living world to a world of paint and canvas, yet while I had him close, he gave me all he could of who he was. His name was Aris." No one moved or spoke. "I am forever beholden to him and I wish to continue my life in his honor, to live and to paint in his name. Aris."

"But," John was stopped before he began.

"That is what must be. It is a decision I have made and it can be no other way."

Reginald and John stared at each other in disbelief. Finally Reginald spoke. "And just exactly how do you propose we do this?"

"Yes," John joined in, "we have already sold so many paintings in the name of Carlos Havarro. What of those paintings?"

"I have thought of that. Those paintings will have more value over time because they were the first."

"That doesn't answer my question. How do you plan on doing this?"

"I have been approached by a very well-known English art critic and journalist. Melanie Fairchild contacted me suggesting an article about my work to be published both in Europe and the States. Her work and opinions are highly respected. If she were to make the announcement in that article and give the reasons for the change, I am quite sure the art world would accept it. I no longer want to be looked upon as a gang banger turned artist. I am an artist and so want to be recognized for my talent and that alone."

John swirled the amber brandy in his glass and sipped it before he spoke. "I can understand what you propose." He looked at Reginald who nodded his agreement. "Alright. It might even add to your artist's mystique." He smiled as he spoke.

"And," John cleared his throat. "And, Aris, I, too, have a surprise for you. The Duke of York has seen your work and would like you to meet with his secretary to discuss a painting."

Sarah gasped and Aris laughed. "I would be honored to meet with his secretary. Just say when."

. . . .

The taxi ride back to London was filled with laughter and

conversation. What could be more appropriate for the Immortal who had spent most of his existence in the presence of royalty than to be welcomed, once again, into the court of Kings and Queens. Yet even though Aris' mood seemed light and happy, his inner thoughts were of the danger in which Sarah was placed every time she left the safety of the Catacombs. The Spanish coven and the war were always troubling thoughts in the back of his mind, but he rarely mentioned it when the two of them were alone. He didn't want to worry her, yet he knew that many of his comrades would end up giving their Immortal lives for the security of their society. The dread of having to be the one who led them to their death was a heavy weight even for his broad, strong shoulders.

. . . .

Kitsuko hated herself for following Aris. Her early training at the monastery and her life as an Immortal had taught her the horrors of obsession. And yet she found herself driven by an uncontrollable hurricane force to claim him, to make him fall in love with her.

Following him to London, lurking outside an English mansion like a thief in the night. Staying just a few cars behind him on the highway. "Who is this weak woman who has taken over my senses?" It didn't matter. Nothing else mattered. Just to get a glimpse of him from a distance, even with the wretched human, thrilled her.

So lost in her thoughts, she didn't see the stop light in front of her turn red. Screeching brakes brought her from her reverie just in time to save her from crashing into the car in front of hers. Not quite so lucky, the car behind her wasn't able to avoid a collision. The bumper caved in on impact and pushed her forward with a crunch. She sat sandwiched between two cars as she watched Aris and his human drive on, oblivious to the accident behind them.

Opening the driver's door, she stepped out of the car. The driver of the car behind her was already assessing the damage. She marveled at his tall, dark good looks as she walked toward him to exchange information. His black eyes flashed as he smiled.

CHAPTER 17

"Alright, Jane. This is our first session so we will commence by taking you into a deep state of relaxation. Then we will find a place in time when you have full memory, working comfortably toward the time when your human memory ends and your Immortal life begins. I can't tell you how many sessions we will need, but I can tell you that I believe we will be able to answer your questions with time." Jane nodded her head in agreement as she rested on Sarah's sofa in her sitting room. "Where would you like to begin?"

Jane closed her eyes as she thought of her human life. There had been so many wonderful experiences in the court of Elizabeth I, the greatest of which was simply knowing the formidable Queen. "I would like to set out when I was maid-in-waiting. It was a glorious time in England and one I cherish in my memory."

"Perfect." Sarah leaned closer to the reclining girl as she began an hypnotic induction. She watched as Jane slowly became more relaxed and entered into a deep hypnotic state.

JANE HOWARD, transcript, Session 1
"What year is it, Jane?"
"It is the year 1586 and I have just begun waiting on the Queen."
"Tell me about Queen Elizabeth."

"*Her Majesty is fifty-three years old. She never shows herself without full make-up and wigs and she has a great many. All of her hair pieces are tinted the vibrant red that was the color of her hair in her youth. I am told by the other maidens who have been in her service longer than I that beneath the wigs her tresses are thin, dull and mostly gray. It makes me sad to think such a powerful woman must hide her true image from her subjects.*" Jane grew quiet and Sarah sat waiting for her to speak. When she did not, Sarah again questioned her.

"Tell me of the court."

"*Ah, the court. What a place of luxury. And a place of courtly love.*"

"Courtly love?"

"*Courtly love is not the same as romantic love. All of the men fawn over her Majesty, writing poems and songs of her beauty and grace, yet all know they will never be her lover. However, there were two that won her heart more than any others. Robert Dudley, Lord of Leicester and Robert Devereux, Second Earl of Essex. Each of these men held a special and unique place in her life.*"

"What can you tell me of these courtiers?"

"*Robert Dudley was the first of the men she loved. He knew the Queen when they were both but children. In their teens, her Majesty's sister, Mary, was on the throne. Mary's younger sister, our Elizabeth, was locked in the Tower of London. The Queen feared her subjects would revolt and raise Elizabeth to Monarch. Queen Mary was hated by her subjects because of her marriage to Prince Philip of Spain and her persecution of the Protestants. Philip brought the Spanish Inquisition to England with him. Any who were not Catholic and would not convert were tortured and burned at the stake at the order of Mary. She became known as 'Bloody Mary,' murdering any who would not bow to the Pope.*

"*Along with his treasonous family Dudley was imprisoned in the Tower at the same time as Elizabeth, yet in a different location. Still, they shared for their lifetime together the experience of not knowing from moment to moment if they would live or die at the command of a mad woman. It bonded them in a way that was unsevered until Dudley's death in 1588. She called him her Robin. He lived for her and loved her all his life. He was her Master of Horse and her champion.*"

"And what of Essex? What can you tell me of him?"

Suddenly Jane grew stiff and began to tremble. Her face contorted and she opened her mouth as if to scream, but no sound escaped.

Sarah responded instantly to the change in the young woman. "Jane. You are safe. You are here with me in the Catacombs. We are in the 21st Century and you are safe and secure."

As if some magic incantation was spoken, Jane's face softened and her body relaxed. Sarah breathed a sigh of relief.

"Now, Jane, I will bring you back to real time." Slowly Sarah brought Jane's awareness back to the Catacombs. When the Immortal opened her eyes, she looked at Sarah and a sad smile played on her lips.

. . . .

"It was so strange. I felt I was there, at court. I could see the people and smell the smells. It was all so real." Jane still rested on the sofa as she described her journey to Sarah.

"It's that way for many people. Can you tell me what happened to you when you began to speak of Essex?"

"I have no words for it. I was suddenly overcome with terror. I know not why. The vision of court disappeared and I was in a black abyss full of pain and Essex was a part of it." She sat up, turning to look at Sarah. "Must we return to that wretched place? I felt terrified."

"Jane, I'm afraid so, but before we do, I'll make you feel safe and secure when you mention him. Would you like to tell me about him now while you are not in hypnosis?"

Jane stood and paced thoughtfully before she answered. "I think not. But, Sarah, I know that Essex was somehow involved in my last day as a human. I must know the circumstances. Whatever we must do, I do gladly. I trust you and believe in you. I place myself in your good hands."

CHAPTER 18

Twenty-five Immortals lined the training floor as Aris and Richard watched Kitsuko teach evasion tactics, spinning and tumbling around the room with ease and precision.

"She really is amazing." Richard spoke quietly, almost reverently.

"Yes, she truly is." Aris had been careful not to be alone with the newly promoted captain since their last meeting.

"Do you think we really are going to win this war?"

"Richard, we have no choice but to win. My concern is our losses. And Sarah."

"Sarah? But she will be safe here in the Catacombs. Henry will watch over her and protect her."

"I have no worries about her during the battle. My concern is if I am eliminated, what will become of her. I know she can return to the states and continue her life, but what if one of the Spanish coven should follow her. What if Mariska survives the conflict? She would hunt Sarah down and kill her and if DeMarco survives, he would change her regardless of her desire. I am being driven mad by the images of her death."

Resting his hand on the arm of his friend, Richard spoke with concern. "That will never happen, Aris. We will all make sure that Sarah is safe now and for as long as she lives. As long as there are

Immortals on the earth, she will be protected."

"And what if there is no more Immortal society?"

As he spoke, the twenty five soldiers leaped as one, twenty feet into the air, spun and landed in the exact same spot where they began. Richard laughed, "With that ball of fire instructing us, I think we may be invincible."

"I hope you are right my friend." He glanced at his watch. "Come, let them train without our eyes on them."

The two Immortals quietly left the pavilion so as not to disturb the concentration of the soldiers.

CHAPTER 19

It was Sarah's first time to venture alone through the corridors and streets of the Catacombs. Aris had planned on taking her to see the Master Keeper of Records, but when he was called to meet with his commanders, he had given her explicit directions to find the Catacombs Library without him. The Immortals she passed in the narrow streets nodded and smiled at her. In her pocket rested the communication device Gabriela had given her when she first arrived so that if she needed guidance, she could reach any of her friends. She knew he wouldn't send her alone if he had any fear that she was not absolutely safe, yet she couldn't help but be a bit nervous to walk alone in the labyrinth of the inner city.

Aris had been pleased when she told him she wanted to visit the Master Keeper of Records. She was intrigued by him as much as he was her. Aris told her he had been with Queen Akira since the early sixteenth century. Sarah had been full of questions, but Aris suggested she receive her answers from Henry himself. She was excited to spend time with such a prominent Immortal renowned for his brilliance. When she reached the library, she was struck by the beauty of its wood paneled and enormous interior. She felt for a moment she had entered a movie set. A lovely blond Immortal woman sat at a long table, books and charts covering its dark wood.

Sarah approached her quietly, but before she could speak, the woman lifted her blue eyes questioningly toward the human. "You are Sarah?"

"Yes, I'm looking for Henry."

"He is expecting you. Aris notified him this morning you would be visiting us." She rose from the table to lead Sarah between shelves holding the grandest collection of volumes Sarah had ever seen. "I am called Millicent and I assist the Master Keeper in the Records Hall. He is waiting in his study to receive you." She made no sound as she walked toward a large heavy wooden door at the back of the cavernous room.

She turned the door's handle and it unlatched quietly opening into a softly lit sitting room. Henry sat behind a huge desk covered with papers and books. Again, he was dressed in a black business suit and a tie. His silver hair was tied back from his face with a thin black ribbon, his eyes sparkled in the light from the lamp on his desk. He stood as she entered and moved to take her hands in his.

"Sarah, welcome. I am so glad you came to see me." Motioning her to sit in a comfortable chair, he spoke. "Would you like some tea?" She noticed a beautiful hand painted tea service on a table next to her chair.

"Yes, thank you." He poured and handed her a cup. "So, what has brought you to the library today?"

"I want to learn more about the Immortals. More about you, if I may."

"What can I tell you?"

"Well, it seems each of you has a story to tell of your human life. May I know yours?" She hesitated but a moment before her words began to pour out as if she had no control over them. "What was your life above ground? How long have you been here and how did you become the Master Keeper of Records?"

He laughed. "You certainly are full of questions."

Sarah blushed. "I am. I'm just so incredibly fascinated by your society, your way of life. It's so foreign from the human world where I come from. There's so much fear and hatred above ground. You have found a peace here that I've never felt before."

"Ah, my life as a human. What shall I tell you?" He settled into the over-stuffed chair across from her. "I was changed in 1519. I was living in France at that time. I was sixty-seven years old. Quite an old man for that period."

"Were you born in France?"

"No, I was born in Italy. I lived in Vinci and became quite well known as an artist and a delver into the sciences. Through my work I met many influential people until at one point, I was requested to travel to the Vatican. It was an era of artistic excellence and I held council with other celebrated creative men of that period. My work was appreciated and I flourished. It was during my stay in Rome that I came to know of the Immortals. A priest who befriended me told me of such a society. He was kind and wise and we had many long evenings deep in discussion on a myriad of topics, some religious, some secular, all intriguing.

"One evening after several meetings, he brought up the tale of the Immortal life. At first, he was timid. He felt I would be frightened at the thought of the undead. Rather than frightening, I found the subject captivating. I wanted to learn more. Over time, he told me all he could about the life underground.

"You must remember, I was a scientist. The more he told me, the more I wanted to meet and speak with an Immortal. At long last, he admitted to me that he was one of the undead. I begged to be taken to the Catacombs; to visit the city underground was my most intense desire. Alas, he would not even tell me where the court lay. Not even the country that housed it. Yet, I continued to ask questions, hoping he would change his mind." He reached forward to refresh the tea in Sarah's cup.

Having refilled it, he leaned back in his chair against the cushions as he spoke. "King Francis had just recaptured Milan and was visiting the Pope. It was then, in 1516, that I met him. The King commissioned me to create a full-sized metal lion for him that could walk. It was a challenge from which I could not turn. I packed my studio and my life to move to France to begin my work on the great beast.

"The priest from the Vatican and I continued our correspondence through letters, yet I regretfully felt unable to question him further about the Catacombs. It was too much of a risk. One of the couriers might read the letter and we would most certainly be tried for witch craft. Only in person could I find out more about the idyllic society he described to me. Obsessed with thoughts of the Immortals, I begged him to visit me until, at last, he agreed.

"He arrived, lodging with me in the manor house provided by Francis I. We spent many nights over wine and candles discussing philosophy, religion and the Immortal life. Still he refused to tell me the location of the court. When time came for him to return to Rome, my mind refused to cease questioning such a Utopian existence. I longed for more discussion, more information. I missed my friend, our conversation, his intelligence and his sense of humor. Our written correspondence continued, but without the freedom to fully express our thoughts.

"In the next year, it seemed my age began to show itself. My joints became stiff. My powerful stride was reduced to a slow shuffle. My hands became arthritic. I could no longer manage my brushes and colors. I sunk into the depths of despondency.

"Again, I wrote my friend asking him to come. I knew my death was near. I prayed it was. To my artist's soul, losing the use of my hands, no longer able to paint, to create, was worse than losing my life. I felt death was soon upon me and not sure what the afterlife might actually bring, I decided to take a precaution just in case heaven and hell might be a true possibility. It became my desire that none other than my dear friend perform the last rites as I breathed my last breath. I begged him to come.

"He came immediately. His presence gave me a brief moment of hope, brought me out of my despair, yet even as I gained strength and was again able to rise from my bed, I knew the end was yet upon me.

"Days passed as I lingered in my decrepitude. We spoke of the Catacombs, of eternal life. As I grew more weak, knowing it was but hours that I had left of my mortal life, I knew of only one way to outsmart death. I begged the priest to give me the gift of Immortality. He refused.

"It seemed there were laws in the Catacombs as to how and when a human could be changed. I wept cold tears of despair as I grew more and more weak.

"King Francis had grown to love me as a true friend. He visited daily to encourage me to heal, yet even he could see that I would not live more than a short time. He shed tears of remorse at the loss of my friendship and my talent. He was a true comrade.

"When I again became too weak to rise and my death was imminent, my dear priest decided I had too much to give to the Immortal race to allow me to die. He told me all of the Catacombs he had kept hidden and offered me the rite of change. I accepted.

"He performed the ritual in my chamber, sending my attendants out of the room each time he worked in the pretense of prayer for the dying. While they were absent, he exchanged my blood, little by little, for his venom. The change took three days and my servants and the King's physicians mistook my agony of changing for death throes.

"As I drew my last breath there was no one in the room save the priest and King Francis. The King held my head in his lap as I succumbed."

Sarah had not moved an inch since Henry began his story. As he spoke his long, white fingers gestured in the air, resembling the wings on a white bird soaring above the earth. To her eyes, he was beautiful.

"In my new state, I was able to lie still through the burial ritual. I was glad for the time to adjust to my new self. My mind, which had always been vast, now had no boundaries. I knew the Creation and the End Times. I knew all the past and all the future. I was almost sad when my friend came for me to take me to the Catacombs to meet the Council. While I lay in state, he had prepared them for my coming. And so, dear Sarah, that is how I came to be what you see before you. Henry, Master Keeper of Records in the Catacombs of King Khansu and Queen Akira."

"You said you were an artist. Would I know your human name if you told me what it was?"

"I believe you just might."

"Are you able to tell me?"

"Yes, Sarah." He smiled a slow mischievous smile. "My human name was Leonardo."

"Leonardo? From Italy?"

"Yes, Vinci, Italy."

An unthinkable thought exploded in Sarah's head. "*Leonard of Vinci? Leonardo da Vinci. No, impossible!*"

"Henry, when did you say you were changed?"

Still he smiled, his eyes sparkling like a naughty child. "I was changed in the fifth month of 1519."

Her heart seemed to stop beating in her chest. She, Sarah Hagan of Chicago, was in the presence of one of the greatest men of all time.

. . . .

"How could you not tell me who he actually is? How could you let me go there and question him as if he were a mere mortal?" Sarah's tone was accusatory as she sat next to Aris on the sofa in her sitting room.

He laughed. "He is not a 'mere mortal'. He is actually Henry, the Master Keeper of Records."

"Well, yes. But Leonardo da Vinci for God's sake. Now it all makes sense. I wondered how the Queen could choose which Immortal would fill such a vital post. But she didn't, did she? He created the post. When he was changed, he already understood the soul of man and the journey that it takes throughout eternity."

"We had no records when he came to us. No written history of our kind or of yours. He is the one who created the Records as only he could." He wrapped his arm around her, drawing her closer to him. "He is our foremost scientist. Just as he developed concepts when he was above ground that were far, far beyond his time, so he has accomplished the same below ground. He is the favorite of the King and Queen and spends a great deal of time in the royal court. He was alongside Akira when she developed the Immortal light, when our communication devices were created. He brought all of his human knowledge and his divine inspiration with him when he came to us. Akira joined minds with him to find the path to develop our society to the level you see today."

"Umm." Sarah leaned into his shoulder, closing her eyes and thinking about her future. Just who else was living eternally in the golden city beneath the ground? As she relaxed against him, the sensation of his solid muscular chest and the spicy, musky smell of his skin made her not care who else was living in the Catacombs. She cared about nothing outside of the moment. All she was aware of was the gnawing ache deep inside of her to hold him and have him take her and make her his.

CHAPTER 20

Afternoon sun beamed through the tall window hewn into the west wall of the throne room. As DeMarco paced back and forth, his moving shadow kept time with the tap of his boots echoing off the stone walls and floor. "What do you mean the human cannot get near her? It was your bright idea to use this man and now you tell me he is incapable of doing his job?"

"Your Majesty," there was fear in the voice of the handsome young vampire standing before his King, "What else could we have done? If any of the members of the Catacombs sees one of us, they will know what we are attempting. And since you are determined to capture the woman, using a human was the only solution. He follows them whenever they are above ground but she is always with one of them. He has no chance against an Immortal."

"Julian, you go to London. You guide him. Stay out of sight, but make sure he does not fail." Furiously, he spun on his heel. "Tell him to make his chance." He bellowed as he stormed out of the room. Just before the door slammed behind him, he turned and whispered, "Or you and he will both answer to me."

Dropping to his knees, bowing his head, Julian spoke. "Yes Sire, I will take care of it."

CHAPTER 21

Gabriela sat on Sarah's bed as the mortal dressed for the art reception that she and Aris planned to attend that evening. "Gaby, it's mystifying. I mean, I feel as if I belong here with all of you. I don't really miss my life above ground; I still think of my human friends and love them, but there is a peace here that I've never known before."

"It is the magic of the Catacombs. It is built on a foundation without fear. Without fear, how can you not be at peace?"

"Well, I don't know what it is that makes me so comfortable here, I just know it feels like home."

Gabriela stood, crossing the room to help Sarah who was arguing with the clasp on her gold chain necklace. The latch was so delicate Sarah couldn't hold onto the tiny mechanism with her fingers and open it at the same time. She had just dropped one side for the third time when Gabriela stepped up to secure it for her. She tilted her head to the side, making sure the clasp was firmly closed as she spoke. "I think it is home for you, Sarah. Aris loves you. Every Immortal who knows you thinks of you as family even though you are human. Our society contains the greatest minds on earth and yet you have taught us something we knew nothing about. We recognize your work with Jane and respect you for your abilities that are new to us.

Yes, Sarah, I think you are home."

"But Gaby, if I became Immortal, what would happen to my human life, my friends, those who may never know about the Immortal society? My heart aches at the thought of leaving them."

"If you remain human, you will lose them eventually anyway. Death will separate you. And, Sarah, you won't have to give them up for a very long time, but as they age and you do not, the separation must occur. You can understand why they must never be allowed to see you as your unchanging self."

"I know. I suppose you are right. If I remain human, we will all die off one at a time anyway. Oh Gaby, I've thought of this from every angle humanly possible. It still comes up human - 0, Immortal - 1. I fully understand that once it's done, I can never go back. I remember one time Aris said something about humans not being able to understand eternity. Well, I certainly can't right now, but I want to. I just know I'm captivated by the Catacombs and the Immortal life. The thought of having forever to explore, to learn. To be absolutely free of fear." She was silent as she thought about forever with Aris. No need to eat or sleep, no death, just eternal life, making love to him and with him for as long as time existed. She turned to face her friend. "Sometimes I feel as if I have no choice but to become what it seems I am already."

Gabriela hugged her. "You will make the right decision but do not change only for Aris. He will remain with you human or not."

Sarah stepped back just a step, a serious note to her voice. "Gaby, I love Aris with all my heart, but if I do this, I won't be doing it for him. Or even for us." She stood silent for a moment, her eyes closed, deep in thought. When she lifted her lashes, her smile was full of confidence. "If I become an Immortal, I will be doing it for me and no one else because it's the only thing I truly want to do."

The two women looked at one another for a solemn moment, then Sarah twirled, laughing, in a grand circle. "Anyway, how do I look?"

Admiringly, her companion answered. "You look like an Immortal already."

. . . .

The soft lighting enhanced the bright spotlights illuminating Aris' artwork. Sarah stood in an out-of-the-way corner watching Aris work the room as Reginald Clinton introduced him to patron after patron, London's elite. His casual grace, the way he made anyone with whom he spoke feel as if they were the only person in the room, was as instrumental in his popularity as his gifted brush strokes on canvas.

Suddenly, as if he felt her eyes on him, he looked at her. Smiling, he excused himself from the small group gathered around him.

"You look beautiful." He touched her bare arm and a thrill ran down her spine. Last minute preparations for the war had kept them at arms-length without more than a moment to spend alone. With the arrival of Kitsuko, battle strategy had become more complex and training more intense. Aris was away from her more than he was with her. She understood, yet missed his warm lips on hers and his strong arms around her. She longed for the conflict to be over, to have more than stolen moments with her beloved. She straightened his dark tie then ran her fingers under the soft lapels of his suit. Her touch thrilled him and he fought his rising desire.

Their attention was diverted from each other by a small group of men and women entering the gallery. Many of those milling about the room turned to stare for just a moment before returning to their conversations. She recognized the face of the tallest man, but couldn't remember where she had seen him before.

"Aris, who is that tall man in the center?"

"Reginald said there was a chance the Duke of York would come this evening. It appears he was right. Come, let us find Sir Reggie." He took her arm as they hurried across the room toward the gallery owner. Sir Reginald was standing deep in discussion with an elegantly dressed couple explaining why Aris' work would be a fantastic investment. They turned toward the artist as he and Sarah approached.

"Good evening." Aris tipped his head toward the group. "Sir Reginald, may I see you for just a moment?"

Reginald excused himself then stepped away from the potential buyers with a sigh. He spoke to Aris. "I was doing so well. What is it? Why did you ask to see me?"

"Look over my shoulder. Is that not His Grace?"

"Good God, it is." Reginald stopped cold in his tracks. "I was told he might stop by, but I thought it just a rumor. And, here he is." Taking Aris and Sarah by the arm, he steered them toward the arriving royalty. "This is the chance of a lifetime. Smile pretty, you two."

As they crossed the room, Sarah was sure she recognized a tall dark-haired man from the last gallery showing. He was lounging comfortably against a wall just as he had been before. She noticed him watching her and when she caught his eye, he smiled then turned away.

．．．．．．．．．．．．．．．．．．．．

Gabriela was curled in a chair enjoying the dancing flames in the fireplace. Sarah sipped tea as they chatted.

"Gaby, he's amazing. He had everyone in that room mesmerized, not just the women but the men as well. And the Duke of York? He commissioned Aris himself. He didn't even leave it up to his secretary."

Gaby laughed. "Well the inhabitants of the Catacombs do have just an extra bit of charm."

"So I've noticed. I'm just so glad he's made such an impact. From the courts of kings to a Chicago gang banger and back again. It's quite a story he has to tell. If only they knew all about him."

"If they knew all about him, they would know all about us and our society would be doomed. He's doing just fine as a twenty-first-century man, is he not?"

"You're right, Gaby. He's doing just fine."

CHAPTER 22

The Catacombs bistro had few patrons so early in the day. Aris invited Sarah to join he and Richard as they discussed travel plans to Spain. Kitsuko sat across from her and after constantly hearing what an amazing fighter she was, Sarah was surprised at her subdued manner.

Even though her words were few, Kitsuko's mind spun out of control. Watching Aris and the attention he paid the human woman drove her mad with envy. In all of her existence, Kitsuko had never had feelings such as those she now had for the handsome Immortal. She was obsessed with thoughts of him, aware of him whenever he was near to her, haunted by him when he was out of sight. Her concentration flew even on the training floor when he entered the pavilion. She couldn't help herself and followed him whenever he left the Catacombs. Again and again she tried to find a way to speak with him alone. He could never mate with a human, that she knew for sure. He was stirred by her. She felt it when she touched him the first time they had been alone together. She smiled to herself as she realized he feared his feelings for her.

"Ladies," Aris stood. "Richard and I have a meeting with the Queen so we will leave you to get acquainted." He kissed Sarah on the forehead, then the two men left the restaurant.

Kitsuko drained her goblet before speaking softly. "And so, Sarah, how is it with you and Aris?"

A little surprised by the intimate question asked by the stranger, Sarah answered evenly. "I'm not quite sure what you mean."

"Well, a human and an Immortal, a love affair that can never be." Her lovely face wrinkled into a hostile scowl. "He needs one of his own kind."

"One of his own kind?"

"One of us, one to share all eternity with him. One who will never change. You will grow old and ugly. You will never have a true mating. You are weak and pathetic." She laughed. "And I will be here long after you are dead and gone." She rose from her chair. "Think on that, human." She spun on her heel and swept from the room.

Shocked by the unexpected verbal attack and the truth that had just been thrown at her, a truth she had been avoiding for months, Sarah picked up one of the empty goblets left on the table and stared into the thick, red liquid pooling in the bottom. Kitsuko's words had been cruel and selfish, yet she was right. In her present state, Sarah would never be a mate for Aris. She was nothing more than a huge weight hanging from his shoulders. Tears pooled in her eyes as she thought of him going off to war and leaving her behind, helpless and useless, unable to be by his side.

. . . .

The clanging noises in the enormous cavern were loud, metal on metal, as the Immortal troops thrust their blades into solid steel mannequins to prepare them for the impact of their daggers against the rock-hard chests of the Spanish vampires. The sounds echoed off the stone walls and reverberated harshly in the ultra-sensitive ears of the undead, yet they continued their drills without ceasing. Aris and Richard stood to one side as they watched Gabriela work with a new arrival, a tall handsome male who lived a human life above ground. Like so many others who chose to live in human society, he rallied at the first call to stand and fight for his society and his Queen.

Richard spoke. "Queen Mariska has sent some of her Council to meet with DeMarco. She wants to discuss a treaty. Aris, we must move quickly. If they come to terms, the Queen and her troops will return to DeMarco. If our Immortals are there in the forest that surrounds the castle, waiting for her, we will take them all by surprise. It will be an advantage beyond words. They will have no time to organize. There will be two armies without cohesion. We will surely overcome the enemy."

"Never think that it will be easy, Richard. And, we will lose some of our people. They will die at the hands of the miserable vampires of Spain." Aris' tone was somber as he spoke.

Richard spoke softly, almost a whisper. "What must be will be. Without the battle, our world and the world above ground will be devastated. Those who will be lost give their existence courageously, without fear."

"Richard, our Immortals have never experienced battle. They have no idea of the horrors of watching their friends die around them, the remorse for dead comrades, and the self-recrimination because they have been left alive. This single battle will change our society for all eternity." He watched as Gabriela corrected the newcomers, working tirelessly toward proficiency in weaponry.

· · · · · · · · · · · · · · · · · · ·

Richard stood alone, the pavilion dark, quiet and empty except for him. Hearing the sound of the heavy door opening, he turned to find Sebastian searching for him in the gloom. As he touched the control panel on the wall, a soft morning light filled the room.

"Ah Richard. I hoped to find you alone." The two friends found seats on the steps leading to the training floor. "I am concerned about Aris."

"How so?"

"He worries about Sarah constantly. I understand his feelings for her, but I fear his thoughts for her stand in the way of our troop displacement. We must travel soon. Councilors of both Mariska and DeMarco are meeting to discuss reconciliation. We must move. Time is of the essence."

"Sebastian, I know he has reservations about leaving her, but I do not believe that would stand in his way as a general. When he is sure we are ready, he will give the command to travel."

"I only hope you are right. We have no time for his love to stand in the way of our victory."

"Be at ease, my friend. Aris knows his duty and he will lead us to triumph when the time is right."

"I hope what you say is true."

"Come, Sebastian, a goblet or two and you will find peace. Aris is our General and we must stand behind him."

"Of that, I am more than willing as long as he is moving forward, not standing still."

Richard threw his arm around the shoulder of his friend as he led him from the pavilion and into town.

CHAPTER 23

Aris and Sarah were to meet Richard and Gabriela for an evening together. Aris had agreed after much deliberation to take her to a Sanguinaria, a blood tavern. He worried she would be disgusted by seeing the Immortals partake of their sacred drink.

Jane told Sarah about the taverns as she was describing life below ground to her human friend. Sarah tried not to think about it, but she knew the drinking of blood would be a basic part of her existence if she chose to change. When Jane explained more fully to her the blood the Immortals drank in the twenty-first century was a synthetic created by Queen Akira and her alchemy, Sarah felt she might accept it more easily. After the Queen came to cherish the human race as having intrinsic value and not simply a herd for feeding upon as she first thought, she spent centuries working with the scientists to create a substance in place of human blood that would satisfy her Immortals. Sarah knew that if she was going to accept the Immortal life, she would have to accept all of it with her eyes wide open. She held tight to Aris' hand as they approached Richard and Gabriela. The couple was sitting at an outside table. She noticed immediately the pewter goblets in their hands. She had always known logically that they were vastly different from her, yet this was the first time she was confronted openly with their most disturbing difference.

"Are you sure you are going to be alright with this?" Aris worried that all of Sarah's bravado would disappear when she saw her friends drink blood, synthetic or not.

"Well, we're going to find out right now, aren't we?"

Richard rose to hug Sarah and seat her next to Gabriela. Soft chamber music played by a string quartet could be heard coming from the open door and windows of the tavern. An attractive young serving man approached their table with two additional goblets.

"One only." Aris spoke quickly, taking the cup from the server and motioning him away. "Please bring a glass of water."

Sarah thought of the many times in the past Aris sat with her friends in Chicago with an untouched glass of water before him as the humans drank wine. Here, their roles were reversed. However, this time the "wine" the Immortals drank was something much richer.

The three vampires sat uneasily at the table. None wanted to be the first to drink in front of Sarah, but each knew if she was to accept them fully, she must see them as they truly were. Gabriela, knowing Sarah's reaction to their drinking blood would be important in her decision to change, was the first. She raised her goblet toward Sarah as she spoke. "To our friend, companion and sister." She tipped the goblet to her lips and drank. The men followed suit. When Aris placed his cup on the table, a tiny red drop rested at the corner of his mouth. Sarah reached to wipe it away then held her finger to his lips. As his soft tongue licked her finger, she shivered.

. . . .

Cuddled alone in the palace Aris had created for her below ground, safe in her bed, Sarah thought about her evening. While she missed him, wishing he could be with her instead of drilling with the army, she was glad for a moment alone with her thoughts. She marveled at her complete acceptance of the Immortals' existence, their way of life. Or way of death. Which was it? Her logical mind interrupted, spoke loudly. "*You are a human. What is wrong with you? How can you contemplate becoming one of them?*"

She had no answers to that question. Nor did she need any. She knew, after their evening at the blood tavern, without any shadow of a doubt, exactly what she wanted. She wanted to become one with this exceptional society, to learn all they knew, to discover and live in a new, a better world. She wanted to live in harmony with these amazing beings. She wanted to stand with them against the Spanish coven, against all adversity. She wanted to love Aris, not just with her heart, but with her soul, with her body, to be able to free the heat and passion she felt that she held back from him, to be with him for all eternity. She knew, without a single doubt or fear, she desired to become an Immortal, not for Aris, but for herself. Kitsuko would find her a very willing adversary for his love.

At complete peace with her decision, she fell asleep with a smile on her lips.

. . . .

Sarah was out of bed and dressed before Jane appeared with her breakfast tray. She ate leisurely, telling Jane of her experience the previous evening in the blood tavern. Yet she kept secret her decision to change. Aris would be the first she would tell and as soon as possible. She wanted to begin the three day ordeal so she could be ready for the vampire war in Spain. She wouldn't allow Aris to leave without her and the time was short before his departure.

"Sarah, do you think we could do another session this morning? Is it too soon after the first one?"

"No, it isn't too soon. Let's do it." She moved the tray aside, and sat on the chair next to the sofa. "Here, lie down and get comfortable."

Jane rested on the sofa, the white wolf curled on the floor next to her. Sarah took out her notebook and pen. "Are you ready to begin?"

"Yes." Jane closed her eyes, sighing softly.

. . . .

Sarah began the hypnotic induction the same as she had for so many years during her career as a therapist above ground with but a single difference. She assured the Immortal that she would feel no human fear of anything that would surface, that she was an Immortal in complete control of any situations that presented themselves and could come out of hypnosis to return to the present simply by opening her eyes.

JANE HOWARD, transcript, Session 2

Sarah noticed that in her first session, Jane had been most comfortable speaking of Queen Elizabeth and so she began their second session questioning her about her time as maid-in-waiting.

"It is but a year that I have been waiting on the Queen. She tells me that my youth and innocence have made her love me very best of all the young maidens. Often she calls me to her privy chamber just to chat and play board games with me. She tells me she sincerely trusts me and so quickly feels as close to me as her beloved personal maid who has served her for many years."

"Jane, tell me more of your Queen."

"In this past year as I watched her reign over England, I saw her use her great wit to overcome the male bias of her Council. Time and again she won them over without them ever knowing they had been had. She would laugh as she told me of her victories. Her ability to rule her kingdom her way, without King, consort or any man to share her power, taught me to have the greatest respect for her. In private, she allowed me to see all the vulnerable sides to her and that taught me to love her."

"Vulnerable?"

"Her Majesty was before the public all her life. In her youth, her fair skin and red hair were legend in all the courts of Europe. Her beauty and her pledge to remain a virgin married only to her people, to her England, made her worshiped almost as a deity by her subjects.

"At fifty-four years, time and responsibility had begun to show on her face and she hated it. Each day as we prepared her for court, she would tell us of the time when she needed neither wig nor white lead and vinegar face paint. She needed not the vermilion for her lips and cheeks. She bemoaned her mirror each morning as if it had no purpose but to show the lines and wrinkles around her eyes and mouth, her yellow and rotting teeth. Many days she spent in agonizing headaches from the decay in her mouth. She admitted to me she was almost glad when her vision began to blur her aging image in the betraying glass.

"She swore me to secrecy before she told me the worst ravage of age; at fifty four she desperately loved a lad of but twenty. It was Robert Devereux, the Second Earl of Essex.

"Oh, I could see why. He was tall, long of leg. Chestnut curls surrounded his beautiful face and he courted her shamelessly. He even challenged Sir Walter Raleigh to a duel over who loved Her Majesty most. It was sad, but the courtiers laughed behind their hands at the Queen's manner in her dealings with the Earl.

"She flirted and batted her eyes at him like a girl. She showered him with gifts, making him one of the richest men at court. She even gave him the tax on sweet wines, which alienated some of her dearest supporters. Essex was hated by the men, yet because of his great beauty and flirtatious complements, adored by the women.

"He cavorted about moving from woman to woman, yet none had the heart or the courage to make his actions known to the Queen."

"Jane, did he show affection to you as well as the other ladies of the court?" Sarah hoped to slowly and comfortably bring Jane's attention to the day of her changing and the role Essex played. The young Immortal paused a long moment before she answered.

"*Yes, he did. On many occasions he approached me and on a few made physical advances to me.*"

"But you never mentioned it to the Queen?"

"*No. Her heart would have been broken to know he was such a treacherous knave. I avoided him as best I could, yet he seemed to be obsessed by a woman who would not succumb to his deceitful charm. Neither his beauty nor his allure could make me forget his supposed love for Her Majesty and I felt a hidden wickedness behind his insincere words. I only saw him when court functions demanded it, otherwise, I avoided all places he was known to frequent. And so, after a time, he began to search me out in the gardens hoping to find me alone.*"

"And did that happen frequently?"

"*Too frequently.*"

Sarah spoke gently as she approached Jane about her personal relationship with Essex. "Jane, can you tell me about the first time Essex found you by yourself?" There was a long, silent pause.

"Yes." Again, silence. "*It was summer twilight as I walked in the Queen's rose garden. She sent me away while she rested in preparation for a masque ball in the evening. The clouds above were a soft fuchsia and gold as a gentle evening breeze brushed my hair against my cheek.*

"*I heard the sound of muffled footsteps behind me. When I turned, there he stood, his head surrounded by a glowing halo created by the vanishing rays of the setting sun. I gasped as I realized who it was and quickly began to move away from him. He reached to grasp my arm as I turned. At that exact moment a huge white owl with an enormous wingspan swooped from an unseen spot in the sky. His talons tangled in Essex's curls and the Earl loosed my arm. I turned to flee without seeing the outcome of the encounter between the man and the gigantic bird. I rushed to the safety of the Queen's chamber and, gratefully, I reached it without further incident.*" Jane chose to breathe when she was in Sarah's presence to make her human friend feel more comfortable and her breath became ragged as she related her escape.

Even though Sarah had given Jane the suggestion she would feel no fear during her sessions, she became concerned when she heard the change in her subject's breathing. Immediately she brought the Immortal to present time, safe at home in Sarah's rooms in the Catacombs.

. . . .

"Sarah, I remember other encounters with Essex fully, yet I only remember the experience of the day of my change in bits and pieces. Must it have been so awful, so horrible that I will never remember?" She bowed her head in sorrow. "I must know what happened."

Her friend stood to take the vampire's hands in hers. "Jane, you will. It will be slow and perhaps painful, but you will remember."

The white wolf whimpered softly as he rose, placing his cool muzzle in the hand of his mistress.

CHAPTER 24

The air was humid and warm as he maneuvered the small boat on the underground river. All the delicate tendrils of blond hair around Sarah's face tightened into tiny spiral curls, wet with perspiration. Aris had planned the day just for the two of them. Showing her some of the beauty of the Catacombs, not just the battle preparation, had been on his mind since their arrival and he was grateful to Sebastian for taking over his duties so he could spend the afternoon with Sarah away from talk of war.

"Aris, why is the air so damp in here? Normally, caves don't feel like this."

Aris smiled as he maneuvered the energy-powered craft silently through the gently flowing current. "You will see. Trail your fingers in the water."

"Is it safe? I mean, there's nothing in the water to bite me?"

He laughed long and loud. "You worry about a river creature biting you when you're holed-up in a city of undead, Immortal vampires who drink blood? You are quite a strange woman, Sarah."

She realized as soon as the words left her mouth, how silly they would sound to him. She obviously no longer feared the Immortals of the Catacombs, yet something living in the water? Well, that was another thing all-together.

"Go ahead, trail your fingers. There is nothing there to harm you."
Alien lighting globes illuminated the river from below as the boat
skimmed soundlessly against the current.

Above their heads was thousands of years old solid iridescent rock.
The cavern through which the river flowed was dark except for the
golden lights shining from beneath the water. Lit from below, Aris
looked strange, even frightening. Sarah wondered how she appeared
to him. Hollows for eyes, shadows for lips. She thought she might
look like one of the vampires from the old black and white 1930s
movies.

She let her fingers dip into the water as it slapped gently against the
sides of their craft. It was warm, almost hot to the touch. No wonder
the air was humid. "Why is the water so hot? And where does it come
from?"

"There is a great deal of water underground. Surface water seeps
down through the rocks creating subterranean lakes and waterways.
This river is one of them. There is a small underground volcano
located west of the Catacombs several miles below our city. The
ground water trickles all the way down to the level of the molten rock,
is heated by the magma then escapes upward toward the surface. Our
hot river water is a result of the surface water and the volcano."

"Oh, I see." She continued to let the warm water flow sensuously
through her fingers. Her mind drifted as they floated in an unearthly
silence, day-dreaming she and Aris were explorers trapped in a
tropical rain forest, their only means of escape this river of no return.

She smiled as she imagined him pulling the boat onto a jungle
river bank covered in reeds and grass. Closing her eyes, she could
almost feel him taking her hands, drawing her to him as he stood
on the river's edge. In her imagination his body was warm and
powerful as he pressed into her. She melted into him, the contours
of his muscular thighs against her. Feeling his manhood swell against
her, tortured by her need for him to take her, her fingers reached to

unbutton his shirt.

"Sarah?" She heard his voice as if from a great distance.

Her vision continued as he stood nude before her, his smooth firm body glistening in the sultry air.

"Sarah? Are you alright?"

Startled back into the present. she thought, "*Just when it was starting to get good.*" She replied out loud, "Yes, I'm fine, just thinking."

"I want to warn you, it is going to become very dark very soon. The underwater lighting will be extinguished for just a moment and we will be in an extremely confined space. There is no need to be frightened. There is nothing to harm you in the darkness. There will be light again shortly and a vision like none you have ever experienced before in all your human life."

As he finished his sentence the tunnel grew black. She lifted her hand directly in front of her face and still could see nothing. She felt the walls pressing in on her. The sound of her breath was loud and strained. It was the only sound she could hear other than the gentle lapping of the water as they moved forward. She reached to find his hand only to have him touch hers first.

"Rest easy, it is only moments before there is light."

As if he conjured it, a blinding light encompassed them, a light brighter than the sun. She blinked rapidly, shutting her eyes tight against the visual onslaught. After a moment, she carefully opened them a little at a time. She found they were in an enormous underground cave; a cave so large the river disappeared into a tiny speck as it flowed to a vanishing point in the distance. The bright light emanated from above them, yet it was so brilliant, Sarah couldn't look at it long enough to find out how tall the ceiling actually was.

She was experiencing sensory overload as Aris steered the boat to the river bank. As she gazed at the landscape on either side of the canal, her breath stopped. Tall monoliths surrounded them. Some appeared at least ten stories tall. They reminded her of the enormous monument stones in the deserts of the Southwest United States. With one radical difference: these mountains of rock were of astoundingly brilliant shades of primary colors layered one on top of the other like ocean wave over ocean wave. She was reminded of Petra in Jordan. Once she had watched a documentary about the Nabatean's two thousand year old colorful hand-carved rock trade center in the middle of the desert. But this cave was even more brilliant and appeared to be older. She had never before seen such intense reds and yellows, oranges and blues of every shade and greens of every hue.

Aris helped her step out of the craft and onto the stone dock. The boat idled quietly in the water, waiting for their return. As Sarah looked around, she found it hard to believe the rocks were such bright colors naturally. Surely they had been tampered with by Akira's alchemy.

As if reading her thoughts, Aris spoke. "Sarah, these rocks were exactly as you see them when the Immortals discovered this cave centuries ago. It has been a place of personal refuge among our kind since long before I came to the Catacombs. It is the Specus Solitudo. The Cavern of Solitude."

A gentle breeze ruffled her hair as she looked at him questioningly.

Holding her hand, he led her toward a path winding through the natural pillars. "We found shafts leading from here to the surface. Air currents flow through them to keep the air in the cavern fresh and clean.

"Sebastian and Henry were exploring this cave shortly after it was discovered by the Immortals many centuries ago. He and Henry were planning the first illumination system for the cavern. In their surveying they found a temple carved into an underground mountain of rock. Or should I say carved from the rock. Pillars and windows and doors. All perfect. All by hand before the time of the Immortals. It is my wish to take you there."

Sarah threw her arms around him. "I don't know if I can take much more beauty, but I'm willing to try. Let's get going." He kissed her gently, then holding her hand once again, moved forward.

They wound their way through columns of blue striated stone, in some places it looked like turquoise and in some, lapis. As they walked the sky above them dimmed until it was as soft and gentle as a sunset. They walked with his arm around her waist and she wondered why his stride met hers even though he was so much taller than she was. She decided it was because they simply were perfect for each other in all ways but one and she had solid plans to change that.

Without warning, they stepped from the path through the forest of monoliths into a huge open clearing. Sarah sometimes questioned the wonders of the Catacombs but if she had, the vision before her wiped all remaining doubt from her mind.

The temple was at least two hundred feet wide, five stories tall, carved without blemish. The columns were plumb, the arches above the entry way perfect. The walls of the exterior matched the colors of the setting sun above ground. Orange. Red. Yellow. The steps leading to the temple were the same color of translucent green that rests just above the horizon at the exact moment before the sun drops from sight.

Her voice was hardly above a whisper when she spoke. "Can we go inside?"

"Of course." Still holding hands, they crossed the courtyard. Side-stepping large boulders and rocks that had fallen in the path over the last centuries, they made their way toward the entrance. When they reached the enormous doorway, Sarah held back.

"Aris, are you sure it's alright if we go inside."

Laughing, he pulled her through the door. "Yes, my love. Come inside and look all around you."

The light pouring through the doors and windows of the hand-carved room made it bright enough that once Sarah's eyes adjusted, she could see perfectly.

She gasped as she realized she was surrounded, floor to ceiling and wall to wall, by beautiful hieroglyphic writing. Each wall and pillar was carved from a different color stone and each surface told a unique story. Mesmerized, skimming column after column of detailed sketches, she realized each wall was covered by a complete chronicle of an event. All of the people drawn were depicted nude; the only backgrounds were natural surroundings. Without clothing to date them and only simple settings without tools or any sign of a culture, there was no clue as to when the carvings were created. "Oh Aris, you were right. How could anyone ever envision such a wonder? By not clothing the people the artist made the stories timeless. They could have been created yesterday or thousands of years ago." She stood in one spot, turning slowly, taking in as much as her human eyes could see. "Are you able to read any of this?"

"No, none of our people have really taken on the project to translate them. Some scant research has been gathered as a hobby by a few linguists, however no one has stepped forward to head an actual project." He smiled. "Of course, we do have eternity so there really is no rush."

With their arms wrapped around each other, they gazed at the walls in silence.

"A timeless story of birth and death." Aris spoke as he pointed to the first carving in a pictograph, a young woman expecting a child. The next drawing showed her ready to deliver. The next, squatting on birthing blocks supported by two other women. In the next, she was lying down, holding the child to her breast. Then, a sweet image of a tiny child sitting on the floor, playing with a ball. And the final tragic drawing of the child lying dead, the mother tearing her hair and beating her breast at her loss. "This story needs no words for the telling."

"So many centuries, Aris, and yet nothing is different. Birth.

Death. Sorrow. Only in your world of the Catacombs is there simply life and joy. Not human life but life everlasting. Life as no human has ever known or could imagine." She turned to face him. "The time to tell you is now. I've made the final decision. I want to become an Immortal. You asked me long ago if I would ever give my human life for love. The answer is yes. You are the only one I have ever loved and I'm not only willing, I am yearning for you, for Immortality at your side."

"Sarah." He reached for her, his eyes brimming with laughter. "Sarah." He kissed her with a passion he had been holding back, waiting until she was ready, praying the day would come when she would give herself to him. He felt her melt against him, the texture of her soft skin beneath his hands; he smelled the warm sweet fragrance of her hair. They stood in silence in their first true embrace. When he could no longer hold back, his lips sought her throat and as he felt the pulse of her heart beat against his mouth, he moaned. Her mouth found his, her heart pounding in her chest, desire ripping all reason from her mind. Her breath coming in tiny gasps, her trembling fingers reached for the buttons on his shirt longing to feel his bare chest against her. Knowing he could not have her while she was still human and using all his vampire resolve, gently, he took hold of her shoulders and moved her away from him.

He stared into her eyes and when he spoke it was quietly, thoughtfully. "I need you to be sure, to be without question. Sarah, it can never be reversed. Do you truly understand what that means? It is a decision for all time. You will suffer during the three days of your changing, a suffering you cannot even conceive. You will feel as if your body is in flames as the human blood burns out of your system. There will be no turning back once we begin. To do so would end your human life and all possibility of your ever becoming Immortal." It pained his heart to caution her. He desperately wanted to take her where they stood, but he loved her too much to allow her feelings for him to cloud her reason. "Sarah, what of Colleen? What of your Chicago life? You cannot just disappear. What will you tell them?"

"I'll tell them we are going to be married and we've decided to stay in London for a while because of your work. They'll not only understand, they'll be genuinely happy for us. I'm sure Bonnie will be fine with taking over my business and my clients. She's been handling them since I've been gone anyway. Maggie can stay on and help her. It will be great for both of them. And, since my human friends won't be able to tell the difference in me, I certainly don't have to give them up. At least not for a long, long time." She gripped his hands. "Oh, Aris. Give me credit for knowing my own mind."

"I do not wish for you to ever regret your decision. I would never want you to change only to fulfill my desire."

"Of course you are an important part of my decision, but you're most certainly not all of it. Aris, I'm not blind. I see the perfection of your society. You live an existence without fear or greed or hate; an existence where you have a choice to live with humanity or not, to enjoy a human life or live only as an Immortal. And, you have the choice to change back and forth any time you want."

She tilted her head as she smiled at him, "By the way, the ability to make that choice? It only lasts for all of eternity. Oh, yes." Her smile grew into a happy laugh. "Yes, and I get to share that eternity with you? I ask you, what human in their right mind would walk away from such an opportunity?"

He held her close to his chest and nestled his lips to her throat once again. The thought of having her for all time, of possessing her at last, nearly drove him mad with love and desire.

. . . .

Gabriela helped Sarah pack her clothes after she finished packing her own. She understood Sarah's need to visit her friends in Chicago before her changing, but this trip couldn't have come at a worse time. Their spies from Spain had reported DeMarco and Mariska were getting close to a possible reconciliation. It seemed Aris had been right when he said their desire to win a victory in London might overshadow even their hateful, arguing natures. The Immortal troops had only a short time left before they must travel to Spain. Gabriela was needed to command her fighting force, yet she was leaving, flying with Sarah to ensure her safety.

Sarah had fought them all to return to Chicago alone. Taking Gabriela away from the Catacombs at such a crucial time worried her. Feeling sure the Spanish coven would take all DeMarco's attention, she believed she would be safe.

The vampires wouldn't hear of it. Richard volunteered, and Kitsuko immediately agreed to share the responsibility of training Gabriela's troops to allow her to travel. Kitsuko was only too glad to have Sarah gone from the Catacombs and a chance to have Aris to herself. It was settled, the two captains would share Gabriela's command until she returned. Still, Aris fretted about Sarah leaving the Catacombs at all even though he understood why she wanted to see her Chicago friends. It was with great reservation that he finally agreed.

"I'm almost finished. Just my toiletries and I'll do that in the morning." She sat on the sofa. "Gaby, thank you so much for coming with me."

"Do you actually think Aris would let you out of the sight of one of us, DeMarco in Spain or not? It would not surprise me if he decided you should not go."

"I know it's a bad time, but we'll only be gone a few days. I just need to see my old friends before, well, you know."

"I know. And I understand. Still Aris will be troubled for your safety all the while you are gone. I will be with you and he knows you are out of harm's way with me, but he will still be worried. Although the truth is I doubt the Spanish coven will be thinking about your whereabouts right now."

"I'm sure you're right." She stood, going through both her suitcases to make sure she had everything she needed. "Looks good here. Guess I'll get some sleep. The plane is before dawn tomorrow." She stooped to kiss her vampire friend on the cheek then crossed to her room. Her sheets felt cool and soft as she climbed into bed and turned off the light. She yawned as she called through the open door. "Good night, Gaby. Soon sleep will be an option, not a demand." She smiled at the thought of an eternity of sleepless nights with Aris.

. . . .

Aris parked in front of the terminal and popped the trunk. Stepping out to open the door for the two women, he spoke gravely. "Alright, now call me as soon as you land."

"Good God, Aris." Gaby spoke as she got out of the car. "This is the third time you told us. We will call you at precisely the moment the wheels touch the ground." She laughed at the painfully concerned look on his face. "Please, stop. I will take care of her and return her to you safe and sound." She hugged him then lifted her carry-on from the open trunk.

He drew Sarah to him, speaking softly into her hair. "Stay within Gabriela's sight at all times. Please, no insane chances." He moved her to arms-length, scrutinizing her face. "In a short time you will be invincible but until then, remember, you are the fragile human woman I love and I expect you to return intact."

She wound her fingers into his thick dark curls, kissing his beautiful mouth as her answer.

Lost in saying their goodbyes, neither of the three noticed the dark rental car parked in the cell phone lot. Kitsuko's Immortal vision watched Aris say goodbye to his human with a smile. A dream come true. Four days alone with him without the blonde standing in her way. She had confidence she could convince him of the folly of his choice of mates.

As she pulled out of the lot to follow Aris back to the Catacombs, she noticed a car just like the one that had crashed into her in London. At first she thought it was a coincidence, but as it passed her, she recognized the driver as the driver that banged into her car. *"That's strange. Could there be any relationship between Aris and that man?"* She put the episode out of her mind as her thoughts returned to the next four days without Sarah.

CHAPTER 25

As Colleen squealed away from the curb at O'Hare International Airport, she hollered over her shoulder at Sarah sitting in the back seat. "What kind of crazy person flies over an ocean for four days." She directed her next comment to Gabriela sitting next to her. "And you? You're crazier than she is to come along." She turned on her blinker and changed lanes. "I don't know why people drive so damn slow on the tollway. Makes no sense to me."

"Thanks for picking us up. I'm kind of sorry the baby is sleeping and Bob is home with her. I can't wait to see her." Sarah leaned toward the window looking up at the familiar skyline. "It seems like forever since I've been in my own apartment."

"Yeah, your little short trip to London turned into a month. You're lucky we all love you. Bonnie's been working her butt off taking care of your peeps and hers while you've been out in la la land."

"Don't try to make me feel guilty. I talked to Bon and she's loving it. She's made enough extra money to finish financing the new sofa and chair she wants."

"Yeah, well we miss you anyway. How come you can only stay for a couple of days?"

"An art exhibit in Spain. The London gallery owner has set up a meeting with a Spanish colleague. We're going there to meet him and see the gallery. Aris asked me to go with him and I don't want to miss it."

Wide-eyed at the name she just heard come from Sarah's mouth, Gabriela turned in her seat to stare at her friend as Colleen spoke. "Who's Aris? I've never heard you talk about him before."

Sarah cleared her throat. "Well, I guess there's no time like the present. Carlos has changed his professional name. He doesn't want to be constantly connected to his gang-banger life anymore."

"Yeah?" Colleen was incredulous. "When did that happen?"

"Well, he's been talking about it for a while. He says he's felt like a different person since his near-death experience. He's living a brand new life and he wants a new name to go along with it."

"Okay. I sort of get it. But where did he get a name like Aris?"

"Someone who greatly influenced him in his life. I really like it."

"I guess it's okay." Gabriela breathed a silent sigh of relief as Colleen accepted the story. "Does he want us all to call him that? I think it's going to be kind of hard if he does."

"He would like it if everyone would call him Aris."

"I'll do my best. I've never known anyone who changed their name in mid-stream before. Is he keeping his same last name?"

"No, he isn't going to use a last name. Look C., it really isn't that difficult once you get used to it. You'll see."

"No last name, huh? That's kind of weird, don't you think?"

When there was no answer to her question she continued. "Like I said, I'll do my best. I promise, but don't get pissed if I mess up now and then." She pulled up outside Sarah's building. "Do you girls want company or are you ready to call it a night."

Sarah glanced at her watch. It was almost one in the morning. "I'm pretty tired, C. My jet is lagging." She leaned toward the front seat to kiss her friend goodbye. "We're going to see you and Bob tomorrow night for dinner, so I think we'll just go in and collapse."

"No problem." She got out of the car to embrace the two tired travelers. "See you guys tomorrow."

As Sarah stepped into the revolving door taking them into the lobby of her building, she felt like a stranger in a strange land.

. . . .

They all relaxed in their chairs as they finished the last sips of wine in their glasses. "That was a great dinner." Sarah folded her napkin and stood along with Colleen and Gabriela to begin clearing the table.

"No, ladies. I'll take care of that. Take the baby and go sit in the living room and catch up. I'm glad to do this." Bob began stacking the dishes as the women slid their chairs under the dining room table.

"That was a far cry from the meals you cooked when the two of you were first married." Sarah wrapped her arm around her friend as the three women left Colleen's police detective husband to take care of kitchen duty. "I remember those little hot dogs wrapped in dough you used to always serve. This was a real adult meal."

"Thank you, I think." Colleen laughed as she poured a splash of brandy into the crystal glasses resting on the coffee table. "Now, tell me everything."

"Why don't you catch me up while we wait for Bonnie and Jack. I'm glad she's still seeing the fireman. He's a really nice guy." She lifted the glass to her lips, the familiar fragrance of the golden liquid made her mouth water.

"This tastes amazingly good, C. You've turned into quite the hostess. What happened?" She laughed as they settled in to hear all about the metamorphosis of Colleen Stevens, hard-as-nails parole officer who would never be tied down, to Colleen Stevens-Drake, loving wife, mother and budding chef. She planned to return to work when Collette began school, but for the moment she was really enjoying being a stay-at-home mom.

The doorbell rang as Bob wiped his hands on a towel and shut off the kitchen light. "I'll get it." He opened the door for Bonnie and Jack. Their greeting was warm and happy as they all settled in around the coffee table. Sarah kept them busy with questions, asking about what she had missed in the weeks she had been away. Bonnie promised to fill her in on her clients when the two of them had time alone to talk about Sarah's business.

"The baby has grown so much." They all turned to look at the little girl sleeping next to her mother on the sofa. Her little mouth trembled in a tiny yawn as she made fists with her miniature hands. "She looks just like you, C."

"Enough about us, we want to hear everything about, well, about everything." Bonnie leaned forward, resting her elbows on her knees. "I mean it, everything."

Sarah told them about the London art world. She explained to all of them the name change of the man they thought they knew so well and was surprised at how easily they accepted her story. She related how Aris was taking England by storm and was invited to show in Spain. Her American friends sat, enthralled with her account while Gabriela marveled at her devious mind.

"And, I've saved the best for last." They all waited for her to speak, each one knowing what she was going to say. "Aris has asked me to marry him. And, I've said yes."

Colleen whooped, jumping from the couch to grab her friend and hug her. Noticing the baby was jostled awake, Bob picked her up and rocked her back to sleep before she began to fuss. Bonnie rushed Sarah and wrapped her arms around her. Jack sat on the sofa, a silly grin on his face. It was a laughing, crying huddled group of women that Bob and a sleeping baby joined in congratulations.

. . . .

All of her friends fit into the booth for brunch at Saul's Deli, Colleen and Bonnie on one side, Sarah and a slightly slimmed down Maggie on the other. Gabriela pulled a chair to the vacant end of the table and sat half in and half out of the aisle. They laughed and joked while they looked at the menus, but ended up ordering their usual breakfasts. The waitresses welcomed Sarah back after her long absence and kept all of the women's coffee cups filled to the brim.

"Okay," Maggie was the first to speak about the up-coming marriage. "You will, of course, be married here in Chicago." Her statement was matter of fact as if there was no doubt at all.

Sarah played with the paper from her straw. "Well, we're not sure. His time schedule is so crazy right now we might just get married in London."

"Is it legal for you to do that?"

"Of course it is. All we have to do is post the banns, wait fifteen days and say our vows."

"Really? It's that easy?"

"Honestly Maggie," Colleen spoke in between sips from her coffee cup. "It isn't the getting married that's hard, it's the getting un-married." Maggie giggled as she looked at the engagement ring on her own finger.

"Well, easy or not," Bonnie joined the conversation, "I think you owe us big for all the years we've put up with you being man-less. You have to get married right here in Chicago so we can give you away."

"I know I owe you, but we don't honestly have the free time right now to plan a big ceremony." An embarrassed smile on her face, she continued. "And I miss him. I don't want to be on this side of the ocean planning something that is for both of us. We're just going to say our vows quietly in the U.K."

Colleen's voice could be heard clearly above the buzz of the restaurant. "No, I really don't think you are. How can you do this to us? And what about your mother? And your grandmother? We all want to be there. Hell, who cares about these guys," she gestured at Bonnie and Maggie. "I want to be there. I was the one who sent Carlos, crap, I mean Aris, to you in the first place." She grumbled, "I don't know why the hell he had to change his name. The name Carlos is perfectly respectable."

"I know it seems hard to call him something different after knowing him as Carlos for so long."

"No, I'll get it sooner or later. We'll all help each other. Aris. It's such a strange old-worldly name. I've never heard it before."

"It isn't so strange. It isn't like he's the only Aris on the planet."

"Don't try to change the subject."

The waitress brought their breakfasts on a huge tray. Gaby stood to make it easier for her to place the plates on the table. When she sat again, the ladies began to eat. Colleen continued talking, browbeating Sarah as she dumped half a cup of ketchup on her home fried potatoes. "Come on, Sarah. We'll take care of everything. All you have to do is let us know when you can come into town for a couple of days. That's all it'll take. We'll make all the arrangements. Nothing fancy, just something simple. We all want to be there, hon. It's a big deal to us too."

Sarah knew her friends were right. If she could survive changing into an Immortal and going through the vampire war, having a wedding in Chicago wasn't too much to ask. "Okay, okay. I'll talk to Aris. I'm sure he'll agree. I do want all of you to be there. Now, can I please eat my breakfast in peace. I'm starving."

With a smile of triumph on her lips Colleen kissed Sarah on the cheek just before she put a huge forkful of scrambled eggs in her mouth.

CHAPTER 26

Try as she might, Kitsuko was unable to find Aris alone until the last evening before Sarah returned. She hunted him down in Sarah's quarters and when he heard it was she outside the door, he took more than a minute to answer her. She knew he was anxious at being alone with her and he proved it when upon opening the door, he stepped into the corridor.

"Sarah is not here."

"I know she is not. I have come to speak with you Aris. May I come in?"

"Perhaps we should walk to the Sanguinaria. We can talk there."

"Please, let us just step inside. I will be on my best behavior. There are simply some things I must tell you and I wish to do it in private."

Opening the door, he showed her into the living room. A bright fire blazed in the hearth and a goblet and pitcher rested on the coffee table. She sat on the sofa and the firelight danced in her dark eyes.

"Would you care for a drink?" She shook her head and he took a seat in the chair across from her.

"Kitsuko, what is on your mind?"

She leaned forward as she spoke. "You know very well. I have feelings for you and I know you return them. I have felt you quicken at my touch. I have felt your eyes follow me as I train. Tell me, you have no feelings for me."

Shocked, Aris took a moment to collect his thoughts before he answered. "Kitsuko, I respect your prowess as a fighter. I am eternally grateful for all you have taught us. You have even given us the edge we need to beat the Spanish."

"I know that is not all, Aris. You feel more for me than just another soldier. Do not lie."

"Yes, I did feel excitement at your touch, but I belong to another. Lust and love are not one in the same. They can be felt separately and together. Your touch excited my body, but my heart, my love belongs to Sarah. It has always been that way and it always will be. I wish to take her for my wife."

"How can you step outside of your own kind to find a mate? How can you love someone so feeble and pathetic? You are a warrior and need a warrior by your side, not a mere human." Tears welled in her eyes as she spoke.

Aris moved to sit beside the now sobbing woman. "Kitsuko, my dear, I have loved Sarah for centuries. It is not an infatuation, but a deep and lasting devotion." He wiped her tears with the tips of his fingers. "What I felt for you in the moment, in just that instant, was pure base desire. My body responded to your touch, not my heart. What you feel for me is infatuation, nothing more."

"No, you do not understand." Her eyes pooled with tears once again. "I love you. It is more than can be explained. It is more than I am. I love you." She reached to pull his face to hers, to kiss him for the first time.

Standing quickly, he moved away from her. "No, you mistake respect for love. Now, I think it is best if you go. Calm yourself and rethink your words. I know you will realize I tell the truth about your feelings. Go and we will never speak of this again."

She stared at him in disbelief, then rose and left the room. She had lost the battle, but the war was yet to be fought.

CHAPTER 27

The international flight left O'Hare Airport on time and as it made its climb to cruising altitude, Sarah leaned back in her seat, closing her eyes against the cabin light. Thoughts of saying goodbye to her Chicago life haunted her. Everything would be different the next time she visited. Everything was already different and then as now, only she and her Immortal companions were aware of the differences. She felt guilty lying to all the humans in her life.

"Am I really lying to them?" she thought. *"No. I guess I'm really not. I'm just not telling them the whole truth."*

Her friends had rallied to Sarah's every need. Bonnie was pleased to take over Sarah's clients. Maggie was happy to stay on with Bonnie, working her usual three days a week. Colleen took over the care and feeding of Sarah's condo so she and Aris had a place of their own to stay when they visited. She knew eventually it would be sold, but at the moment she was grateful she wasn't hurried into a decision.

Her mother and grandmother had cried when she left, but were at least satisfied there would be a wedding ceremony state-side.

Now that her human world was relatively well taken care of for the next few months, she could concentrate on her new world—on her changing.

While she was away Aris had petitioned the Council for permission to take her for his mate. They granted it gladly. Once an Immortal, they knew she would never betray their society. Once she changed, there would be no human alive who knew of the existence of the Catacombs.

She was excited to learn that on her return to London, she would attend Immortal catechism to familiarize herself with the Law as well as what was expected of her in her new culture. She was thrilled to begin her new journey, yet she felt anxious when she faced the reality of the price to be paid and the physical pain her decision would bring her as she made the transition from human to vampire. "*If others have stood it, I can as well.*"

As if reading her mind, Gabriela reached over the armrest and squeezed her hand. "We will all be there for you."

Sarah knew the Immortal spoke the truth.

. . . .

Passing time with Sebastian, Aris waited for the hour to drive to the airport to retrieve Sarah and Gabriela. The two friends sat in the Sanguinaria, each with a half-full pewter goblet on the table before them. Aris spoke softly as he questioned Sebastian. "But how did you know you would find the strength to stop?"

"When it was time for Emily's changing, I felt much as you do right now." He spoke of the changing ceremony between he and his mate, a human he met and loved at the royal court of Tudor England. "I shall not lie to you, my brother. To check the flow of sweet human blood after so many centuries of doing without it is more difficult than you can possibly imagine. But you will find a way. If I was able to do it, you will."

Aris buried his head in his hands. "But how? Her scent, just the feel of her pulse against my lips drives me mad. It takes all my will power not to take her and I have not even yet tasted her blood." He raised pleading eyes to his friend. "I am in terror of my dark side. Please, Sebastian, tell me how to not drain her of her life?"

"When the time comes, your love for her will overcome your blood lust."

"I sincerely hope you are right, Sebastian. I pray that you are right."

CHAPTER 28

Anger crackled in his voice as DeMarco spoke to his exiled captain. "So you come crawling back, Esteban? You think I need you? You and that bitch I called my Queen?"

Kneeling before DeMarco, ignoring his slurs, Esteban spoke quietly, convincingly. "We have need of one another if we are to win this battle. The Queen travels now to join you here at the castle. She brings her troops to join with yours."

"Coming here? To my realm?" His temper raged out of control. "I banished her and she is coming here against my orders? I will eliminate her for all time." He threw open the door, shouting into the corridor. "Guard. Guard." Looking over his shoulder, he shouted at Esteban. "And you along with her."

Bowing his head and with a shaking voice, Esteban responded. "My Lord, please listen to reason. We are two armies with the same enemy. Apart, we will surely fail. Together, we are invincible. The Diaries are our objectives, not war within our own coven. Please, listen. The Queen comes in peace and to prepare to march together with you to London. She has a contrite heart and wishes to be by your side once more."

"She has no heart." Allowing for the truth in Esteban's words, the King regained control of his anger and as the guards entered the throne room he motioned them away. "However, there is legitimacy in your words, Esteban. I will think on it. Go. Tell the Queen to make haste."

"Yes, my Lord." Esteban rose, leaving the room with a smile on his face at having accomplished what the Queen swore he could not do.

CHAPTER 29

"I'm so glad you're going to be my teacher, Henry." Sarah was slowly getting over her initial shyness with the Master Keeper of Records. They sat opposite one another in one corner of Henry's office in the library. The shelves behind his desk were stacked with papers, books and several strange looking devices that she had never seen before.

It had been very difficult for her when they met. Because he was the Master Keeper, he knew her Soul Chart. He knew everything about her. Not just in her present life, but in all her past lives. She wasn't proud of everything in her past. At the beginning of their relationship it was challenging for her to overcome her embarrassment when she was with him, but it was becoming easier and easier as she grew to know him better.

"As am I. It is a rare treat to welcome a new member to our society. You, my dear, fit so well as it is, the transition will come easily to you."

"Henry, tell me about Specus Solitudo? Aris said there had been some research done on the hieroglyphs."

"Yes, some. Why?"

"I find it fascinating. The carvings are made by humans, that's obvious by the subject matter, yet they're far below ground, carved into solid rock from a time before even the Immortals were here."

"We have no idea how old the carvings might be. None of us has taken the project to heart as of yet. We have nothing but time you see, so there is no hurry." He smiled.

"Henry, I want to learn all I can about the temple. It fascinates me. I want to find out about the people who lived below the ground in that cave. Where they came from, who they were."

"Once you are changed, you will have all the time in the universe at your disposal. With your curiosity, I feel sure you will find ways to keep eternally busy."

. . . .

Sarah hurried down the corridor, thrilled with her meeting with Henry. As she rounded a corner, she saw Kitsuko walking toward her. When she neared, she stopped, blocking Sarah's path.

"So, human, you have found the courage to change. It will make no difference and as a newborn, your skill will be limited. You will always be a detriment to Aris. Why do you not just give him up?"

"Why do you hate me so?"

"Why? Why does Aris go outside our society to find a mate? Why does he feel the need to turn you when our world is full of women who would love him?"

"You mean you, don't you? Listen, Kitsuko, Aris and I are destined for one another. You can do all you want to try to take his love from me. It will never happen. Immortal or not, we are pledged for as long as we are in existence. Why don't you just give up your desire for him? It will never be fulfilled."

"I would take your life right now if it would drive you from his heart. But the sorrow of loss would just deepen his love for you. I will wait. You will not have the courage to make the change, to suffer and die for the man you think you love. You will grow old as a human and I will still be here, waiting for him. One day he will grow tired of mourning your loss and I will be there. So enjoy your time with him for one day he will be mine." She laughed out loud as she pushed by Sarah continuing down the corridor toward the training pavilion.

Sarah continued on her way, shaken and lost at the thought of Kitsuko's prophecy.

CHAPTER 30

Late morning found Sarah, Gaby and Jane seated on Sarah's bed in her rooms in the Catacombs. They had just chosen her clothes for the changing ceremony, arranging them on a tall chair in the corner so they could admire them. The lingerie and dress were in soft shades of blue silk fashioned in the style the underground Immortals wore; a long dress fitted at the waist, the skirt flowing in soft ripples to barely skim her ankles. The sleeves were long and fitted, the bodice cut deep, squared off so the Queen would be able to anoint her chest without difficulty. Soft blue silk shoes rested on the carpet beneath the chair

Sarah was propped against pillows, staring into space. Kitsuko's prediction clouded her mind. She longed to be changed, to be a part of the Catacombs, to have the ordeal behind her. Still, she had some unanswered questions about the actual act of changing and she desperately wanted to ask, but held back worried she might make her friends uncomfortable.

Gabriela and Jane sat Indian style across from one another on the foot of her bed. The white wolf curled on the floor near his mistress. Their conversation was stilted, uneasy. The two Immortals were concerned they might say something about her coming ordeal that would frighten Sarah more than they knew she already was. They had all been laughing and joking while they dressed her and arranged her hair, a joyful dress rehearsal. But now that their tasks were complete, the silence between them was heavy.

"Look, I have a great idea. I honestly don't want to sit around here like this. Aris is with the commanders until evening. What do you say we go above ground today. Just for a little while." She swallowed hard. "It may very well be my last look at London as a mortal."

"You two go ahead." Protectively Jane folded her arms across her chest. "I have not been above ground since I came to the Catacombs and I have no desire to do it today."

Gabriela rose, taking her young friend's hands to pull her from the bed. "Come with us. We will make sure you are alright, but if you want to come back below, we will return immediately." Her voice issued a soft challenge. "Come with us. It is for Sarah. It is a day she will remember forever and Aris will worry less if there are two of us with her. Be with us."

Sarah stood next to them. "Please Jane. Just for a little while. If you're uncomfortable in any way, we'll come right back. Besides, aren't you the least bit curious about life above ground?"

"I hear about it from others. I have little memory of life out of the Catacombs and less experience with humans. This is my home. I think I will stay here today." She smiled at Sarah.

"I understand, but please, just for a little while, come with me to say goodbye to the only way of life I've ever known."

Jane decided that Sarah's request was more important to her than her own shyness. "Oh, alright. When shall we go?"

Gabriela answered. "I have a training session this morning with my troop. Can the excursion wait until afternoon."

"That will be fine with me. Jane?"

"One time is as good as the next. At your pleasure."

"I must leave you two. Richard and Aris had the troops early this morning. I give the next drill. I will return after we finish our practice."

Sarah rose to hug her friend farewell then turned to Jane. "We have a few hours until she comes back. Would you like to have a session while we wait?"

Jane's eyes lit up. "Yes. That would be wonderful." She settled in, reclining, her head resting on the pillows. Sarah found a comfortable spot next to her on the bed. The wolf changed position so he could see his mistress even while she was lying down.

Sarah recited the familiar induction and within moments Jane was in a deep hypnotic trance.

. . . .

JANE HOWARD, transcript, Session 3

"Tell me Jane, where are you now?"

"I am in the Queen's chambers."

"What year is it?"

"It is 1587."

"What do you see as you look around you?"

"The Queen is furious. She rails at her oldest friend and closest confidant, her secretary, William Cecil called Lord Burghley, yet he stands unflinching before her."

"Jane," Sarah questioned softly when her subject hadn't spoken for a few moments, "can you tell me why the Queen is so angry?"

It has just been made known to her that her cousin, Mary, Queen of Scots, has been executed. You see, while Her Majesty did jail the Scots Queen, she had no intention of executing her. Mary was sent to the Tower because, finally, the Queen's Council found proof that she intended to murder Elizabeth and take over the throne of England. They presented letters from Mary commanding some of her closest supporters to proceed with the assassination of the English Queen. Cecil pressed Elizabeth to sign the death certificate to rid the English throne of a dangerous adversary.

It was my charge to wait on Her Majesty directly after she signed the document. She signed, yes, yet she swore to me she had no intention of destroying her cousin. It was not simply filial love that stayed her hand. She believed that once a sovereign, any sovereign, had been executed the door was flung open and no monarch would ever be safe from being put to death from those who opposed them. A woman of great integrity, her conscience and concern for the future battled her logic to kill the woman who would usurp her throne.

Her Council knew her feelings and, without her knowing, commanded the execution of Mary of Scots. It was told to the Queen that Mary died poorly. It took three strokes of the axe to sever her neck and when the headsman held up the severed head of her decapitated adversary, her tangled red wig separated from her balding scalp, exposing a few lonely gray tresses. The grimacing face bounced across the scaffold floor, landing at the feet of her beloved dog. The animal raised its muzzle to the sky howling mournfully.

On the morning Cecil brought the news to Her Majesty, she went mad, pulling great handfuls of hair from her head. In her great fury she smashed precious piece after piece of glassware against the stones of the fireplace as she screamed at Cecil that he had committed treason. She commanded her guard to take him to the Tower then fell in a heap on the foot of her bed, her body quaking, tears pouring from her eyes.

"What have those fools done? They know not what corridors of death they have opened for any who oppose their rulers." She pounded the great mattress with her small fists as she shrieked the words. "What have they done?"

I sought to sooth her. "Your Grace, listen. Hear the cheers of your loving people. England is safe from any invasion from the north, from any furtherance of the Inquisition and Your Most Gracious Majesty is safe on the throne." I sat beside her on the bed, brushing her hair away from her tear-stained face. "It was done without your final command. You are free from guilt." Wiping her eyes, she sat upright. "She commanded her men to murder you in your own palace. She was a Catholic and bound to cause England to follow the Pope. How can you beat your breast at her end?"

As if defeated, the Queen's head drooped onto her chest as she spoke softly. "Oh Jane, do you not see? The boundary has been broken. An anointed monarch has been executed. The Crown will forever more be at the mercy of those who surround it." She fell back onto the bed, another torrent of tears streaming from her eyes, sobs tearing from her throat.

For three days she passed no food. She neither slept nor spoke. Leaning against the huge pillows stacked at the head of her bed, she stared straight before her. I wondered at what visions her staring eyes conjured. Was it the horrific death of her blood relative? Three gruesome strikes of the axe. Did she visualize the crimson sleeves and petticoat her enemy wore to her death to proclaim her martyrdom for Christ? Whatever Her Majesty saw in her minds-eye that morning took her vitality, her very soul from her.

On the third day, Cecil stood outside her chamber surrounded by her palace guard. He pounded hard on her door, calling to her, telling her the Council waited upon her decisions on many urgent matters. The government was at a standstill. They could not move forward without her pronouncements. He requested she put her mourning aside to return to her duties as sovereign while there was still a kingdom to rule.

I was astonished at the transformation in her at the mention of her duty to her people. Her eyes became clear. She rose from the bed standing tall, looking directly at me. "Jane, what is keeping you? Call Perry and the other ladies to attend me and dress me. England cries out for its Monarch."

I jumped to my feet, my Queen restored, standing before me in all her royal glory.

Her ladies attended to her toilette, preparing her to meet with her heads of state. Once painted, wigged and dressed, she left her chambers recovered, ready yet again to Queen it over England.

We were all relieved. The siege of sorrow had ended. I tidied her privy chamber with the help of her other maidens. Working quickly, we completed our task with much time to spare. Happily each of us went our own way, relishing in the few hours we had to ourselves while Her Majesty attended to affairs of state.

A beautiful crisp sunny February day tempted me to walk outside on the castle grounds. Dressed in heavy velvet fur-lined robes and leather fur-lined boots, I crossed the threshold into a frozen wonderland. The black bark of all the barren trees surrounding the palace was covered in sparkling crystal ice. Rainbows reflected on the snow-covered ground as the sun bounced off the glassy surfaces. My breath was visible in little puffs of steam as I hurried down the path to keep warm.

Suddenly, peeking from the trees on the edge of the forest surrounding the palace, the face and massive rack of antlers of a snow white stag caught my attention. He was enormous, as tall as a small horse, powerful yet sleek and graceful.

Slowly he stepped from the forest toward me. My breath stopped in my chest lest I frighten him away. As he took a few steps closer, I raised my palm to greet him.

"Ah Jane." A loud masculine voice boomed behind me. "At last I find you."

I turned only to discover the owner of the voice was none other than Lord Essex. He lurched toward me and I knew he was drowning in drink.

"Here, dear Jane. Let me kiss you." He lunged for me. Just as his hands grasped my arms, the great stag rushed toward us, antlers displayed for battle. Essex put me behind him, stepping between me and the huge animal thundering toward us. Without waiting for the outcome, I turned, running as fast as I could toward the palace. Racing up the steps to safety, I glanced behind me.

The buck had stopped short as soon as I was free of Essex. It was as if his charge was to protect me. He stood, his head tilted to one side, watching me. Essex watched me as well, but it was a wicked determination I saw in his eyes. With great relief I stepped inside the palace doors, closing them tightly behind me.

As Jane told the story of Essex, her body stiffened, her lovely face twisted into an unsettled scowl. Seeing her discomfort, Sarah released her from the trance and quickly brought her subject back to present day, to the safety and comfort of the Catacombs.

. . . .

"Sarah, things are coming back to me in a much more clear way. I had forgotten the white buck. He was so beautiful." Jane gazed into the fireplace as she remembered the frosty morning so very far away in her past. "Essex always frightened me. The other maids were taken with him, yet I always seemed to see through the false face he wore for the court." She turned to face her friend. "I remember that fright while I am in hypnosis."

"Jane, I feel sure we'll find the answer to your question about the day you were changed. You see, you're not afraid to let go in your hypnotic trance even though you sense danger, so the subconscious mind is free to share all the information that it holds. And it holds the events of that day. We are simply pulling down the veil that separates you from the memory."

"I am without fear because I trust you, Sarah. I know you would never allow anything to hurt me."

"I promise you, you will always be safe with me." Sarah marveled that an Immortal would seek assurance from a mere human, and she was grateful she was able to give it.

CHAPTER 31

As Aris made his way to the Sanguinaria, he passed the training pavilion. Kitsuko sat on the steps to the training floor, her shoulders slumped, her head held in her hands.

Concerned for her, he entered the pavilion, calling her name to get her attention. She glanced up and seeing it was he, smiled, raising her hand in greeting.

"Aris, we must talk."

"Alright." He sat a few steps below her wary of being too close. "What is it?"

"You have made clear your love of the human, your desire to make her your mate. But what if she decides not to change? What will you do if she decides to remain human?" Her words pled for an answer that would give her hope.

"Kitsuko," he sighed then continued speaking. "I take Sarah for my true and only love, human or Immortal. You must understand there will never be another for me. If she lives a human life and dies, I will mourn her for all eternity. There can never be another for me."

"How do you turn your back on Immortal love? I will be here for as long as you. We share the same warrior spirit. She will never be as strong as I am, Immortal or not. How are you able to choose her?"

"The choice is made. You must let go of this desire you have to share your life with me. It can never be."

Her heart broke with unshed tears as she realized his words were true. They sat in silence for a time and when she spoke, it was with resignation. "Then I must leave the Catacombs. My work here is finished, the training complete. I cannot stay here and watch you. My love for you is too deep for me to see you care for another."

"Kitsuko, you do not have to leave. The people of the Catacombs respect you. You have shown us the methods to aid our victory. The skills you have shared with us are invaluable. Stay. Fight with us."

"No, Aris." She rose. "I must leave. I return to the Himalayas, to the monks. Tell your human she will see me no more. Farewell." With her head bowed with regret, she quietly left the training pavilion.

. . . .

Walking toward the blood bar, Aris marveled at his conversation with Kitsuko. He felt sorrow at her leaving and deepest regret that he had been the reason for her to go, yet he knew her decision was for the best. Although Sarah had never spoken about Kitsuko, he could sense an animosity building between them whenever they were together. He hoped the little warrior would find peace once again in her monastery in the mountains.

The three males slid into a booth at the Sanguinaria, Aris first, then Sebastian. Simon sat facing them, making soft spoken intimate conversation easy for them.

"What news do you bring us from Spain?" Aris motioned the barkeep to serve three goblets, which were brought immediately.

Simon sipped from his cup, then spoke. "The King and Queen have negotiators speaking about reconciliation even as the Queen is en route to join the King. Her army is held up in a mountain pass in an enormous snow storm. They must wait until it ends before they can resume travel. Even though the two Monarch's Council members fight constantly among themselves, resolution is imminent. It is imperative we move quickly."

"We are almost ready." Aris replied. "The troop carrying the weapons to Spain leaves soon. Once they are in place, we are free to travel."

"Have you been able to turn this peace-loving race into a society prepared to kill and to die for their Queen?"

"Ah, Simon, such a painful question. None will really know the meaning of war until they feel the life ebb from their enemy at their own hand, until they see their own people lying dead, an impaler protruding from their chest." He shook his head. "Are they ready? That, only they can answer."

The three Immortals sat without speaking, each lost in his own vision of the battle to come. Aris kept his concern for the outcome silent; he banished his fear of the future if they were not victorious. Determined that he would do all he could to lead them to triumph, he refused to think of what would happen to the earth if they failed. He forced his thoughts away from the horrid aftermath of a lost battle and retuned his thoughts to the present.

"I must tell you," Aris spoke first, "Kitsuko is leaving the Catacombs. She feels her work here is finished and she wishes to return to the mountains." He felt no need to share her true reason with his friends.

"She has been a great aide to our cause. We will miss her, but I understand her need to return home." Sebastian turned to question their spy. "Now Simon, tell us of the terrain, of the castle."

Simon opened the folder resting on the table before him. He withdrew and unfolded a map of the area he was about to describe then spun it around to face his friends.

"As you know, it is in the north of Spain in Catalonia." He pointed to a spot in the mountains. "It rises on the slopes above the Val d'Aran valley about 350 kilometers from Barcelona."

"To be honest, Simon, when we came to get Sarah the first time, we paid little attention to anything other than getting her out of the tower and out of Spain. Anything you can tell us will be a help."

"There is the overgrown road through the forest surrounding the castle, the road you traveled to find us and Sarah, and there are two other entrance roads to the rocky outcrop where the castle stands." His finger traced the two distinct lines on the map. "They are dirt, strewn with fallen trees and boulders. They leave the forest to converge on a barren stone plateau at the entrance to the courtyard. The outer curtain of walls are held in place by six small towers. These towers are manned twenty-four hours a day by the King's guards. In the courtyard are the entrances to the main buildings and what is left of the large tower from which you carried Sarah.

"The castle is in disrepair, but still a fortress. Our greatest hope is to ambush the Queen's forces in the forest before they reach the safety of the castle walls. We have information they will travel the northeast road. Our people will trek from the southwest, circle around behind them and attack from the northwest after they enter the woods. Are we all agreed?"

"All will be ready within a few days at most. We will begin our journeys in groups and pairs. Some will stay in Barcelona while others find their way to the forest that surrounds the castle. Keeping the numbers of the Immortals in the forest to a minimum until the day we fight will cut our chances of being seen. When our lookouts know the Queen's retinue is close, those in Barcelona will join us. We will attack while they are still working their way through the woods to the castle. We will defeat them. Once the Queen's forces are taken, those left inside will surrender."

"And what of those, Aris?" Simon asked. "What of those who surrender?"

"If they swear peace, we will bring them to the Catacombs. They will take the Blood Oath and be watched with a close eye for centuries to come to be sure they are true."

"What of those who do not wish to follow the Immortal law?"

Aris glanced toward Sebastian before he answered. "They will be impaled and burned. There will be none left who oppose peace." He thought of his words to Sarah at what seemed such a long time ago. "*The only victor in any war fought for any purpose is death.*" He never thought he would once again be the instrument.

CHAPTER 32

Because she was yet a human, Sarah's eyes were still blindfolded every time she entered or left the Catacombs. Gabriela held her arm to guide her and keep her from stumbling as she led her down corridor after corridor through the underground labyrinth. Quite suddenly, the air changed and Sarah knew they were outside. Stumbling over a rock as she walked, she breathed in the afternoon air.

She heard the door of a car open and felt the guidance of her friend as she was seated in the passenger seat. The driver's door slammed shut as the engine roared to life. Sarah felt the forward motion of the vehicle and soon after, the sounds of the city. The black scarf that had been tied around her eyes was removed.

"I'll sure be glad when you won't have to do that anymore. You know that even if I could remember the way, I'd never tell anyone."

"I know that. It was a pledge Aris made to the Council in order to bring you below. We do not take our pledges lightly."

Sarah marveled at the natural light above ground. It was exactly the same as the Immortal light below.

"I wish Jane had come with us. I thought she might."

"Her wolf."

"What do you mean?" Sarah didn't understand her friend's words.

"The wolf cannot come above ground. The sight of him would raise havoc. The two of them have never been separated since they arrived in the Catacombs. Leaving him even for an afternoon was something she could not bear to do."

"She's a lovely, strange girl."

Gaby laughed. "Yes, she is strange even for an Immortal." Sarah had missed the smell of grass and flowers so they decided to take an afternoon walk through Regents Park. Gabriela found a parking place and the two women stepped from the car.

"Gaby?"

"Yes."

"Do you remember being human?"

"Yes, I have a memory of my human life. Why?"

"Well, are you much different now than you were then."

Gabriela laughed out loud. "Just a bit, don't you think?"

Sarah smiled in return, but her voice grew more serious. "I don't mean your Immortal self. I mean your human self. When we lived in Chicago, you lived completely as a human. Does it feel the same in your Immortal humanity as it does as a mortal? I mean, oh, I don't know how to express what I want to know."

"I believe I understand. You wish to know if you will still be yourself or if your basic traits will change. No, they will not change. That is the reason we are so careful about those we allow to become Immortal. To give the power of eternal life to one who is humanly evil results in the vampires of the Spanish coven. Devils. The Council is thorough in its investigation. Only once has anyone fooled them. That was DeMarco and he came to the Catacombs already changed into a drinker of blood. Our Council had nothing to do with giving him eternal life."

"So you're saying I'll be pretty much who I am except I'll have super powers."

Gaby gave her a hug. "You will be exactly who you are, super powers or not. Being Immortal will not change you, just your destiny." She kissed her friend on the cheek as it began to drizzle. They ran for a nearby restaurant to share one more afternoon above ground while Sarah was still human.

. . . .

Her long dark hair damp from the drizzling rain, Kitsuko stood in a darkened doorway across from the restaurant. The late afternoon sky was heavy with dark, rolling clouds as she waited. She was determined to find a way to have a final conversation with her rival, still hoping to frighten Sarah into giving up her desire to become Immortal. In her besotted mind, if Sarah was out of the way, she believed she would be able to win Aris.

As she waited, she noticed the same tall, dark-haired human she had seen in the past when she was trailing Sarah and Aris. He lingered under an awning covering a doorway next to the restaurant. As she watched, a taxi pulled to the curb and another man got out and stepped beneath the shelter out of the rain.

She knew in an instant the newcomer was a vampire. Her curiosity stirred, she moved in the shadows of the buildings toward the end of the block. Crossing the street, she made her way to a telephone booth just out of sight of the two men. She pretended to make a call as she listened to their conversation with her vampire hearing.

In muffled tones, the two men discussed their plot to kidnap Sarah, to take her back to Spain to DeMarco. Their plan was to be accomplished that very evening while Sarah was above ground. The vampire had plans to kill Aris. His death would demoralize the Immortal army and Spain would march on London. When all the plans were laid, the vampire hailed a taxi and disappeared into the rainy night.

CHAPTER 33

As the clouds separated and drifted away, the star-filled sky and the lights on Tower Bridge reflected on the choppy waters of the Thames. Sarah and Aris wandered down the street along the river hand-in-hand.

"We have had so little time together since you came to stay at the Catacombs. We have hardly had a moment alone to speak since your decision in the cavern. I want to know what you have been thinking about your changing."

They stopped walking, leaning against a metal railing along the sidewalk. A double-decker bus passed them and drowned out her answer.

She waited a moment, then repeated. "My thoughts fly all over the place. Sometimes I'm terrified. Sometimes I'm elated and can't wait. But all the time, I know in my heart it's the only thing I can do, the only thing I want to do."

"You are sure?" His dark eyes questioned hers.

"Absolutely sure. I have questioned myself up and down. I have never been more sure of anything in my life. I want to become an Immortal. I'm driven by the desire to feel what you feel and see as you see. I know your world is different and I know the only way I can experience it is to become what you are. I want it desperately. I want you desperately. I am willing to do whatever I must to be with you." Her laugh was nervous as she turned to walk once more. "Still, I have to admit, it's a little scary. I really hate pain."

"Sarah," He took her arm. "You must understand the full extent of the ritual. You say you hate pain. How do you feel about abject agony? You will burn as the venom enters your blood stream. Your body will feel as if you have fallen into the core of the underground volcano. You and you alone will have to withstand the fire. I cannot help you." She trembled at his words. "You must understand the ordeal you will suffer to change.

"Each time I draw your human blood from you, you will feel an exquisite bliss. Then, when the venom enters, the scalding begins. As the intolerable blaze in your flesh and bones subsides, again, I will draw your blood. Again I will spew venom and there will again be unspeakable pain. You will suffer this ritual for three days, Sarah, three times each day. At dawn, high noon and moon rise. Are you sure?" His voice was anxious. "Please understand, you must be sure. Once we begin there is no turning back; we must persist or you will die. The only way out of the pain is to go through it."

"Aris, I'm already just a little more than petrified. You can't make it any worse with anything you tell me. Besides, being scared isn't enough to stop me. Determination overcomes fear. I told you and I'll say it as many times as I have to in order for you to believe me, I'm sure." Her tone was sharp and her words clipped.

"I am not attempting to frighten you, Sarah. I am telling you the facts of changing. It is not just the pain. There are risks involved."

"Risks?"

"I am a vampire. I was nursed on human blood and have not had it for centuries. Add to that, I am in love with you and want you desperately. When your blood fills my mouth, I fear I will not be able to stop. I fear I will drain you and kill you." He hung his head, shamed by his own weakness.

Lifting his face to hers, she spoke softly. "You'll stop. I trust you. Besides, Aris, I'd rather be dead than not share eternity with you. Remember our life when I lived as Elizabeth in the court of Henry VIII? I gladly breathed my last breath when I thought you were lost forever. I would do it again. I would give my life for love." She laughed. "And I'm going to in just a few days." A little shiver ran down her spine when she thought of the short time left to her as a human.

She had a list of things to do before she breathed her last breath. Calling all of her Chicago friends was on top. It made her sad every time she thought she could never tell them the truth. She loved them all. She loved her life as a human. Yet, since she met Aris and saw the life in the Catacombs, it just wasn't enough anymore.

"Are you sure you won't wait until after the battle? I am only able to remain with you in the Catacombs for a day, two at most, after your changing before I must travel to Spain. We have put our journey off as long as we can and still use surprise against our enemy. It drives me to madness to leave you so soon."

"No, I won't wait. Besides, I'm coming with you."

He spun on his heel to stare at her as if she were mad. "Are you insane? You will be but a newborn. You will have no training in combat. You will not even have full control of your faculties. Sarah, it is out of the question." He turned, holding her arm and began to walk once again.

"It is not out of the question. Do you actually think I would let you and Gaby and the rest go off to war while I stay home? I'll be an Immortal. I'll be able to do all the things any of you can do. You, Richard and Gaby can teach me everything you know about attack warfare on the plane to Spain and I'll be ready to fight when we land."

He scowled at her. "You plan to learn all about warfare in the time it takes us to fly to Spain?"

"Super powers, remember?" When she realized he sincerely planned to keep her in England, her voice changed from playful to stern. "Aris, I'm coming."

"This is not up for discussion. If you do not agree to stay in the Catacombs until we are safely returned, I refuse to change you until the war is ended."

"You wouldn't dare?" Her outrage was clear in her tone.

"I would and will. Sarah, I will not risk an eternity without you. I wouldn't risk your life as a human. Why do you think I would risk your future as an Immortal?"

Realizing he held all the cards, Sarah changed her approach. "Aris, be reasonable."

"I am being reasonable. And logical. It is you who refuses to see the truth." He took her hand as they began to walk. "We will speak no more of it." Sliding his arm around her waist, he stooped to kiss her sweetly. "Now, come. Let us find a restaurant for your last human meal above ground." It was obvious the conversation was closed for the evening.

She let him lead her down the street allowing him to win the argument, but she knew their own personal war was far from over. Once she was changed, there would be no keeping her from the battle against the Spanish coven.

. . . .

The kidnapper waited silently in the alley behind the restaurant. Julian waited in a car across the street cell phone in hand, ready to signal his partner when Aris and Sarah left the restaurant. Their plan was solid. The human would walk toward the couple and just as Julian pulled to the curb, he would bump into Sarah, grab her and throw her into the car. Julian would leap at Aris with a stiletto ready to pierce his heart before tossing his dead body into the trunk. The rain had begun once again in full force. The steady downpour had emptied the street of foot traffic and there was no one in sight. They would work quickly and easily accomplish their task.

They weren't aware of the one link in the chain of events that would alter their well-laid plot. Kitsuko. Silently she crept toward the waiting man. One quick twist of his head and he would be dead, no longer a threat to Aris. She was sorry that Sarah's life would be saved in the process, but her Aris would be safe.

Unaware that Julian was there and had seen Kitsuko as she entered the alley and realized immediately she was an Immortal, she stayed in the shadows to keep out of sight of the human. The vampire's footsteps were silent as he followed close behind her.

Carefully watching the kidnapper as he checked his cell phone for the text message telling him it was time to move, Kitsuko prepared to attack. As he glanced at the display, she leaped on him, twisting his head into an unnatural position. She heard his neck snap as he sank to the ground. Just as she turned to run from the scene before anyone might see her, she felt an exploding pain that began in her back and raced into the center of her heart. The last image she saw was Julian standing over her, his stiletto dripping with her Immortal venom. Her last word was the name of her only love. "Aris."

Julian dumped the body of the dead human in the trash bin behind the restaurant, and then gathered Kitsuko's body to take to the countryside to burn. No one would ever know the fate of the Immortal female that had given her all for love.

CHAPTER 34

Sarah wasn't hungry for breakfast after the huge Indian meal she had eaten with Aris the previous evening. She made coffee in the butler's pantry and was sitting down on the sofa to read some of the material on the Blood Oath Henry had given her when there was a light rap on her door.

"Come in, it's open." She turned to look over her shoulder to see who had come to visit. "Jane, good morning. Come, sit with me while I have my coffee."

Jane closed the door, crossing the room to sit next to Sarah. The white wolf trotted at her side and sighed as he settled in next to her feet. "Did you and Gabriela have a pleasant time above ground yesterday?"

"Yes, it was beautiful. Then Aris met us and Gaby came back to the Catacombs. He and I spent the evening in London. I ate more yesterday than I think I ever ate in a week in Chicago." She laughed as she patted her little round stomach. "It was my last hurrah with human taste buds. I didn't want to waste a moment."

"So now I see why you did not ring for breakfast this morning." She shifted uncomfortably in her seat. "Sarah, do you have any free time today to do a session? I feel we are so close to answers and it will be tumultuous here for the next few days, first with your changing, then with the Immortals traveling to Spain."

Sarah could see the pleading in her friend's eyes. "Of course. Let me finish my coffee. We can do one this morning."

Wrapping her arms around Sarah, Jane hugged her and kissed her cheek. "Thank you so much. I have thought of nothing but our sessions since we began them. Each one brings me closer to the truth."

Sarah placed the empty cup on the table before rising to find her notebook and pen.

. . . .

JANE HOWARD, transcript, Session 4

It was July in 1588 and the Spanish were once again upon us. An Armada of ships was heading for England to defeat our navy and take the throne from our Queen. King Philip had engaged three thousand monks to chant for their victory and the Catholic Pope had admonished all his people in Briton to rise up against the Queen, to fight alongside Spain when they took the shores of England. Yet Elizabeth stood strong in her belief that her people would never betray her or their beloved country.

Every shipyard in England worked day and night building ships to add to the existing English fleet which, along with those of Hawkins, Drake, Raleigh and a few other privateers, equaled under one hundred. The three hundred galleons of the Armada placed the odds at three-to-one. With ten thousand sailors and twenty thousand handpicked fighting men coming from Spain, what chance did the boys and men of Sussex, Essex and Kent have?

Reports showed the Duke of Parma, said to be the most skillful commander in Europe, also waited on England's doorstep with his own fifty-thousand fighting men. More ships were added daily as his shipwrights built them faster than the spies from Her Majesty could count.

The Earl of Leicester, still in London, begged Her Majesty to repair to Windsor for her safety. The Queen believed if the Spanish were not held in the Channel, nowhere in Briton would she be safe. She admonished him to take Essex and Raleigh and be gone to join the fighting forces. Robert Cecil, her faithful secretary, was the only close advisor who remained with her.

In the middle of the night she called me of all her maids to attend her. I watched as she paced and swore and prayed. Never had I seen her so beside herself. "Jane. Jane. What is to become of us? How am I able to be strong for the country when I am so frightened myself? Help me, dear girl. Help me." Sobbing, she fell in a heap on the floor tearing at her thinning hair. Her tears stained her pale green silk bodice as I cradled her in my arms. She cried herself to a restless sleep, tossing her head and murmuring guttural sounds deep in her throat as if fighting the war in her dreams.

Her time of rest was short before she stirred. She sat upright and stared at me with embarrassed eyes. "Speak not of this, Jane." Standing, she straightened her clothes. "Call Parry to repair my hair and face. I must go among my people."

I hurried from her chamber to call the rest of her ladies. As I was leaving, Robert Cecil entered. I heard him tell Her Majesty the ships of Spain had been sighted. The three hundred galleons of the Armada stretched seven miles across the entrance of the Channel like a great crescent obscuring the horizon. Huge ships built like towers, so heavy that it appeared the wind was powerless to drive them forward. Our fighting vessels appeared small and insignificant as mice against tigers.

Soon the battle was at hand. Each hour Her Majesty was brought a dispatch from the fighting. She warned her captains they must keep the fleet from meeting Parma at Calais. She admonished them to hold fast.

Then, alas, news arrived that the ship of Her Majesty's cousin, the Lord Admiral, had been surrounded by galleons. My Lady screamed in fury, smashing a precious vase into the stone of the fireplace. With flailing arms, she chased the messenger from her chamber. "We shall overcome, we shall overcome." She shouted the words again and again until her voice became a hoarse whisper. She sat, staring at nothing, for a very long time. At last she rose from the chair.

"Send a messenger to my commanders. Victory or death." She turned to her privy chamber to kneel and pray for an English triumph.

It seemed for a moment, God took heed. At the turning of the dawn tide, while the Spanish wiped the sleep from their eyes, our little ships danced across the water, threw a line to the Admiral's ship and towed her to the safety of the open sea.

Still, storms raged. At last, first blood. One of the war galleons and Philip's treasure ship surrendered, but what honest advantage were a mere two of three hundred ships gone? And still they lumbered on toward Calais and the waiting Duke of Parma.

Our only plan was to send fire ships to torch the Spanish fleet before their crucial rendezvous with Parma. As the man in charge of creating the English convoy from hell, Walsingham worked tirelessly in Dover, presiding over the fitting of merchant vessels no longer fit for commercial sailing. They were stripped of their canvas and masts, then covered with tar and pitch. Burning, they would sail into the heart of the Armada bringing death and destruction to the Spanish flotilla. A good plan it was, yet God seemed to have shifted His eyes from the English and answered the prayers of Philips' praying monks. The weather turned. The fire ships were trapped in Dover, held fast by a changing wind. Dressed for battle, trapped in the harbor, they shuddered and trembled, their aging wood creaking against the raging squall.

When the Queen heard the news, she was beside herself. In my time of service, I had seen Her Majesty wild with anger, yet never had I seen her so desperately furious. She sent dispatch after dispatch, each one countermanding the one before. It seemed all was lost. I did my best to calm her. I forced her to eat and drink, telling her she must stay strong for her people. Elizabeth lived for England and so at last, she heard my plea.

Then, a dispatch from Drake arrived. He, Hawkins and eight others pledged ten of their best sailing ships. The finest of their four-masted schooners were to be set ablaze; sails, masts, rigging and all. It was said Hawkins wept openly at the sight of his vessel burning in front of his eyes.

The ten ships sailed straight and true in perfect formation right into the midst of the Armada. A messenger brought the news to Her Majesty. The Spanish seemed vanquished, their vessels alight and the crews bombarded by fusillades of molten lead. Those that had not sunk or been capsized now limped out to sea, running from the fray. There was great joy as the English knew victory.

Yet the triumph was short lived. The first of the Queen's champions to return was Raleigh. Exhaustion showed in every fiber of his being as he reported. It was possible their enemy might simply regroup at sea and attack London by sailing up the Thames River while, still, the Duke of Parma waited to attack from Calais.

The door of her chamber burst open. My Lord of Leicester entered, Essex trailing close behind. My Lord appeared old and tired compared with the youth and vigor of the younger man. He shook his wearied head in resignation as he spoke. "Parma launches his troops with or without the Armada. All our ships are chasing after the Armada. The Channel stands open to him. We are without defense."

Silently, the Queen pondered the faces of her two loyal captains. "The sea be damned, to the land defenses now." She paced in silence. Halting, she faced Leicester. "Go to our troops. Cheer them as my Lieutenant-General. I will join you at Tilbury to speak to them as their Queen and champion."

"Your Majesty, you must not. The Spanish have come to put you off your throne. The Pope has given license to every Catholic in England to take your life. You must not walk among the ranks. You will not be safe among the men."

"I have nothing to fear from treachery from my own people. Let tyrants fear. I have always believed in the loyal hearts of my subjects. I go to live or die among them."

Leicester's eyes shown with tears of pride as he bowed a courtier's bow. He rose up, love pouring from his eyes as he stared into hers. "My Lady, you may have the body of a frail and fragile woman, but you have the heart and stomach of a king."

"Go now, my Lords. Prepare a place for your Queen. I will walk among my men and live or die with them battling for the soil of our precious England."

Never had I been more proud of her. She sent for her ladies and we dressed her in all her finest. She swore that if her men were to give their lives up for their country, she would give them something to die for.

She rejected gown after gown as we paraded them before her. At last she chose a gown as white as a dove's breast. The robe she chose was of the softest white velvet. Then pearls. Hundreds of pearls around her neck, around her waist, dangling from her ears and encircling her fingers. Her wig was sprinkled with them—as plentiful as snowflakes on a winter morn.

We were awed to silence as she stood before us, warrior and Queen. Her last garment arrived from the Armory just before we set out to Tilbury. A silver breast plate. As we closed it around her, we marveled at the fit. It was small, as if made for her. We surmised it might have belonged to her dead brother, Edward, when he was but a boy. A shimmering silver helmet was carried on a white satin pillow by a page also dressed in white. And now she truly looked the part of the Faerie Queen.

We set out for Tilbury. The countryside, the hills and valleys in between, was covered with the men and boys who had rallied behind their Monarch. When we arrived, her commanders stood in wait for her, Essex at the side of the Lord of Leicester. All eyes save his were on Elizabeth. I saw him watch me as I attended her. The lust in his eyes frightened me and I was glad none other than I saw. He licked his lips and smiled, the grin wicked and demanding. Quickly I turned away to assist my Queen as she dismounted to walk among her men.

She touched first one on the shoulder and then another. She spoke with such passion her voice cut through the wind like a knife. Her pledge of her life and limb, to live or die in the dirt with her subjects, brought cheers and shouts of 'Gloriana.' They pledged their lives, their souls to her as she wept openly.

Essex swept her off her feet and praised her courage and fire, yet when he placed her gently back on the ground, his passionate eyes found mine. I hurried away to prepare her tent for her accommodation.

It was a sleepless night for us all as we waited to hear of Parma. Would he march on without the force of the Armada behind him or would he turn back?

Finally, at dusk the following day, a messenger arrived. He brought joyous news that Parma had dispersed his men and was sailing back to Spain. When the men heard, their triumphant cries could be heard late into the night. "God bless the Queen."

Later I was invited to dine in victory with the Queen in Lord Leicester's tent. A feast was laid before us that rivaled any at court. Suckling pig and beef and the deepest ruby wine. Satiated and a bit light-headed I begged to return to my sleeping quarters. A tent had been pitched close to the Queen's so her ladies were at hand to attend to her at a moment's notice. On my way to my bed, I stopped in front of a campfire abandoned as, one by one, the exhausted men found their sleeping pallets. All was quiet save the soft crackling of the timbers as the flames burned low. The sounds of the royal party some distance away were faint as a soft wind was blowing through the leaves.

Suddenly from behind, a powerful arm reached to encircle my waist. Frightened, I turned to face a drunken Essex. His eyes were glazed and his breath rank as he tried to kiss me. I fought him, clawing at his face, beating at his chest. The slap to my cheek was hard and sent me flying to the ground. He grabbed my wrists and pulled me to my feet. Holding both my arms in one of his big hands, he grappled with my skirt trying to rip it off. Sobbing, I begged him to let me go. My pleas seemed to incite his lust all the more.

Through the quiet of the night, a near-by sound of drunken voices singing off key reached his ears. They were moving toward us through the darkness.

"If you mention this, I will kill you." His eyes were slits as he released me and retreated into the shadows.

· · · · · · · · · · · · · · · · · · ·

"Sarah, I feel we are close. And you were right, I feel no fear as I relive these events in trance. You have made me feel safe. I am truly confident I will know what occurred on the day of my changing. Thank you so much for this time today."

"I would have continued, but your voice sounded exhausted. Don't worry. We'll find out everything you want to know. After all, Jane, we will have nothing but time." She smiled as she hugged her Immortal friend.

CHAPTER 35

It was the morning of the Changing Ceremony. Sarah sat, wrapped in her robe, waiting for her friends to come for her.

Jane and Gabriela would take her to a special chamber in the palace for a ritual bath, her last as a human. When she thought of the ordeal before her, she shook and her heart raced. She tried telling herself she would think about it later, but there was no 'later.' The time was now, the hour upon her. She sipped her coffee, feeling the heat of the liquid on her tongue, tasting the bitter flavor of the brew and the sweet of the sugar she added to it. *"Just like today,"* she thought. *"The sweetness of everlasting life and the bitterness of the ordeal before it. I must not think of it now, I'll never go through with it if I think about it."* She wiped her brow, damp with perspiration.

A soft knock interrupted her thoughts. She rose to open the door. Standing in front of her were her two Immortal friends and she hugged them in welcome.

Gabriela and Jane sat patiently while Sarah finished her coffee. Chatting aimlessly, each woman knew the only thought on any of their minds. Sarah's changing.

Unable to delay any longer, Sarah slipped her feet into the soft shoes she chose to wear as she began her last human journey. Wrapping the long blue silk ceremonial robe more securely around her, she,

Gabriela and Jane began their long walk through the corridors to the palace. The streets of the underground village were empty as if in tribute to what the inhabitants of the Catacombs knew would be her coming ordeal. Each of them knew first-hand the excitement and the fear of the changing day.

The palace gates were flanked by a waiting honor guard who accompanied them to the bathing chamber, a large room lit only by hundreds of candles. A huge tub carved from solid rock and polished until it glistened in the candlelight sat in the center of the room. The walls were hung with the finest of tapestries. Flowers filled every corner. Sarah felt she was in an hypnotic trance of her own as the three women moved toward the scented water of the bath.

They disrobed their human friend and began to anoint her nude body with an overpoweringly fragrant oil. It was both heady and calming. Their hands on her skin soothed her frightened mind and her breath slowed, at peace as she stepped into the water. Lowering her body into the warm perfumed liquid, she was sure she must be dreaming. How could she, Sarah Hagan, who had never truly faced the complexities of human life, be stepping forward to embrace human death? Her breath grew short as her fear returned.

Gabriela sensed her anxiety. She began to comb through Sarah's golden curls. Jane massaged her neck and shoulders until all of her muscles relaxed and she sank gratefully to her chin in the water. Her mind drifted and she felt so serene that she almost slept.

After a time, Jane touched her shoulder. "It is time, Sarah. Here, let me help you from the bath."

Her damp body glistened in the candlelight as her friends, once again, massaged scented oil into her skin. This was different. Her skin felt strange, slightly numb. Her hair was combed and her beautiful blue dress slipped over her head. Once again, she stepped into her shoes ready to go before Queen Akira, ready to see her beloved and join him for eternity.

Walking on either side of her, Gabriela and Jane accompanied her into the great audience hall where the chosen one hundred Immortals waited to welcome her to the changing ritual.

. . . .

Aris' boots echoed on the stone outside the audience chamber. Sebastian held back a smile. He had never seen his friend so agitated.

"But what if I am unable to stop? What if I kill her?"

"Be calm, my friend. Your love will keep you from being overcome with blood lust. You will not kill your soul-mate. Good God, you have waded through time and space to find her. You have wooed her and won her. Do you actually think that after all of this, you will drain her dry?"

The pacing stopped as he turned to face Sebastian. "I only hope. I have not tasted human blood for centuries. Before my life as an Immortal, I was a brutal warrior. I killed with a heart overflowing with joy. Sebastian, what if that warrior returns? I fear my own nature. I was a killer as a human, a killing machine as a vampire. Only you and the Immortals showed me a different way. Oh God, what if that nature is not gone, just in hiding?" He buried his face in his hands in torment.

"Aris. Enough. Your nature is not evil. The Spanish vampires are evil, not you. You took the Blood Oath and have lived by it since the day you swore you would never take another human life by drinking blood. You have lived in honor. Even in your rage against those who killed the man who lived in your host body. When you took their wicked lives, you did not drink their blood. Please, brother, be calm. On this day your devotion that lasted over five hundred years is returned by the human that grew to love you now. Be at peace. This is your wedding day."

Aris threw his arms around Sebastian's shoulders, thanking him for being such a friend. Sebastian patted his back then turned him to face the door to the audience chamber as it slowly opened. Richard stood in the doorway, smiling. "Come, Aris. It is time to greet your bride."

Chapter 36

They entered the audience chamber through opposite doors. The one hundred Immortals chosen to attend the ceremony parted, stepping aside to form an aisle for the lovers to walk through. Sarah's eyes glistened with anticipation as well as something else. He knew it was fear. Compassion filled Aris' heart as she drew near. He knew his own terror. Could he stop once he began to drink from her? How could he bear to see her suffer by his own hand? Would he be able to continue her torture for three days? If he was unable to complete the transfer of blood to venom, he would lose her forever. He was torn by his own quarreling emotions; deepest dread for the pain he would cause her, abject joy at eternity with her by his side. It was another moment since he had known her he was sure he was going mad.

When she reached his side, she looked into his eyes and smiled while reaching to take his hand in hers. The open trust she felt for him began to dissolve all his horrors. He would overcome any wildness left in his nature. He would bring her to him with all the tenderness and adoration that he felt for her. At last, she was here with him. His joy was greater than he could have ever imagined as they knelt before Queen Akira. For this great occasion, King Khansu was present. It had been centuries since any of the court had seen their King. His withdrawal had been complete until today. And there he sat on the dais with his Queen to honor their union.

Sarah had not been expecting both the King and Queen and she gripped Aris' hand hard as she faced the royal pair. "All is well." His whisper was heard by no one but his mate. Breathing deeply, she softened her hold on his fingers.

A beautiful young vampire male stepped onto the dais carrying a golden vessel encrusted with jewels. It rested in the center of a gilded tray. Holding the tray in both hands, he knelt on one of the blue velvet cushions on the floor. Akira took the ceremonial pitcher from him. As she raised it above the heads of the two being joined, the young man backed from the room.

Aris nodded to Sarah to kneel on the cushions before the Queen. She bowed her head as Akira drew near. Tilting the vessel, she slowly poured a few drops of the warm scented oil onto the shoulders of the waiting human. Massaging slowly, gently, she repeated the first lines of the Changing Ritual that had been used since the first human had chosen to become Immortal.

"I relieve you of the burden of the sorrow of killing to live, a life for a life."

Sarah was grateful that she would never need to take a life to live. She was grateful for the alchemical blood that would sustain her for eternity as she lifted her face toward her new Queen. For a moment, she thought she saw compassion in the eyes of the Immortal monarch as a few drops of oil were sprinkled onto her forehead.

Akira pressed gently as she made small circles with her fingers, rubbing the oil into Sarah's human skin.

She chanted, "To open your mind to the knowledge of the millennia held in the memory of your chosen one."

Aris reached to take Sarah's arm, raising her to her feet. She stepped from her shoes as she lifted her skirt to her knees. Akira poured small drops of oil onto her feet. "That you may walk with the pride of an Immortal through all eternity."

Khansu rose from his throne to step closer to the couple. He reached to touch each one on their brow in his blessing; first Sarah then Aris. Akira did the same. Now joined as mates through the Immortal ritual the couple bowed, then backed from the room. The moment was now at hand for them to be joined by blood. Sarah fought to keep her knees from buckling as they walked toward their chamber.

Chapter 37

Her hands were cold as he led her along the corridor to the changing suite. After a short walk, they stopped in front of a tall, ornately carved wooden door.

He turned to face her, taking her chin in his hands he stared deeply into her eyes. "I love you, Sarah. I will not leave your side until you are changed. I will suffer your pain as well as your ecstasy. Three days and then, Immortality."

She stood on her toes to kiss him softly. "I am ready. Let's begin."

. . . .

Immortal light glowed softly from wall sconces that encircled the room. An enormous canopy bed, a tall backed chair and a covered tray resting on a small round table were the only articles to be seen. Sarah shuddered when she realized what lay beneath the cover. Cold stone walls were adorned with tapestries in muted colors and, while the furniture was sparse, it was regal. Sarah couldn't drag her eyes away from the great bed.

"Lie down, my darling." Aris led her to recline on the soft white silk pillows. The bed curtains were sheer and white, a cocoon for her metamorphosis. The bedclothes were all white, a virgin's bed prepared for her ordeal.

Slowly, she laid back. He brushed the hair from her forehead then kissed her tenderly. "Rest. When you are ready to begin, I will draw first blood." He sat quietly staring at her. He was frightened she would change her mind and not go through with the changing and at the same time, terrified of the beast he feared still lived inside him if she did. He had never desired her more.

Tears pooled in her eyes. Her mind told her to run away. *"What have I done? What am I doing here?"* She turned to look at Aris and she found her answer. She was joining her soul-mate for an eternity of love; she was becoming a part of a society that called to her from a place so deep inside her she couldn't resist. Still frightened but just as determined, she closed her eyes as she reached to draw him to her. "Just hold me for a little while."

He lay next to her, wrapping his arms around her, feeling her tremble with fear. Stroking her hair, he whispered soft crooning words of love, his breath warm against her ear as he spoke. His lips brushed her throat, gently at first then more ardently, causing a sudden rush of desire to swell in her and transform her fear into a demanding need for him. Winding her fingers through his raven black hair, she drew his mouth to hers, her breath coming in short gasps.

Abruptly Aris pulled away from her and rose, sitting on the side of the bed; his back toward her, he held his head in his hands. "Sarah, I want you more than you can understand. It is taking all my unearthly strength to control my desire." He composed himself before turning to face her. "Do you not see, I must maintain control every moment until you are Immortal? I must not allow any thought to enter my mind except my responsibility for your changing."

She stared at him silently, then spoke. "I do understand." She touched his hand. "I'm ready. Please, let's begin now."

. . . .

The first drawing brought pleasure too great for her to stand. He gently licked the pulse in her throat, spreading his venom on her skin to ease the pain of his teeth penetrating her flesh. The sensation of his soft lips and warm tongue brushing against her tender neck returned her to a swoon of wanting him. She moaned softly, tilting her head to expose more.

Aris had undressed her with care, wrapping her once again in the ceremonial robe she wore to the bathing ritual. Puzzled at first when she saw it draped across the foot of the bed, Sarah realized either Gabriela or Jane must have brought it for her. Thoughts of their love for her gave her courage.

The sensation of his lips on her skin was enticing until, suddenly, a brief sharp stab of pain shocked her as his canines grew long and sharp and he bit into her. And then, rapture. With each sip he took from her, she felt she would explode with pleasure. The sensation of his sucking her blood filled her with a longing she had never before known. It was as if her very soul ached to receive him. She reached her hands to caress him. She raised her breasts to him, uncovering them in the soft light of the chamber. Her nipples were rosy and erect, her desire evident before him. It seemed but moments to her when he drew away.

She opened her eyes to look at her lover. His eyes were glazed, a drop of her blood on the center of his full lower lip. He shook his head as if coming back from a daze as he licked it away. He sat next to her for only a moment.

"Now, my darling. Prepare." Once again his lips sought her throat.

But not joy. Horror. Searing, burning horror. Each pulse of her heart as it pumped the venom through her body brought a new onslaught of flame. At first it was her throat. Then it spread like a wildfire in the wind. Her arms shook. Her fingers curled into claws as she dug them into the bed. Her moans turned to cries of agony. Aris' heart ached at her pain, yet still he poured his venom into her.

Was it days, was it weeks? When would he stop? She writhed on the bed as she lost herself in her anguish. She felt him pull away and yet still she burned. She knew she was turning to cinders. Somewhere through the cloud of torment, she realized this was but the first.

"My love, the burning will grow less soon. Breathe slowly. Soon it will begin to subside."

His words were true. After what seemed an eternity of suffering, the pain grew less and less until it quieted. He watched over her as she fell into a deep sleep drugged senseless by the potency of his venom.

He was horrified. It had taken all he had in him to stop. The taste of human blood, of her blood, had driven him close to frenzy. Only his deep love for her saved her. And now, he must do it again. And again. Eight more times in the next three days he would be tempted. Eight more times he must watch her suffer. He buried his face in his hands and thought of Sebastian to bring him courage. If his friend could withstand the temptation, so could he. He would find the resolve to continue.

. . . .

Each time, it became more and more difficult to stop. As his mouth filled with the enticing red fluid, he fought courageously to control his desire to gorge himself on her. Sebastian believed in him. Sarah trusted him. Other Immortals had trod his path and known victory. Again and again, he pulled away from her, his head reeling. His mouth dry and demanding more. Again and again, he filled her with his poison, changing her human body into one that was invincible, one that would last through the end of time.

Each session of the drawing and filling brought greater pleasure, more unbearable pain. By the morning of the third day, the bed was wet with her perspiration, her robe shredded and lying on the floor.

Her only moments of sanity were the moments of sleep that overcame her after the misery passed. The pleasure was almost as unbearable as the suffering. Never had she felt with such intensity. Never before had her body cried out for peace as it did now. She was unable to speak. She was weak, unable to even turn her head. Carefully holding her in his arms, he prepared for the next withdrawal. The sound of her beating heart thudded in his brain. It would beat until the last of his venom filled her and there was no longer human blood in her vessels. Then and only then would the torment be ended. He closed his eyes and prayed to whatever god might hear him that he could complete his task.

At dusk on the third day, he held her as she trembled and quaked in her final death throes. Then, suddenly, she grew rigid. Her heart stopped beating. Her breath ceased. She lay as if dead in his arms. At long last, her lids fluttered. She opened exhausted eyes to look at him. Finally, she smiled.

. . . .

Aris cradled Sarah in his arms as she became aware of her Immortal body. He remembered his own awakening, his astonishment at his Immortal form, his driving hunger. Knowing how overwhelming the experience was to a changeling, he allowed her to explore her new world in her own time as he lay quietly next to her.

Her first jolt came as she opened her eyes as an Immortal vampire. Her vision was so sharp she could see the individual sunset beams shining from the light sconces on the wall. She looked at her arms in wonder. Each tiny blond hair was as clear as an individual star in the night sky; her skin, smooth as satin to the touch, porcelain perfect to the eye. Her fingernails were perfectly shaped and shined as if they had been polished. As she lifted her hand to stroke his face, she was amazed by the grace of her movement.

Staring into his eyes, she realized for the first time the true depth of the soul hidden deep within the Immortal man holding her in his arms. For the first time she realized the true joy of eternal love. Raising himself on his elbows, he leaned toward her. As his warm lips touched hers, a tender thrill made her shiver. She nestled closer to him, pressing into him with her nude body. As she felt his muscles tense beneath her hands, the thrill exploded, desire flaming in her as she had never felt it before. Unquenchable. Undeniable.

Tenderly he stroked her forehead, her cheeks, as he spoke. "Not yet, my darling. There is a greater ritual that must come before."

Laying her back onto her pillows, he drew the bedclothes to cover her. Bewildered for only a moment by her easy control of her need for him, she shifted her awareness to feel the weave of each individual thread in the sheets. She could smell the fragrance of the white cotton, of the very fields of Egypt where it had been woven. Giving in to the pure sensation of bliss, she reached to rest her hand on his chest.

Closing her eyes, the light coming through her eyelids made visible all the tiny individual vessels that ran through them carrying his venom, giving her this exquisite gift. As they lay quietly and she slid her hand across his velvety skin, she realized his chest wasn't moving. Then, with a second jolt, she realized she wasn't breathing either. Her chest lay as quiet as his.

Sarah knew before her changing that breathing would be her choice, not a demand of her new form. She knew her human functions would only operate if she chose, yet the experience was still shocking as she focused on the total silence within her body.

Without warning and with a vengeance, the silent void exploded within the very core of her being. Small at first, yet powerful, dark, frightening. The void changed shape and intensity into a craving, a demand, a desire even greater than her desire for Aris. A desire that blazed with an agony that even her changing hadn't brought.

She was barely able to groan his name in supplication. "Aris?"

Understanding her need, he uncovered the tray resting on the bedside table. He reached for a goblet to hand to her. She sat up and took it from him, gripping it tightly with both shaking hands. She closed her eyes as she raised it to her lips. It had a familiar scent that momentarily bewildered her. Then she recognized the smell of rust that was carried in blood. Without a second thought, she brought it to her mouth, tipped it and drank the contents to the bottom.

It was warm and thick like pudding, yet not sweet. Salty. Salty and rich. It tasted like nothing she had ever tasted before. She savored every drop, rolling it in her mouth for a moment before she swallowed. At last, when the goblet was empty, she opened her eyes. She felt a moment of embarrassment as she handed it back to him.

"The need to drink will return several times today. It will be overpowering. We will stay in our chamber and I will be here with you to feed your first hunger as an Immortal." He brushed her curls away from her forehead. "Now, stand and walk. Take your first steps in your new life." He stood, taking her hands in his. He helped her rise from the bed, wrapping the soft blue bathrobe around her. As her feet touched the silk of the woven carpet beneath them, she sighed with the tactile pleasure of her every step. She felt each stitch caress her toes as she walked across the floor. She felt the creative hand that sewed them, the days spent in the life of the human that went into making the rug. At a complete loss for words, she stood in one spot slowly turning in a circle to survey her surroundings.

The candles adorning the dressing table were lit and each candle flame danced, alive and warming to her new senses. She could taste color. She could smell sound. Would she ever grow accustomed to this new world?

Aris interrupted her musing. "Your ordeal is finished." He took her hand, leading her to a bathing chamber. An enormous, tall glass shower stall stood in the center of the room. He turned the handle and jets of hot, steamy water shot from hidden spouts, fogging the glass and running in twisting rivers down the shiny walls. She could see each droplet of water creating the fog. Smiling, she dropped her robe on the stone floor.

"I will be just outside. There is a clean gown for you behind the door." He stepped out, leaving her to explore her new body.

As she turned to step into the shower, she noticed a tall mirror on a silver stand resting against the wall. As she drew near to it, she laughed out loud at what she saw reflected back at her. All her tiny wrinkles and physical imperfections were gone. Her complexion was as smooth and glistening as marble. Her body was lean, yet muscular, powerful. Her hair thick and rich, her eyelashes as full as brushes. The image before her was one of beauty, of perfection. She was the very picture of an Immortal.

. . . .

What did she feel? What did she not feel? Every inch of her skin was a bare nerve. Every sensation new, delicious. The hot water pouring down her back ran in rivers of delight. She watched the water as it swirled in a circle of froth, then disappeared down the golden drain. Each individual soap bubble reflected light more brilliant than the finest diamonds as they spun in the whirlpool on the floor of the shower. Her red toenails reminded her of the liquid in the goblet and her desire to drink returned. Quickly, she stepped from the shower. Every nub on the thick fluffy white towel massaged her skin as she dried. Wrapping her bathrobe around her, she hurried to Aris and the pewter goblet. The bedding was changed and inviting as she laid down next to him.

Chapter 38

The first hours of Immortality were filled with overwhelming sensation and drink after drink. She felt her body growing stronger, her senses more acute. She realized she had the ability to change from human awareness to that of her kind, an Immortal being. She laughed as she played games with Aris, enjoying her newfound abilities. He kept her close, resting with her on the huge bed throughout the day, replenishing the life giving liquid whenever she had need of it.

Everything she experienced was a hundred fold greater than any of her human experiences. A thousand, no a million fold. It wasn't peace she felt, but a restfulness greater than any she had ever known. Exploring the new depth of feeling and understanding her Immortal existence gave her, she experienced a rekindling of her lust for knowledge, her desire to learn, her desire to be more than she was, more than a human mind could understand was possible. Her love for Aris was greater than all the love she had felt for all the people in all her human life as she watched every move he made, marveling at his heavenly beauty. When he reached to fill the goblet from the pewter pitcher resting on the bedside table, her eyes followed him as if he moved in slow motion. The rustle made by the cloth of his shirt as his arm brushed across the sheets thrilled her. The sounds of each individual drop of the liquid splashing into the goblet excited her. Her eyes glowed as she watched the fluid flow into the cup. The taste was of heavenly nectar as she swallowed the ambrosia. If he had worried at her disgust at what she must now do to stay alive, all was washed away as he saw her reach hungrily for it, draining every drop of the crimson fluid.

At long last, she knew her body had received enough. She rested in his arms at peace. He thought she had fallen into a human slumber when she caressed his cheek, turning his face toward hers.

As they stared into one-another's eyes, she felt she was floating on a cloud of joy; indescribable joy. Endless waves of bliss filled her as she sank deeper and deeper into the black depths of his eyes, his soul.

He whispered. "Sarah, you are my only Immortal love. We are both innocents in this experience. Our coupling will be the first of its kind for both of us."

"I'm so glad." She stroked his face, his skin smoother than the richest velvet she had ever touched with human fingers.

"Lie quietly, my beloved." She watched every movement of his nude body as he rose from her side to sit cross-legged next to her on the bed. "Close your eyes." The shadow of her long, thick lashes covered her cheeks as he kissed the tops of her eye lids.

He began to glide his hands over her body, her legs, her torso, her arms. Bit by bit he caressed her, his touch skimming her skin like delicate warm smoke emanating an otherworldly fragrance that she felt rather than smelled.

She could feel his hands lifting away from her skin, still moving, floating just inches above. A sensation of bliss overwhelmed her. Her very existence melted into the energy flowing from his hands. It filled every pore of her, every cell of her body, every neuron of her brain. Suddenly she knew all that he knew, all that he had ever experienced. She felt the pain he suffered at his changing; the loneliness he felt when he thought he was the only one of his kind. She met the wild beast that roared inside him to this very day. She felt his guilt, his sorrow for the evil he had done in his past. She felt the joy that was his because of her love. She felt the very essence of him enveloping her, enlightening her, their very beings permeating one another. When it was finished, she lay quietly absorbing all that had just occurred. She realized he had just taken her through her final transformation. He had given her the knowledge that all Immortals shared, the knowledge of the ages.

. . . .

She marveled at the stillness of her body as they lay looking into each other's eyes. When he reached to draw her closer she heard as well as saw his movement. She wondered at her patience, desperately wanting him to make love to her, yet relishing every slow-motion moment of discovery they shared.

She watched as his long powerful fingers cupped her breast. Hard as she tried, she could find no fine line where he began and she ended. Even their external bodies seemed to meld into one, a shared pulse of energy between them stronger than the beating of a human heart. As he stroked her tender nipple, she leaned her head onto the pillow and closed her eyes. She realized that in all her human life, she had never even imagined the depth of feeling she was now experiencing.

His thick lips pressed into the hollow at the base of her throat. She felt the bow of his mouth rise and fall as, time and again, he kissed her tenderly. She felt rather than smelled his musky fragrance, filling her with such sweet desire she almost cried out. His kisses traced her skin to the soft, dark hollow between her breasts.

As his lips found their mark, the sensation of Sarah's yielding flesh caressing his cheeks drove him to crave more of her. He steadied his desire as his hand slid from her erect nipple, over her smooth abdomen, to its resting place on the blond nest of curls covering her woman's mound. Having his mate lying next to him and offering herself to him in a way he had never before experienced opened a whole new world of wonders to him; feelings he wanted to explore slowly. To cherish.

"Aris." He lifted his eyes. Her lips were parted, moist, inviting. He moved to kiss her.

At first their kisses were sweet, gentle, exploring. Slowly he outlined her mouth with his tongue until she stopped him by drawing it inside. The taste of him made her want to devour him. Their kisses grew deeper, more fiery, driven by months of denied passion.

While he could still contain himself, he drew away from her, turning her to face away from him. Curling around behind her, he lifted her hair to expose her pale, tender shoulders. He would mark her as his mate. His searching lips found the nape of her neck. She felt she would faint with longing as first his lips and then his teeth trailed softly across her skin. The very essence of her being cried out to have him take her.

Slowly, Aris' bite became more demanding; his canine teeth descended and broke Sarah's delicate skin. The penetration was superficial, a shallow bite, yet the sensation of him marking her drove her into a frenzy. Before either of them knew what had happened, she twisted away from his grip then spun toward him. Throwing herself on him, she overpowered him, slamming him face down on the bed. He fought to get free as she held him, unable to control the fierce madness driving her to taste his venom. Sarah ripped at the back of his neck with her newly pointed teeth. Waves of rapture drowned his reason and for an instant, he thought he was lost. Even though the venom that ran through his veins fought to respond to her primal demand, he knew that once he touched her, he would lose control to the animal within him; he feared he would harm her. From a source he didn't know he had, he found the strength to hold back.

He grabbed her hair, dragging her off his body. Twisting to face her, he took hold of her. Scarcely controlling the drive to ravish her, he held her securely by the shoulders. Her eyes were glazed and her lips were covered in the venom she had drawn from his body. "Sarah. Sarah." His voice demanded she return to her senses. "Sarah."

"Oh Aris, Aris. What have I done?" Her shoulders sagged and she hung her head. "What have I done to you?"

"Nothing, my darling. You have just marked me as your mate. Here, see? It's almost healed already." She leaned to look where he pointed at the back of his neck. There was nothing there but two small rows of red teeth marks. She knew she had ripped him open.

"But I know I tore your flesh. I taste it in my mouth."

"Immortals cannot be killed other than by impaling, but the human-ness of our bodies can still be injured. But, you can see, the injuries heal almost instantly."

"What happened to me, Aris? Why did I do that?"

"Immortal passion. You are only just changed and cannot yet control it." Drawing her close, he whispered. "And darling, I am quite glad that you cannot." He kissed her deeply.

Settling close to him, Sarah closed her eyes, giving in to all the new sensations of their first love making. She disappeared into their kisses, their caresses, their whispered words of love.

Their hands stroked each other's bodies as if they were blind and only able to see through their heightened sense of touch. His skin felt as smooth as marble warmed in the sun. They breathed together as if this most human act of love-making made it necessary. Their breath was heavy as he slid his hands under her, lifting her to receive his aroused manhood. She watched as he entered her only to be lost once again to sensation.

As he moved inside of her, Sarah was overwhelmed by wave after wave of endless bliss. With each thrust he dove deeper toward her heart, toward her very soul. With each thrust, her body opened more fully to take him in. He spoke words to her in a language she had never before heard, yet she understood. Without doubt, he spoke words of eternal love.

Their melding together went on and on, a never-ending dance of rapture until she felt she was no longer made of flesh. She was the embodiment of the pure desire that possessed them both.

Without warning they each froze, as if turned to stone. Their breathing ceased simultaneously. An essence ejaculated from him into her only to return to him once again. Over and over, time and again, the exchange occurred, body to body. Soul to soul. They shuddered, convulsing, reaching a state of ecstasy only accorded to the gods. They felt death and birth. Joy beyond dreams. They floated on a cloud of endless bliss, and then were silent, unable to speak or move. They lay enraptured in one another's arms, each made whole by the sacrifice of the other.

. . . .

Sarah lay spent in Aris' arms, her legs wrapped around him, her head resting on his chest. He brushed her damp curls from her face, kissing her eyelids gently. "You must rest. This is all so new for you. It is too much to absorb all at once."

She sat up quickly. "No. I must learn all I am able to learn as soon as possible. When do we leave for Spain?"

Aris drew her into his arms once again. "Darling." His words sounded strained as he spoke. "You cannot come with us to Spain. You are but a newborn. You have no control of your powers. You do not even recognize all of them. We are on the doorstep of our journey. If you work night and day, you will still not be ready to fight those bastards in the Spanish coven. You must give up the notion of coming along."

"Absurd." She tore herself from his arms springing from the bed to her feet. "It is not a notion." Her voice was determined as she wrapped her robe around herself, tying the belt around her waist in a square knot. "I will learn all that I can and then I am coming with you."

Drawing his eyebrows together, his tone grew harsh. "You do not understand. You will be helpless against the soldiers of the Spanish army. You will stay here with Jane and Henry. There are a few hundred Immortals who will remain in the Catacombs to protect what is ours in case any of the enemy should escape us to come here. You will watch with them."

Pacing angrily, she spoke, her words clipped and short. "If I am strong enough to defend the Catacombs, why do you say I am not strong enough to face the Spanish?"

"Sarah, please." He grimaced. "Let us not have this discussion now. Our friends wish to see you, to wish you welcome into our world." He turned her to face him. "Let us get dressed and meet with them at the Sanguinaria."

Seeing the resolve in his eyes, Sarah dropped the subject, but she knew, one way or another, she was going to Spain and nothing was going to stop her.

· · · · · · · · · · · · · · · · · · · ·

They were all sitting around a large table laden with gifts, tall silver carved pitchers and goblets. When Sarah was ushered to the table, Aris at her side, they stood, applauding her. Gabriela was the first to reach to embrace her new sister. Then Jane. Richard and Sebastian waited their turn to welcome her as a member of the Catacombs. When they all had kissed both her cheeks, she turned to face Henry.

"My dear." He wrapped his long arms around her, holding her close. She had always wished her human father had shown her affection, but he never had been demonstrative of his love. This new Immortal mentor filled the empty space in her heart as she accepted his welcome. "We have so much work to do. When will you come to me to begin?"

Sarah knew it was subterfuge. Aris had arranged to have Henry ask her to begin work with him immediately. Her mate thought it would take her mind off Spain, however he had no idea how determined she was to do her part for the Catacombs.

"Soon, Henry. Soon."

Packages wrapped in lovely paper and tied in colorful ribbons were stacked in a pile in front of Sarah. Jane motioned to them as she spoke. "Open them, Sarah. After all, today is your first birthday." They all laughed as Sarah reached for the tallest box.

When the last present was opened and the gifts of jewelry and clothing from the Catacombs were placed neatly in a pile on a chair, Gabriela filled the goblets. She raised hers to her new sister as she spoke. "Welcome to the world of the Immortals, Sarah. You have brought us great joy."

All her friends raised their cups in welcome. Then, all the Immortals drained the liquid to the last drop.

CHAPTER 39

Sebastian, Aris and Sarah rested on a bench along the rail of the training pavilion as they watched the latest arrivals work with the impalers. Aris had led the session and now they watched as the Immortals spun and lunged in mock attack. Off to one side a group of four worked on deflecting an enemy's blows. Echoes of the loud groans and thuds the soldiers made when they were thrown to the ground rang throughout the cavern.

"Is Demetri certain Mariska's army is en route to the castle? Has he seen them actually move out or was it word-of-mouth? It could be false information. It certainly would not be the first time."

"Demetri did see them leave the caves and head south. They need DeMarco's army. Our people overheard the Queen and Esteban talk. We are certain they are heading to the castle to join him and march to London." Sebastian's tone was stern. "We are out of time. We must begin to send our troops immediately."

"Come," Aris rose, drawing Sarah to her feet. "Sebastian, gather the captains for a final meeting with the Council. We leave tonight."

With a heavy heart, the newly-wed couple silently walked the length of the corridor to the Council Chamber. Aris gathered her into his arms, whispering into her hair. "Go to your chamber. I will come to you before I leave."

Drawing away from him, she raised her eyes to meet his one last time. Fighting tears she turned and hurried down the hall, determined more than ever before to fight by his side in Spain.

. . . .

All members of the Council were in attendance as were all eight captains. Aris and Sebastian had the floor.

"Travel arrangements have been finalized." Aris' words were clipped and his sentences short as if there wasn't enough time to express all the necessary information. "The uniforms have all been distributed. Each warrior has made the decision as to what should be done with his remains if he should be overcome in battle."

"How will you be told of their decisions?" questioned Bartholomew.

"A zipper compartment in the breast of their leather jackets will hold their request. We will abide by all decisions made."

Bartholomew nodded in agreement.

"The runners delivered the final weapons to the forest surrounding the castle a few days ago. They guard the arsenal and wait for the rest of the army to join them."

"Aris, are they honestly ready?" With the time of departure just hours away, Bartholomew could not help but think about the Immortals that wouldn't return. "What is the chance of victory?"

"Ask the captains, Bartholomew. They will tell you."

Gabriela rose to face the Head Council. "They are ready. More practice would do them no more good. They are strong and willing. They are Immortals." She spoke with pride in her troops.

"Psychologically, they are sound. It is not a war of aggression, but of defense. While each soldier despises the need to kill another being, they know we have no choice." Richard paced in front of the long table as he spoke, then came to a halt. He was silent for a long moment before speaking with deepest conviction. "I believe they will do what is required of them by our Queen."

"Then go." Bartholomew moved around the table to shake the hand of all those who would risk their very existence to keep the Catacombs and London safe from harm. "Go and return quickly to celebrate your victory."

. . . .

Aris held Sarah close for a moment, then he kissed Jane's cheek, preparing to leave their chambers. The final hour of his travel to Spain was nearly upon him. The troops who would fight in the forest had left and were en route to Spain already. Aris would depart with those who would fight DeMarco at the castle after a final meeting with the remainder of his captains. Leaving his mate filled him with dread, but his responsibility to his commanders was overpowering. Before he left the room, he assured her he would return for a final farewell.

As the door closed, Sarah turned to Jane sitting next to her on the sofa. "Jane, I know you trained to fight even though you are not traveling with the rest of the Immortals."

"Yes. Everyone trained, even Henry. We are all very able to use the weapons of impalement. If the evil ones make for the Catacombs, we will be ready."

Touching her friend's hand, Sarah whispered. "Jane, you must teach me. I must go with Aris. I can't stand staying here, not knowing what's happening to him."

A pained expression crossed the young woman's face. "I cannot. He has forbidden it. He forbade any of us from showing you the use of the weapons. You must not leave the Catacombs. You are just newly born." The white wolf, sensing his mistress's sorrow, whimpered as he laid his head on her knee. She reached to stroke his brow.

"Jane, you don't understand. I can't let him go without me whether

I'm trained with weapons or not. I'm going to Spain and I will stand beside him and fight to my extinction if need be."

"Sarah, be reasonable. It is too late at any rate. The first groups have begun to travel. They will all be there by week's end. There is no time." She lifted her hands in supplication. "Please, Sarah, you must listen. It is not going to come to pass. You must wait here with the rest of us. They will come back." Even though she knew to the contrary, Jane spoke with conviction. "Aris has no fear they will lose the battle. He is sure of victory."

"Yes and I'll be there to share in it." Sarah smiled as a plan formed in her mind.

"Alright, Jane." If Jane had known her better, she would have been wary at her giving in so easily without a fight. "I suppose I do understand. I am just a newborn and not ready to fight a war." She laughed and changed the subject as she returned to sit by her friend. "So, we have some time to kill, don't we? Why don't we do a session. You were so close to the truth the last time you were in trance. What do you think about that?"

Relief bubbled in Jane's voice as she spoke. "That sounds perfect. Shall we begin right now?"

"Yes, I think now would work very nicely."

· · · · · · · · · · · · · · · · · · · ·

JANE HOWARD, transcript, Session 5

It was an autumn morning perfect for the hunt, cold and crisp, the sun shining brightly and the sky dappled with a few brilliant white clouds. A biting wind blew as the Queen's hounds barked and strained to be off while the riders waited for the stewards to bring the stirrup cups. The courtiers, too, were impatient, yet we knew the mulled wine would warm us against the icy chill of the morning and so we waited to be served. My mount whinnied, pawing the ground, ready to race across the meadows in the chase.

A sound caught my attention as I reined my horse, holding him tight to keep him from making way before the others were ready. It was Essex on his huge black stallion. He greeted the other nobles and their ladies briefly then made for my side, reaching me just as the steward came along. Wrapping the reins around the pommel of his saddle, Essex leaned to reach for two cups from the tray. First mine. It appeared that he would spill it, yet he did not. I took it from his hand. Then he raised his in a toast to the morning and the Queen. I drank the warm wine. It had a strange taste to it, but I thought it might be some new spice the kitchen had added to enhance the flavor.

The fanfare was played and we began to trot. Soon we were away from the palace grounds. Suddenly I became dizzy, my head swam; I felt I might faint. Pulling up the reins, I halted my horse. The other riders were far ahead when we began so no one noticed I had fallen back even farther. I closed my eyes to stop the spinning of the ground beneath me. Without warning, I teetered in the saddle as my horse began to move. Holding tight to the pommel to steady myself, I opened my eyes. There sat Essex with his hands on my reins.

"Never fear, fair maiden." His eyes flashed wickedly as he licked his full lips. "I will take care of you." His laugh was evil as he reached to pull me from my horse and onto his. He held me tight to him as we galloped toward the nearby forest. I tried to scream, but the words were lost somewhere between my spiraling brain and my tongue.

In what seemed the blinking of an eye, we were at the forest's edge and he was pulling me from the saddle. He threw me on the ground, ripping at my riding skirt.

In that instant, I found my voice. As I opened my mouth to scream, he slapped me hard across the face. Fighting my way through the fog, I bit his hand as he covered my mouth.

"Bitch," he cried as he lifted me by the front of my riding habit. He hit me again and again. My head swum and I tasted blood on my tongue. "I'll beat the fight out of you. In a faint or awake, I will have you today."

Suddenly a loud, ferocious growl sounded just behind him. As he threw me back to the ground, my head crashed onto a sharp rock. I could feel the blood rushing from the wound to saturate the ground around me before all went dark as I lost consciousness.

Yet I remember. Her words were clear, strong, without fear as she told the story. I remember. Yes, even through the blackness, I remember. It was a white wolf. It was Hawke. He raced from the forest, and slammed his huge body into Essex, knocking the knave from his feet, tearing at his clothes, his flesh. As Essex reached for his knife the wolf tore at his hand. A scream broke the otherwise silent morning as the great animal ripped his teeth through the arm and wrist of my attacker. A river of blood poured over his white ruffled sleeve. As Hawke lunged for his throat, Essex knew he was beaten. Jumping on his horse, nursing his wound, he rode away shouting curses over his shoulder.

The wolf watched me for a moment before slowly approaching me, whining deep in his throat. In my stupor, I felt no fear. His soft warm tongue licked my face. He tilted his head as if he were examining my wounds.

I must have been dreaming because he changed right there before me from wolf to man. A tall white-skinned, white-haired man with eyes the color of lavender flowers. He was nude and the morning light shown on his muscular body. He looked like a marble statue in the Queen's garden.

It had to have been a dream because he scooped me into his arms and ran like the wind itself into the forest. I know not how long or how far he ran until, at last, he stopped, laying me gently on the ground. We were in front of the mouth of a cave and he gathered grasses and branches to make a bed for me just inside the cavern entrance. When he had settled me, he once again transformed into the white wolf and rushed into the cave. I know now he could not have entered the Catacombs in his human body. I know not how he became aware of the Immortals or how he communicated to them to come to my rescue, to save my life, but he did. When he left me lying there, my world was dark and empty.

And there all memory of my human life ends. There is no other recollection except the torment of my changing. When I awoke, I was an Immortal. No more human and through no wish of my own, it was then I began my life underground.

Sarah sat quietly staring at the huge white animal resting on the carpet next to the bed. The wolf raised his massive head from his paws and stared back.

. . . .

"What a strange feeling I am having." Jane slowly opened her eyes once Sarah ended her hypnotic trance. "It is as if a veil has been lifted. My mind is clear, yet how can this be possible?"

"Just lie quietly and rest for a moment." Sarah spoke as she moved toward the door to wet a cool cloth in the bathroom basin.

Jane spoke quietly from the sitting room. "Sarah, what do you make of it? Was I dreaming? How could a wolf become a man and then a wolf again? I must have been delirious to have such a vision."

A strange deep male voice could clearly be heard through the open door. "You were not delirious. A wolf to a man. A man to a wolf. And now, a man once again."

Sarah rushed through the door to see a tall white skinned man wrapping the bedspread around his naked hips as Jane lay on the bed, eyes wide and mouth hanging open in shock.

CHAPTER 40

"Have no fear. No harm will come to you." He stood before them, a living representation of Michelangelo's glorious white marble statue of David. All except for his intense lavender eyes. Neither of the women could move or speak, frozen in time and space.

"Please." He was perfectly still so as not to frighten them further. "Please, trust me." He turned to face Jane and raised his hands in supplication. "I have protected and loved you for centuries. I am no different in this form than as your beloved wolf. Please, Jane, have faith."

Sarah was the first of the two Immortals to speak. "Who are you?" Her thoughts were spinning. "How did you do that?" She shook her head to clear her mind. "What do you want?"

"I will answer all your questions. Just tell me you know I will do you no harm." He stared into Jane's eyes as he pled for her faith in his assurances.

Her voice was a whisper as she answered, "I believe you."

. . . .

The three of them were silent as they sat in front of the fireplace. Sarah brought Hawke a robe belonging to Aris, Although Aris was tall, the sleeves were several inches too short, his smooth muscular forearms exposed in the firelight. Sarah thought she had become accustomed to the beauty of the Immortals, but this man, this god among men, was more glorious than any living being, human or otherwise, she had ever seen.

"I have been watching over you, Jane, for centuries."

"I knew you were some sort of magical creature when you did not grow old in your wolf form, but remained vital and strong throughout the ages. The Keeper of Records told me that many centuries ago and I accepted it. But what are you, man or wolf?" Jane's voice was barely above a murmur when she questioned him.

"My kind has been called by many different names throughout the ages, but in your time, I am known as a shape-shifter. I am and can be all animate things."

"But where did you come from?" Sarah didn't think she could ever be shocked again after learning about the Immortals, yet here she sat amazed. Incredulous and full of questions, she realized just how wrong she had been. "Can you change shape at will?"

Hawke spoke slowly, thoughtfully. "First, from whence I came. A place on earth before recorded time." He sat silent for a trance-like moment as he remembered his creation. "The two who created me were sorcerers, a woman and a man, my mother and my father. There are many recorded shifters throughout history who have been created through mystic means, yet I was the first of the albinos. The first and the last. The only one of my kind. A freak of nature even among wizards' offspring.

"My wicked creators had a plan when they conceived me, to use my shape-shifting ability to change my form to spy on the rulers of our land. They told me it was a game and so, to gain their praise and love, I became very, very good at it. A playful innocent, I changed into cats and dogs, roaming the palace and easily hearing all conversation without being noticed. Telling all that I heard, I enabled my foul parents to wreak havoc on the land. The devils went on a killing spree the likes never known before or since.

"When I saw all that occurred, when I recognized I had been created as a weapon of evil, I fled the kingdom. Months and years I roamed until, at last, I found a forest that offered safety and peace. There I lived for centuries, eons on all fours, ages on the wing, becoming any creature I wished for as long as I chose. Yet always the pure white color of snow, always different than all around me." He whispered. "An owl. A stag."

Jane gasped. "You." Each of the animals rescuing her from Lord Essex at Elizabeth's court had been white; she realized each had been Hawke. "A wolf," she murmured. "And now a man."

"Yes, a man." Moving with caution, Hawke knelt next to her, touching her hand with the tips of his fingers. She shivered. Quickly he withdrew, lowering his eyes from hers. "I became your champion the first moment I saw you in the garden of the royal court. I watched you as you grew from an innocent child into the full beauty of a grown woman. I watched your loyalty to the Queen, your acts of love. How could I not pledge myself to you?"

As he lifted his gaze to hers, their eyes met in a sudden mutual, deep awareness surpassing any physical form they presented to the world, an awareness of the connection of their very souls.

Quietly Sarah slipped out the door, shutting it softly behind her.

CHAPTER 41

The troops waded through the mud created by the melting snow. The steady sloshing sound made by their boots muffled their voices as the Spanish warriors marched double-time to keep pace with their leaders. The soon-to-be-depleted human herd staggered in a daze behind them.

Oblivious to the cold and the great distance they had traveled, Mariska and Esteban covered ground quickly, never slowing their pace. An enormous sleek black wolf trotted easily on Esteban's right, completing the trio of decadent beauty.

Grumbling under his breath, Esteban kept pace with that set by his Queen. When at last he spoke, his words were clipped, accusing. "I did not think you would give in to DeMarco so easily. I thought you said there would be terms, a position for me in the high court." His voice was low, sinister. "I still do not understand why I must step down from your side. We can kill him and take over his troops." His words grew menacing. "Why do you persist in the thought you need him? Have you no faith in me?"

"Be still! Your constant hammering at me is driving me mad."

"Do not speak to me as if I were a child." He grabbed her arm, spinning her to face his threatening glare.

Her red lips curled back over her teeth exposing her fangs, which had dropped. "Take your bloody hands off me if you want to stay whole."

His hand dropped from her arm before the last word left her mouth. She was centuries older than he and that much stronger. He had no desire to battle her. He knew exactly what the outcome would be.

She turned from him and resumed their journey. He hurried to join her, matching his steps in time with hers.

When her anger had subsided, Mariska remembered how much she really needed Esteban, not just for the battle. It was imperative she have a strong-appearing male to rule as co-regent once they took the Catacombs. She would always be more powerful and she knew she could always outsmart Esteban. He was easily manipulated and she would always be in control He was perfect for the job once she had eliminated DeMarco. After a time of silence, she gave a long sigh and turned to him. "Esteban, I believe in you as a General. I have told you that time and again. But we are too few alone. We are but half the army we will be when we join with DeMarco's troops. Together we will have greater numbers than our enemies. We will be undefeatable. Without DeMarco's warriors, we will never even reach the Catacombs.

"We arrive at the castle at dawn. You will organize the troops while I placate DeMarco. We leave as soon as you have made everything ready to travel. Once we defeat the Immortals, I have no intention of sharing the Diaries with him. We will use him, kill him and his precious human and take the Catacombs for ourselves."

"And who will rule beside you, Majesty?"

"Who but you, my General."

. . . .

Julian sat on the cold stone floor of the castle, stunned by the violent blow delivered by the King.

"You fool," he shouted, his face contorted, his words reverberating off the walls and tall ceilings of the throne room. "How could you have allowed them to escape?"

His strength returning, Julian slowly rose to his feet. "I had to dispose of the Immortal. I couldn't..."

Another crushing blow drove the warrior to his knees. He bowed his head before his sovereign, anticipating more.

"Get up. Get out of my sight. Prepare for the arrival of the Queen and her troops. This time you had best be sure to perform your duty or you will burn. If Sarah and Aris are killed, you will join them in death. Your duty is to bring them to me in one piece and uninjured." His voice dropped to a menacing whisper. "Do you understand?"

"Yes, my Lord." Julian stood, hurrying from the room before DeMarco could strike him again.

The King smiled as he thought of the thrill of personally eliminating his rival. Never again would the Immortal male stand in the way of his having Sarah. Once the Catacombs were his, he would eliminate Mariska and take Sarah as his Queen. He spun on his heel, crossing the room to stare out the window and contemplate eternity with the only woman he ever loved.

CHAPTER 42

"Gabriela, you have to help me." Sarah leaned across the table, speaking discretely yet passionately to her friend. The Sanguinaria had only a few customers, but still she spoke in fervent whispers. "Don't shake your head at me. I'm going, with your help or not."

"Sarah, Aris will be thinking only of your safety, not of the army. You must not even consider going to Spain." Gaby took hold of her friend's hands as if she could hold her in the Catacombs by sheer physical force alone. "You will be lost and our society along with you. What you suggest is madness."

"Madness be damned. I'm going." She freed herself when the server brought their goblets of Alchimia Sanguis. She lifted the pewter mug and drank. Her Immortal friends had been amazed at how quickly and easily Sarah had adapted to drinking the alchemical blood. She licked her lips, placing the mug on the table as she continued.

"I am Immortal just the same as you. It won't be any easier for me to be destroyed than it will be for you to be destroyed. Or any others of us for that matter. Either you help me learn how to use the damn impaler or I'll just figure it out on my own."

"Even if you become proficient, Aris will never agree." Sarah could tell her friend was beginning to waiver. Her tone became more pleading, less demanding.

"He doesn't have to. I'll tell him I'm staying here then leave once everyone else is gone. I'll travel to Barcelona alone and join you at the castle. It will be too late for him to send me back." She rose from the chair with determination. "I'm going to live or die with the rest of you. And that is it." She turned to walk away.

"Wait. I will help you." Standing, Gabriela sighed deeply. "Aris will finish me himself for this, but I will teach you how to fight." She took her arm to lead her from the Sanguinaria. "Come, let us begin immediately, but I still beg you, please reconsider."

Sarah smiled as they hurried down the cobbled street toward the armory.

. . . .

They stood deep in one of the underground forests, hidden in a circle of low, full bushes unlike any Sarah had ever seen before. Green and leafy in appearance very much like bushes above ground, yet these moved of their own accord, their branches and leaves rustling as if a wind blew through them. A soft whispering sound could be heard as if even the undergrowth was cautioning the newborn.

The impaler rested heavily in Sarah's hands as Gaby helped her find the perfect grip for balance and impact. Interlacing her fingers over the top of the handle, she lunged forward on one leg, plunging it with all her Immortal strength again and again into the target Gabriela had slipped from the armory. Tireless, amazed at her own stamina, she felt more powerful, more ready for battle with each strike.

When, within an amazingly short time, Gabriela was satisfied her friend could attack and win, she taught her new defensive movements using the weapon. As she had done with everything since her first day as an Immortal, Sarah responded as if it were all quite natural, as if she had been fighting wars all her life.

"Enough of this. Now, you learn to climb."

"Climb?"

"Yes," Gaby spoke as she guided her friend toward an enormous tree just outside the circle of brush.

"Here, place your hands on the tree."

A strange surge of energy filled Sarah as her palms rested against the soft, warm bark. It was as if she became one with it, as if her hands and arms were nothing more than a limb that grew from it. Almost faster than the eye could follow, she shimmied to the top, resting on a large branch. Laughing, she looked down at Gabriela and leaped to the ground, landing without so much as a sound or puff of dirt.

"You are as ready as you will be in one day. Come, let us leave the forest. Aris will be returning from the last meeting with the commanders and I do not wish for him to have any idea what we have been doing."

"You go on Gaby, I want to stay and practice more. I'll be there before he arrives."

Reluctantly, Gabriela nodded yes as she turned to make her way back to the village. She could hear the sound of the impaler impacting the target over and over again as she left the forest.

. . . .

Aris had expected a fight from Sarah when he told her she couldn't accompany them to Spain. He had been surprised and relieved when she agreed to stay behind without too much argument and glad she so readily listened to reason. He hurried to their rooms to spend their last few moments together before his departure.

When he entered their chamber she was fresh from the shower and chatting quietly with Jane, the white wolf resting at his mistress' feet.

The women decided to keep the secret of the shape-shifter between them until after the war was won. It was agreed Hawke would return to his animal form, remaining that way until the Immortals returned from Spain. Only they knew of the existence of the man inside the wolf's skin.

Sarah embraced her mate as Jane rose from her seat. Aris kissed their friend lightly on the cheek as she wished him a safe and successful journey. Bidding them goodbye, she and her four-legged champion took leave, closing the door quietly behind them.

"Now, my love. Come, let us sit." He motioned for Sarah to join him on the sofa. "I leave within the hour. We gather tomorrow near the forest of Spain." He sensed her nervousness and did his best to ease what he thought was her fear for him. "Rest easy. We are a family and fight as one. They are all enemies among themselves. Our impalers are superior to theirs because of Akira's runes. We fight as an army, they as rabble. Be at ease, sweeting. Ours is an easy victory." He spoke words to quiet Sarah's concern, but deep inside he knew that many of his comrades would perish in the battle and he himself could be destroyed. "I will return to you in no more than two days." He reached for her.

"Yes, as you say, an easy victory." Her words were cut short as Aris' lips sought hers. Their kiss was raw. Demanding. She buried her face in his neck, inhaling his fragrance to better remember it, tasting his skin. Aris held her away from him, locking her features in his mind's eye. Then he pulled her close again and wrapped his arms around her, to memorize the feel of her against him. They sat quietly, entwined, until it was time for him to leave her.

Aris kissed Sarah quickly, looked at her one last time, and closed the door behind him.

CHAPTER 43

Jane paced the floor in front of the fireplace in Sarah's sitting room, her wolf heeling at her knee. They moved back and forth, beating a path in the carpet as Sarah watched from her seat on the sofa. When Jane spoke, her words were brusque. "What kind of madness made you think I would let you go alone?"

"Jane, it's for your own good. I'm sorry, but I must forbid you from coming with me."

Jane's voice rose in exasperation as she turned to face her friend. "You forbid me?" Hawke whined as he touched his cool muzzle to her hand and, without thinking, she rested her fingers on his wide brow.

"You never venture out of the Catacombs." Cautiously, Sarah kept her tone even as she replied, hoping to get her friend to agree to stay behind without an argument. "Why would you travel to Spain?" She changed her tact adding another reason to her plea. "And you're needed here. All of you who stay here will be vital to the safety of the Infinity Diaries if any enemies escape and come to England."

"A few hundred Immortals will be left behind to guard the Diaries. I am not needed here." As Jane finished speaking an idea flashed through her mind and she knew she would win. She remained silent for a moment as if in thought, then she spoke. "But I can see how I could be important here. Yes, perhaps you are right.

I should stay in England."

Sarah laughed knowingly. "Oh, I get it. You stay here until I leave. Then you get on a plane and follow."

"I wonder why that sounds familiar?" A mischievous smile lit Jane's eyes. "But you see, either way I am going to join you. You can help me through the ordeal of going above ground by allowing me to accompany you or you can leave alone, sentencing me to the terrors of traveling among humans unaided."

Sarah responded in kind. "When, my dear Jane, did your path of innocence turn to one of treachery?"

"When, my dear Sarah, you led the way." Jane kissed her companion's cheek before leaving to gather their black leather uniforms to wear as they traveled through the mountains of the Pyrenees in Spain.

· · · · · · · · · · · · · · · · · · ·

"We agreed you would remain a wolf until after the war." Jane packed a small carry-on bag for her trip to Spain as she snapped angrily at the tall albino man standing beside her. He was wrapped once again in a bedspread and still looked exactly like a statue of a Greek god.

"And so it would have been had you not decided on this fool's errand." He took her small hands in his and stopped her from moving about the room. "Here, sit for a moment." Leading her to her sofa, he motioned her to the cushions.

"Alright Hawke, but I am going with Sarah." Her anger melted as she looked at him, even as her resolve deepened. "I could never allow her to go alone."

"Jane, I cannot accompany you into the world. A wolf? An enormous albino? Either way I am a spectacle. I beg you, do not go to Spain. Without you I have no reason to live. You are my sun and moon, the reason I eat and sleep. If anything were to happen to you, I would cease to exist."

Jane reached to run her fingers over his smooth cheek. "There is nothing to fear. By the time we reach Spain, the war will be over. Henry told me if he did not believe that, he himself would keep us from going."

He stood, drawing her to her feet. "I will exist in a living death until you come back to me. I will show my shape-shifter self to the Council and beg to marry you. I will renounce my mystical power and go through the changing to become an Immortal if I must to become your true mate and be with you for eternity."

"Be without fear, my love. I will come back." He lifted her into his arms and cradling her like a child he kissed her gently.

CHAPTER 44

Jane's hands trembled as she worked to buckle her seatbelt. She wondered if Sarah hadn't been right, if she shouldn't have stayed at home in the Catacombs, but it was too late. The 'Fasten Seat Belt' sign was lit and the flight attendants were working their way through the cabin making sure everyone was belted in and their electronic gadgets turned off. Finally, after watching several failed attempts, Sarah came to her aid, strapping her to her seat.

"Thank you." Jane brushed her hair away from her face then, without thinking, gripped the armrests so tightly she left an indentation where her powerful fingers had been squeezing. "Oh no." Seeing what she had done, she folded her hands tightly in her lap, keeping them still for the rest of the flight, her unbeating heart filled with gratitude it was not a very long one. They would land in Barcelona in under two and a half hours where a rental car waited for them at the airport, the thought of which set Jane trembling again.

The taxi ride to Heathrow Airport had been terrifying. Horrible, harsh, blinding lights coming at her from every direction. Deafening blaring horns hurt her ears, making her very teeth ache. Humans everywhere covered the sidewalks like ants on an anthill, blindly rushing, never even seeing each other as they passed. The peaceful village of the Catacombs was all she had known, that and sixteenth century England. Suddenly, she was thrust into the midst of an age confusing and frightening even to those who were born to it.

"Put on these headphones, lean back and close your eyes. It will all be over soon." The voice of reason spoke to Jane in the form of her friend and she did exactly as was suggested.

. . . .

"Sarah, what will we do when we get there?" The trees on the side of the road were a blur as the rental car sped down the dark highway.

"I have no idea, Jane. I've never been to a war before." Sarah stared out the windshield as they raced through the pitch black night, their bright headlights glaring back at them from the surface of the blacktop. *"I'll think about it later."* She tried repeating the mantra she had used all her life, but found it had lost its magic. Later was now; preparing couldn't be put off another minute. In less than an hour's driving time, they would arrive at the edge of the forest where they would leave the car to proceed on foot to the castle.

Understanding the newborn's need to be with her mate, her desire to stand by her friends, and the fact she would go to fight with or without his help, Henry had been persuaded to map their journey. He was confident the war would be over before they arrived so he laid out their trip for them. Red marker lines on the map indicating back roads where their high speed would go unnoticed, a green marker line from the highway through the forest to the stronghold of DeMarco and Mariska.

Sarah shivered when she remembered her last encounter with the King and Queen of the vile Spanish coven. But she hadn't been an Immortal then. She hadn't had the gifts of speed and extraordinary vision. She hadn't had an indestructible body. Only direct impalement to the heart would stop her now. If that were to happen, there would be no suffering, only death. She carried a letter, as all the Immortals carried to Spain, telling what was to be done with her carcass if her heart were pierced. Jane carried a similar letter. Both women knew what might happen and both were driven to risk everything for their Immortal family.

CHAPTER 45

The Immortal troops chosen to ambush Mariska and Estaban in the forest and attack DeMarco and his army holed up in the castle arrived in pairs and small groups. Once assembled, the troops from the Catacombs moved silently through the trees, Sebastian at their head, Gabriela at his side. Upon reaching the crossroad, they would each take the path laid out by their spies. Gabriela would lead half the troops to hide just outside the walls of the nearby castle, and the other half of the soldiers in the charge of Sebastian stayed behind, soundlessly climbing the trees along the path. Each one dressed in a uniform of black leather, impalers in their belts, stilettos tucked neatly in their boots, their outlines disappearing against the dark bark and in the dense foliage. Motionless, Sebastian's warriors lay in wait, some sitting on their haunches, with their backs against the tree trunks, others lying on their stomachs, with their impalers already in hand. The rest disappeared behind rocks and brush, easily hidden from their unsuspecting opponents. The smell of wood smoke from the fires burning in the turrets of the castle floated in the air, fires lit to welcome the returning army. All of the Immortals waited in silence for the sign from Sebastian.

The moon-lit sky above was just beginning to change from night to dawn when the first of the Spanish coven appeared. Patiently waiting until the vampires were surrounded above and below by his army, Sebastian prepared to give the signal.

At the perfect moment his battle cry echoed through the trees, joined by the answering shouts of the Immortals as they leaped to meet their enemy.

The two armies collided in combat, their cries echoing through the crisp early morning air. "Esteban!" Mariska cried out as a leather clad Immortal landed in her path, impaler ready to pierce her heart. As he drew back to deliver the death blow, Esteban spun, stabbing him from behind and striking a direct hit to his heart. He sunk to the forest floor, his Immortal venom flowing from his wound. "To the trees," she shouted. "Kill them where they stand."

Many of her coven leaped to the branches, racing to eliminate as many of their adversaries as they could before they faced one another on solid ground. Bodies from both armies rained from above as those hiding in the rocks raced to join the fray.

Seeing an opportunity one of the vile vampires flipped from a high branch, landing directly in front of Gabriela. Suddenly, the vampire was not alone. Gabriela found herself surrounded, unable to get away, and isolated by the pack. She met the eyes of one of the females as she approached. They glowed with anticipation of the kill. Gabriela laughed. If she were to die, they would not take her without a fierce fight. Her powerful hands grasped her impaler; she began to spin where she stood. She struck out again and again, her arms reaching out like the spokes of a wheel. Vampire after vampire dropped in unrecognizable heaps at her feet. At the moment she thought she was safe, a stiletto flew from Esteban's hand penetrating its target. Gabriela crumpled to the ground.

The sounds of combat in the forest were heard by Aris and Richard as they waited just outside the castle walls. Aris shouted, "Now!" His division charged the keep, impalers and stilettos at the ready. They were met by their enemy racing from the courtyard to join the battle, they could hear raging in the trees beyond the fortress walls.

Arms and legs flailed as the two armies clashed ferociously. Shrieks and screams cut the cold morning air as both vampires and Immortals met their brutal end.

Those left alive from Sebastian's division raced in fierce pursuit of Mariska's troops, who were advancing toward the castle and the reinforcements. The battle filled the courtyard with bodies. Barely any open ground was left on the battlefield. Taking advantage of the already burning fires, Richard began tossing the Spanish coven's dead and wounded into the flames. The smell of burning vampires joined the stench of spilling venom and death.

Having cleared a small space of ground, Richard turned to rejoin the fight. Esteban stood before him, a malicious grin on his face. "Your female is dead. I killed her with the same hands that will end your puny life."

Richard threw back his head as he screamed in grief. Taking advantage of the moment, Esteban spun his weapon over his head, preparing to let it fly into the heart of his enemy.

"Your aim is as foul as your stench. I live, devil." Gabriela, covered by her own venom and with her wound not yet fully healed, threw her stiletto straight for his heart. Her aim was true and he fell to the ground. Shoving her foot onto his chest, she wrenched the weapon from his heart, picked him up by one of his legs and threw him into the flames. For only a moment, her eyes met Richard's before they both raced toward the castle where Aris battled his way to what was left of the tower bridge.

As Aris neared the great door, he saw Mariska dash inside pushing even her own soldiers out of her way. He knew she was running to her mate and he was determined to get there first. Leaping onto the remnants of the tower wall, he climbed hand over hand, impaler in his belt, stiletto in his teeth. As he climbed over the wall, he saw dead Immortals and vampires strewn in the rubble of the bridge.

Aris rushed toward the door that led to the throne room, stepping on dead friend and foe alike, but before he could reach it, DeMarco leaped out.

Seeing his rival, his enemy, before him, DeMarco's eyes lit with the fire of something deeper than hate. "At last!" He edged his way around the bodies lying on the stone walkway, dagger in his hand, loathing in his heart. "You will die and she will be forever mine."

"Come and get me." Aris stood, legs apart, muscles bulging, as he prepared to fight the demon that wanted to claim his mate. Before either could strike the first blow, Mariska burst through the door. She laughed as she joined the King and they danced the dance of death with Aris. Had he faced either one alone it would have been no contest, but together, they formed a most formidable team. DeMarco leaped over the dead bodies and drew close behind him. As he spun to deflect DeMarco's dagger, Mariska plunged her own into his thigh. Venom flowed from the deep wound in his leg, pooling on the stone beneath him. DeMarco's weapon missed its mark, but a huge gash rent Aris' shoulder. While his wounds were not fatal, he was weakened by the loss of venom and sunk to the ground.

CHAPTER 46

"Look, there is the turn-off into the forest Henry marked." Jane looked closely at the map then pointed to huge boulders painted with thick yellow phosphorescent stripes marking the end of the road. Sarah pulled the car into a cover of trees and heavy brush. Quickly they changed from their traveling clothes into black pants, boots, sweaters and tight leather jackets, the uniform of the Immortals, pulling skull caps tightly over their heads to cover their blond hair. They were quickly ready to travel on foot through the cold mountain air.

One final glance at the map was all it took before Sarah broke into a run. Jane followed close behind. Their legs moved faster than Olympic sprinters, jumping tree stumps and enormous rocks. Soon the sounds of the raging battle rang in their ears, urging them on.

As they cleared the forest, the red glow from funeral fires, already burning, added to the brightening light of the morning sky. Sarah stopped short. Jane tripped over her friend as they both stood with their mouths open, staring into the milieu before them. Far from being over, hand-to-hand combat surrounded them. Recovering from her initial shock, Jane rushed forward, grasping and drawing an impaler from the heart of a dead vampire. Tossing it to Sarah, she stumbled over another weapon lying in the dirt, this one with the runes of Akira clearly marked on its shaft.

"Now, Sarah." Turning, she raced toward the castle wall. The stench of battle surrounded them as the two Immortals dashed for the portcullis leading to the castle courtyard. All around them were sounds of death. In the center of the keep there was a fire burning, turning to cinders the bodies of the dead.

An enormous dark-skinned vampire jumped in front of Jane just as she entered the courtyard. Swiftly, without thought, Sarah flung her impaler through the air. It made a sickening thud as the stiletto point punctured the chest of the male. He shrieked as he grasped the handle of the weapon protruding from his chest. It had just missed his heart. Jane grabbed a huge log, slamming it into his shins. He shouted curses as his legs gave way and he fell to his hands and knees. Taking advantage of his fall Sarah rushed forward. Leaping into the air and smashing the bottom of her boot into his face, she toppled him onto his back, grabbed the impaler, pulled it out of his chest and plunged it deep, directly into his heart. Thick liquid burst from the wound, splashing Sarah's face and clothes. A deep hissing sound escaped from his body as he lay without moving.

Wiping her face with her jacket sleeve, Sarah turned to search for Jane. She caught sight of her friend racing across the courtyard toward the castle. Above her head, what appeared to be the remnants of the tower bridge extended from the crumbling wall. The span ended in thin air. The tower that had supported it lay in rubble beneath it. She froze at what she saw on that bridge.

DeMarco and Mariska had cornered an Immortal against a pile of fallen stones. Sarah cried out as she recognized the trapped male. It was Aris. He fought like a demon, but the two vampires were working together to wear him down. They laughed as they took turns worrying him and jabbing him, cutting him with their weapons.

Without thought, Sarah jumped for the piling holding up the bridge. She began to climb like a spider, clinging to the rock as she raced up the wall. Her newborn strength and speed left Jane trailing behind her in their climb.

Jumping over the low stone wall edging the bridge, Sarah readied her weapon. Furiously Aris fought DeMarco. As he ducked to evade the point of the King's impaler, Mariska raised hers high, preparing to stab him in the back.

"Mariska!" Sarah shouted her name, causing the Queen to halt mid-strike. She whirled to face the furious voice. Just as she turned, Jane climbed over the stone wall directly in front of the Queen. Mariska laughed as she plunged the sharp metal point into the Immortal's chest. She hit her mark. Jane crumpled to the ground. As if turned to stone, Sarah stared unmoving.

Mariska jerked the weapon Jane carried from her dying hand. Sarah knew what the vampire planned, yet still she stood frozen in horror unable to move or protect herself. Rushing her, the blade held high, the Queen let out a high shrill shout of victory.

Turning from Aris and seeing Mariska lunge forward, DeMarco leaped between the Queen and Sarah, taking Mariska's raised blade in his own heart. His last word as he sank to the ground was the name of his only love: "Sarah."

Aris lay gasping, for a moment unable to rise to her aid, a huge open wound in his shoulder, his thigh ripped from hip to knee. No longer immobile, Sarah pulled the impaler from the gaping wound in DeMarco's chest and prepared to meet her adversary. With a frenzied battle cry and one fatal jab, she felled the Queen. As Mariska's knees buckled beneath her, Sarah grabbed her by the hair. Pulling the impaler from her heart, she sliced the dead vampire's throat with its point, wrenching her head from her shoulders. Holding the gory mess high above her head, she screamed for the warriors to see their dead Queen. Her wild voice cut through the battle sounds, silencing all those below as they raised their eyes to the bridge. The sun had risen as they fought and they could see clearly the tableaux on the bridge.

Standing tall, the head of the dead Queen held high, Sarah shouted for all to hear. "It is ended. Look here. Your Queen and your King are dead. The Immortals commit their damned souls to the fires for all eternity."

The combatants stared at her in silence as Aris rose to his feet, his wounds closing even as he moved toward her. He dragged the body of the King to the edge of the bridge, lifting the corpse to prove to the vampire warriors they no longer had either leader.

"These are the terms of surrender." He spoke slowly, clearly, first in English, then Spanish. "All who step forward to take the Blood Oath, to swear to abide by the Laws of the Catacombs, will be saved. You will return with us to England to live among us in peace. Any who wish to turn their backs on our terms will die without mercy." He waited while his words settled among the crowd.

At last, dropping their weapons, three stepped forward, two men and a woman. They were covered in dirt and venom. One was spitting something vile from his mouth.

"Three of you? Only three?" Again, he paused. "This is my last offer. Step forward in surrender or die." No one moved.

Lifting the body of DeMarco over his head, he flung it onto the rocks below. "Kill them all." His command rang clearly through the now silent night. "Kill them all, leave none standing." He turned in time to see Sarah fling the head of the dead Queen from the bridge to join her mate in the flames of eternal death as the sounds of the battle below the bridge began again.

. . . .

Aris wrapped his arms around Sarah as she held the head of her dead friend in her lap. She removed Jane's black cap, running her fingers through her soft blond hair and touching her unmoving lips.

"She didn't want to come." Sarah's words were thick with grief as she buried her face in her hands. "She didn't want to come and now she's gone."

· "Sarah," Aris spoke gently. "Sarah, Jane loved you. She could never allow you to come here alone. And you, of all people, know she never wanted Immortality. It was a bitter gift to her. She told you she wished she had died a human death. Now she has peace."

"No, not yet. We don't know what she chose until we find her death request." As she spoke, she reached into the zipper pocket of the dead woman's leather jacket, drawing from it a small folded piece of paper.

She read it, then handed it to Aris. It read: "Grieve not, dear friends, burn this body. Give me peace I have not known these hundreds of years. From dust I came and to ashes I return. To Sarah, know that you have given me moments of memory that brought joy and understanding to a poor Immortal who was lost before you came. Thank you with heartfelt love. Jane Howard."

Aris and Sarah stood. Aris lifted the body of their beloved comrade and the couple left the bridge, carrying their cherished friend to the fire where she would find the eternal peace she craved.

As he lowered her body into the purging flames, Sarah was sure she heard the distant howl of a wolf.

· · · · · · · · · · · · · · · · · · · ·

It was two nights and two full days before the Immortals had burned all the dead and cleared the battlefield of all traces of combat. The three that surrendered, Garret, Stefano and Martha, had been put under guard to wait quietly in the ruins of the tower where Sarah had been held prisoner in what seemed to her to be another lifetime.

It was early on the morning of the third day. Aris and Sarah stood next to one another as they watched out the window of the castle throne room. Richard, Gabriela and Sebastian had just said goodbye to the remaining commanders and were making their way across the courtyard to take the three surrendering vampires back to the Catacombs.

"It's really over." Sarah leaned her head against Aris' shoulder as he wrapped his arm around her waist.

"Yes. You are safe at last."

"I've been safe since the moment you came into my life." As they stood in silence waiting for their friends, her mind drifted back to the first time Aris manifested during her hypnotic session with Carlos. It seemed so many lifetimes ago. She questioned the existence of the Immortals then. Now, she questioned the existence of her own human life. She had been so overwhelmed by the events of the past few weeks; it had been days since she had even thought of Chicago and her human friends.

When Sarah finally did think of them, she knew she must telephone Colleen and her mother as soon as they returned to England. She didn't want to cause anyone any concern for her well-being and it had been several days since she had spoken to anyone in the States. She considered calling while they were still in Spain, but thought better of it. There were too many events to put in order in her mind and process before she spoke to any mortal.

"We are ready to travel. Gabriela and Richard have gone to collect the three." Sebastian spoke as he entered the room. Aris and Sarah turned from the window to greet their comrade. "Everyone is on their way home. It is time for us to return."

"Yes, our flight from Barcelona is later this evening. We will be leaving shortly. We all look forward to being home." As Aris spoke, Gabriela entered the doorway.

"All is ready. Richard waits with the guards and the defectors." She kissed Sarah on the cheek and embraced Aris. "We will see you at home."

They said their goodbyes as Sebastian and Gabriela left the room.

Sarah wrapped her arms around Aris as she spoke. "I miss Jane so much. I keep wishing she and Hawke were waiting for our return."

"Jane is at peace, her request met. We must accept her decision and be grateful that we knew her gentle spirit."

"Yes, just as I am grateful to have you." She lifted her eyes to his, then closed them as his tender lips touched hers.

CHAPTER 47

Only one table sat vacant in the crowded Sanquinaria. Aris and Sarah made their way through the gathering of the celebrating Immortals to claim it. As they settled into their seats Richard and Gabriela entered, waving in recognition. Stopping a waiter as they hurried by, they ordered their drinks before joining their waiting friends.

"Have you heard? The three will take the Blood Oath tomorrow?" Richard shared the news as he and his mate settled into the chairs that awaited them.

"No. So soon? We have only been home for a few days," Aris answered.

"Yes, but they have been questioned without ceasing by the Council and Henry since their arrival. Garret has been the main spokesperson for the three. He told the Council that he and Stephano and Martha had longed for a peaceful existence before the war. They had planned for some time to desert the Spanish court when the time was right and somehow make their way to the Catacombs. All three swear they fully understand the code of ethics we demand of our citizens. All three say they will vow to abide by the Blood Oath for all of eternity so Bartholomew sees no reason to delay. As Head Council, he will present his request to Queen Akira."

Aris sipped from his goblet, his voice troubled when he spoke. "Queen Akira. Yes. Sebastian told me she was furious that I allowed for surrender. He says she will call me to audience before the Blood Oath can take place."

"What will you tell her?"

"I will tell her the truth. I will remind her both you and Gabriela originally came from the Spanish coven. You took the Blood Oath and you have lived a perfect life ever since, never looking back to what you once were. I was unable to eliminate every vampire without giving them a chance to find a better existence. There was no other way except to offer them sanctuary if they chose to change."

Gabriela spoke. "What is a wonder to me is only three came forward."

"I must be honest and say I was amazed that even three would be willing. I still wonder if this is not subterfuge." Aris reached for Sarah's hand resting next to his on the table. Interlacing his fingers with hers, he continued. "They lived a savage life. They know no better. Even when they swear, I will not be content to trust them for many centuries. Remember DeMarco? He fooled even Henry. No, even though I gave them the chance to denounce their past, I will keep watch over their actions for a long time to come."

The waiter brought their refreshment to the table and the conversation turned to Hawke.

"Henry said the white wolf howled for many hours then was seen no more." Richard handed Gabriela her drink. "When the army returned to the Catacombs, they spent a day and night searching for him, yet there was no sign that he was anywhere to be found."

Sarah thought of the howl she heard at the moment Jane's body was laid to rest in the fire. She knew no one would ever see Jane's beloved companion again. She squeezed Aris' hand, knowing the man as well as the wolf would wander alone throughout time.

. . . .

Aris paced the floor as he waited to be shown into the audience chamber. Time and again since he joined the Immortals, he had been called before the Queen. Each time he felt sorrow at having disappointed her. He felt it once again. Whatever punishment she dealt him would be accepted, yet he knew he did the only thing his honor would allow.

He, too, had lived as a rogue before his enlightenment so very long ago. He was flooded with memories of that distant time; memories of the field in Spain when he was a commander for Charles I, memories of his first glimpse of another like himself. He recalled his delight at meeting Richard and Gabriela when they told him there was another way, when he learned of the Catacombs. He remembered the peace he felt when he joined their society. It was the first time in his life, human or vampire, he had lived in harmony with others.

Yet despite the solace offered by his new existence, he had once again become a rogue. He broke the Blood Oath when he killed out of hatred first Cardinal Wolsey and then Katherine, first wife of Henry VIII. Anne Boleyn had used and tricked him, but the blame still was his for betraying the Immortals. He had been forgiven, yet he never forgot what it was to be driven to use all the powers he had to do evil once again. He planned to vow to the Queen he would watch over the three new members to their society, scrutinizing their every move.

"Come, my friend." Sebastian entered the chamber, holding the door for Aris to stand before the Queen. Aris shuddered as the door closed behind him.

Kneeling before Akira, Aris lowered his head in contrition.

"Stand. You have once again disobeyed my orders." He rose to his feet. "Why do you cast your eyes away? Look at me." When he looked into her face, he was shocked to see she was smiling.

"I have called you here to chastise you, yet the entire Council has begged for mercy for you." She shook her head as if at a child who had been disobedient. "You allowed those three to live because they swore they wanted a better life. I do not agree with your decision, but you have proved to me that you truly do have compassion. You have proved by your actions that you are sincerely contrite for your transgressions to the Law that happened so long ago. I am now sure I made the right decision to acquit you for your crimes."

"My Queen." He knelt before her once again, bowing his head in gratitude.

"Rise. You need not humble yourself before me, Aris. I know that without you, our society would have been extinguished. You were the salvation of us all." She raised herself from her throne to step close enough to him to place her long fingers on his cheek.

"I have never known human love, but I believe that may be the very thing I sense within myself for you. I have no understanding of emotion, yet emotion must be this sensation I feel when I contemplate you as a child of mine." She returned to her throne. She sat for a moment before making the request that had been her reason to call him before her.

"Aris, King Khansu has retired from public life. He no longer wishes to reign as Sovereign over the Immortals, yet our society has never been without a King. I have conferred with the Council and the Master Keeper of Records. We are all in accord. We wish you to continue to lead your people as you did in Spain. We wish you to become co-regent to rule beside me as King of the Immortals." Frozen in shock at her words, he neither moved nor spoke. "Aris, what say you to that?"

"My Queen." His voice was a stunned whisper, "I am not prepared to take such a step. I am not worthy of what you offer."

"You are more than worthy, yet I understand your hesitation. Go. You must speak with your mate. You must give it great thought. I await your decision." She rose and quietly left the room.

. . . .

"I don't understand what all this means." Sarah sat next to Aris on their enormous bed. "King of the Immortals? What does that make me?"

"You remain my mate, the one who advises me and walks by my side."

"But, does that mean you can never leave the Catacombs? What about your life above ground as an artist? What will become of that?"

"I spoke with Bartholomew for hours questioning exactly what my duties would entail. Queen Akira will be the true monarch. Mine will be a title conferred upon me as an honor for all I did to save our Immortal society. I will be no more than another advisor to Her Majesty."

"But your art? What of our life above ground, my life above ground?"

"I will continue painting and showing in galleries. We will continue on above ground until you no longer can be seen by your human friends. At that time, we will withdraw from mortal society for as long as we so desire. You understood before your changing that one day you must do just that as your human friends age and you do not. Nothing will change for us until that time." He held her in his arms, whispering softly. "We are Immortal, my love. We have eternity together. Pretending to live your earthly life will be just a moment in time. Have no fear. I am with you always."

. . . .

"Our flight arrives on Friday." Sarah spoke into her cell phone as Aris paid the taxi driver. "We're on the way to meet the art gallery owner right now to make sure everything is taken care of while we're in the states."

"What time will your plane get in?" The excitement in Colleen's voice made Sarah smile.

"Don't worry. We'll take a taxi to my apartment."

"Oh no you won't. Bob and I are coming to the airport. I can't wait to see you. It seems like it's been forever. Will I even recognize you?"

Sarah winked at Aris as she replied. "Well, I'm glowing so I may look just a little different."

"I can't wait to see you. We've arranged a quiet ceremony at our house on Sunday afternoon. Your mother and grandmother are coming and John Marshall is arriving on Saturday so he can be there as well. Bonnie and Jack and Maggie and her guy are coming. That's all so don't worry, only really close friends. Everyone is so happy for the two of you. So what time does your plane arrive?"

"Okay C, okay. We land at two thirty in the afternoon. I'll call you when we're on the ground so you don't have to wait around for us."

"No way, we'll be in baggage claim. I can't wait."

"Neither can I. See you then. Love you."

"Here comes the bride." Colleen was laughing as she broke the connection.

"I hope you're up for all of this." Sarah held Aris' hand as they walked toward the door of the gallery.

"I actually am looking forward to it, but I think we may need to rewrite the vows a bit. There will be no sickness or health, no better or worse and most of all, no death to part us for all eternity." Then right there on the London street he wrapped his arms around her and kissed her, drawing her close, feeling her Immortal body meld into his for all time.

THE END

CPSIA information can be obtained at www.ICGtesting.com
Printed in the USA
BVOW04s0201200115

383995BV00004B/8/P